RUN ALL NIGHT

Fred Anderson

I

1

"Hey Sanchez."

Maya looks up from the tire she's spraying with gel shine. The voice belongs to the sales manager, a turd with a weasel face and an aggressively white grin wrapped in a cheap gray suit. He steps a little closer, taking the opportunity for a peek down the front of her coveralls while she squats. She straightens, wondering if he uses the same product on his slicked hair she's using on the blackwalls. Wondering if a shot of the stuff from the bottle in her hand would be enough to blind him.

"Yeah?" she says.

"Got a delivery for you, up in Tuxedo Park." The grin widens, becomes sharky. "Never gonna believe who to."

She's curious. The Park is the nicest neighborhood in Atlanta. Celebrities and big business billionaires, movers and shakers. Deep pockets filled with big tips. "Who?"

"Tony Soprano."

She sets the gel shine on the rack and peels off her latex gloves to clean the sweat off her face with a towel. It's the middle of the afternoon at the height of summer in the deep south. The shop is like a sauna despite the humming barrel fans overhead.

"Who?" she says again.

"You never saw that show? *The Sopranos?* For real?" He pitches his voice, affecting a Jersey accent. *"Cunnilingus and psychiatry brought us to this.* Figured you'd be all over that quote, being someone who likes to pay lip service to the ladies and all."

Now the grin morphs into a leer, and in her head she

3

hears the tinkle of porcelain veneers scattering across the wet concrete like shards of glass. Maya knows the show. Young doesn't mean uncultured. Her father fed her a steady diet of classic films and TV while she was growing up. It beat having to raise her.

She just looks at him, waiting. Silence almost always works with his type. Just like six months earlier, when she first started the job at the dealership. He had come sniffing around, hinting that if she went out with—and slept with, she was sure—him, he could get her moved out of the detail shop and into the air-conditioned showroom. After she ignored his advances, he had decided she batted for the other team. Hence the comment. She has not disavowed him of the notion. It makes her work life easier. Besides, she likes the job, likes to get her hands dirty uncovering the beauty hidden in the old cars.

After a few seconds the grin falters, then evaporates. He says, "Never mind. Guy's name is Moretti. Everybody says he makes his money with the mob. Importing coke, and I don't mean the kind you drink. He bought the Challenger in bay two. Wants it brought to his house by five. Isaiah can follow and give you a ride back. Be sure you share any tip with him."

He starts to walk away but pauses, bends to examine the glossy black coat on the '69 Z28 she's been working on. Buffs at an imaginary blemish with the wear-shined elbow of his jacket and checks his reflected teeth. What a chode. She rolls her eyes and heads for the restroom to change back into her street clothes for the drive, and to find Isaiah, who has a habit of disappearing whenever anyone from management makes an appearance. Working in the coveralls is like being locked in a hotbox, especially this time of year, but the dealership provides them and it saves her from spending money she doesn't have. However, she won't wear the shapeless outfit off the lot, not when she's delivering to the kind of man who would drop six figures on a muscle car and potential tips are involved. You have to use your assets to your advantage, and the fitted tee and jeans will assist nicely.

Ten minutes later she has changed and returns to the shop, where the sleek yellow car waits. The '71 Challenger exudes raw power and aggression that trigger something visceral in her. Everything about it commands attention, from the wide chrome grill to the sloping roof to the flared fenders. She can't wait to get behind the wheel. Peeling a sheet of protective plastic from the roll on the supply rack, she spreads it over the vinyl driver seat. From the same rack, she retrieves a flimsy cardboard floor mat —CAPSTONE CLASSICS is stenciled on it in big bold blue letters —and slides it into place. Despite being more than twice her age, the interior of the Dodge smells fresh off the assembly line. When she turns the key, the elephant under the hood awakens with a low rumble of raw unbridled strength that seems to resonate in her very being. The clutch is heavy, hard to hold. All the gauges are good. They better be, as much as this thing must have cost to restore. Probably four or five times what she makes in a year.

Maya drops the pistol-grip stick into first and eases the car out into the sunshine.

2

The antebellum house in Tuxedo Park is an alabaster Greek Revival behemoth on three lushly landscaped acres, all columns and windows and sprawling wings, surrounded by an iron security fence taller than Maya by two feet. Each ebony spire curves outward at the top and is sharpened to prevent intruders from climbing over. Definitely the sort of fence a drug runner would have.

It's obscene.

The entry is gated but open. She drives between the brick pillars and rolls toward the house at idle speed. A gardener prunes rosebushes in a flower garden to her left, gathering the colorful blooms into a basket. He waves as she passes. She parks the Challenger under the *porte cochère* at the front of the mansion. In the ensuing silence she becomes aware of the sound of running water through the open window. A sparkling stream flows among the landscaping, too pristine and perfect to be anything but man-made. She shakes her head, thinking of the old line about the rich not being like the rest of us. Truer words.

Isaiah creeps up the drive in his beater Hyundai, which looks out of place among all the opulence. She nods to him before climbing the stairs to the front door with the packet of documentation for the Dodge. Before she can ring the bell, the door opens. The handsome man who steps onto the porch is in his fifties, and bears more than a passing resemblance to a young Al Pacino. His shirt and slacks and blazer have obviously been tailored to accentuate his wide shoulders and narrow waist.

They do it well. A look of surprise flickers across his face at the sight of her, there and gone. He extends a hand.

"Dominic Moretti," he says warmly. There is the slightest hint of an accent. His grip is strong, the flesh soft and smooth.

Maya tells him her name and hands over the paperwork and keys. She wonders just how stupid the sales manager must be, going with *Tony Soprano* when *Scarface* and *Michael Corleone* are ripe for the taking.

"So how does she handle, Maya Sanchez?" he asks. He smiles as he looks past her at the Challenger.

"Like a dream. Wish I had one of my own."

An eyebrow lifts as his gaze returns to her. "To be honest, I didn't expect them to send someone so young. I thought only old men like me still drive stick."

"I learned on a stick, and wouldn't drive anything else. Give me control over convenience any day."

"Exactly!" he says, clapping her on the shoulder like they're old friends. "So many people don't understand the relationship between man—or woman—and machine a stick provides. You know your way around cars?"

She shrugs. "Not enough to be a mechanic, but yeah. I like to do what work I can on them. *Love* to drive them. Deliveries of classics like this are probably the best part of my job."

"Want to come on the inaugural drive, see what this baby can do?"

Maya considers, not sure if he's trying to flirt—and ew, gross, he's so *old*—or just being friendly. When he opened the door, he hadn't given her the once-over the way men usually do. No lingering gaze at her chest, no sense that there was a *bow-chicka-bow-bow* soundtrack playing in his head. She likes that. Being friendly, she decides, or at least not overtly skeevy. Plus, she's still on the clock. Getting paid to cruise around town in a ride like the Challenger beats sweating her ass off in the shop any day of the week. And, keeping the customer happy probably means a better tip. She knows how to take care of herself if he tries anything.

"It's gotta be quick," she says, hooking a thumb over her shoulder. "My ride back to Capstone is waiting."

Moretti looks past her at the sputtering hatchback. "How about I drop you off instead? You good with that?"

"Sure." But she's already second-guessing her earlier conclusion. Something about this suddenly feels like more than friendliness, even though there's no lecherous vibe coming off him. None she can detect, anyway.

He dangles the keys. "Get her turned around."

While she reorients the Challenger, Moretti approaches the Hyundai. The two men have a short discussion, then Moretti takes out his wallet and extracts several bills. Isaiah gives her an inquisitive look. She nods, mouths *it's okay*. He accepts the cash and backs down the drive.

She opens the door to give Moretti the wheel, but he says, "You drive."

Not good. It's one thing to courier the Dodge across town to deliver it; the dealership insurance covers those drives. But once paperwork and keys have exchanged hands, that coverage ends. If she has an accident now, she's on her own. Hell no, even though she would just about kill to drive the thing again. Just fixing a scraped fender on this beast would cost what she makes in a month. Maybe more. She opens her mouth to decline and he stops her.

"It's insured. My collector's policy covers all my vehicles, no matter who's driving." He opens the passenger door and slides in beside her.

"That said, please don't wreck," he adds, smiling.

"It's not *me* I was worried about."

3

Moretti runs his fingers over the glowing dash. "You detail her?"

"Sure did," Maya says. "First one of the day."

"Outstanding." He inhales deeply. "Don't think I'll ever get tired of this smell."

Rush hour traffic is beginning to pick up. Maya looks forward to getting away from the congestion, to put the Challenger through its paces. Within reason, of course. Fishtailing into a guard rail or going nose first into a tree would nix any chance of a good tip, she suspects.

"If I could bottle and sell it," she says, "I'd retire by thirty."

She checks the mirror, signals, and slips around a little old lady puttering along ten miles an hour below the speed limit. The woman looks like a child behind the wheel, barely able to see over it. They make small talk until they're out of the city, mostly about muscle cars and Moretti's collection. The metro area falls behind and with it, much of the traffic. Maya takes the exit for highway 140.

"Give her a sip," he says, as they merge into an even lighter flow. "See how she likes it."

Maya puts the pedal down and the Challenger leaps forward with a throaty roar. The force pushes her back into the seat. She upshifts into third and hits it again. The RPM needle swings toward the red line, and the car screams down the highway like a banshee. Vibrations from the chassis rock her to her core. Her stomach feels like it's about a quarter-mile back. Clutch in, down into fourth, clutch out. The engine gulps air through the hood scoop and there's a burst of acceleration. Trees flash by to either side.

She lets everything fade away until there's nothing but driver and car and road. A twitch of the wheel pulls them into the passing lane, thundering past a lifted pickup that seems to be standing still. They ride in silence for several miles, threading in and out of the sparse traffic. When she glances over at Moretti, he's watching her drive, and a rush of heat goes through her core. She lets off the gas and the engine loses its bestial sound. The Challenger begins to slow. Everything comes back into focus. Her heart pounding from the exhilaration, Maya whoops and slaps a hand on the dash.

"*Damn*, this is a fine ride," she shouts, her cheeks hot. For just an instant she wishes Moretti *would* make a move on her, then the feeling passes just as quickly as it came. She cuts her eyes to the side. He's still watching her, intently. "Sorry. I got carried away."

"Don't be, it *is* a fine car. And you're a fine driver." He twists in the seat, so he's facing her. "I have a proposition for you."

Shit. He really *is* about to try to get in her pants. A skeeve after all.

"Oh yeah?" she says, in her most noncommittal, uninterested way. Calculating how long it will take them to get from here to Capstone. Wondering if she can delay his advances for that long. Waiting for his hand to come snaking across the vinyl for a squeeze of her thigh. Or worse.

"I want to hire you to deliver a car for me."

Surprised, then suspicious, her eyes narrow. She says, "I already have a job."

He chuckles. "I'm not trying to poach you from Capstone, Maya. This would be a one time thing. The car is a gift for my son, down at LSU. He got himself suspended from the football team at the end of last season because of his GPA. Too many parties. He's busted his ass in classes all summer, playing catch-up. I got a call from his coach today—he made his grades and the suspension is going to be lifted. I want to surprise him."

Maya whistles. "This is one hell of a surprise."

"Jesus, no, this car's for *me*," he says, and now he laughs. "I love my son, but he's not getting this baby. I'm giving him a Trans Am we restored together last summer. It was our thing. He must've put two hundred hours into it. Maybe more."

She's beginning to wish she'd turned down the ride and gone back with Isaiah. The last thing she wants is to drive halfway across the country to deliver a present to a spoiled rich brat. Even if it *is* a Trans Am. So long, nice tip.

"No thanks," she says.

He straightens in the seat, his whole body stiffening. "Aren't you even going to ask how much?"

"Nope."

They're in a place called Norcross now, out in the eastern sprawl of Atlanta, going south. The Challenger passes under an overpass and the highway name changes to Jimmy Carter Boulevard.

"Two grand," he says. "It's not even eight hours to Baton Rouge. Drive down, give him the keys, drive his old car back. Easy money."

"Sorry, no." But she's thinking about how two thousand dollars is six weeks of rent.

"Three thousand."

She scowls. "Why are you so desperate for me to do this?"

He clears his throat, shifts uncomfortably in the seat again. "Well, it's not *you* so much as the time constraint."

"That makes no sense."

"Alex—my son—doesn't know his final grades yet. Doesn't know he's back on the team. He'll get the news in a meeting first thing tomorrow morning with his coach, and I thought it would be nice if the car was there waiting when he came out."

4

"You want me to drive to Louisiana *tonight*?" she says. Almost screams. "Jesus, no!"

"Five thousand dollars," he says quietly. "And I'd be forever in your debt."

"Even if I wanted to, I couldn't. I have to work tomorrow."

"Let me take care of that. As much money as I've given your boss over the years, he owes me. I'm pretty sure I paid for at least one whole wing of his house."

Maya thinks about all the different things she could do with five grand. Pay off her credit card, for one. That comes first. The debt hangs around her neck like an albatross. Then get a new bed, maybe, replace the thrift store special she sleeps in now. Or a couch, one that doesn't hurt her butt to sit on for more than ten minutes. Or put some into savings for a rainy day. So many choices.

But most of all, the money would give her room to breathe. To for once not feel like she's drowning. Like life is something to be enjoyed, rather than a grind. She gets by, sure, but more often than not dinner is beans and rice or spaghetti because they cost the least.

"If you leave in the next couple of hours, you can be in Baton Rouge by two or three tomorrow morning, local time. I'll reserve you a room at the Cook—it's an outstanding hotel, right there on campus—so you have a chance to catch some sleep before you drop it off."

The movie in her mind shows her settling into a luxuriously

soft bed. Chocolates on the pillow, sheets with a thread count higher than her rent. The whole nine yards. Sleeping like a baby ... then waking the next morning to find the Trans Am gone, stolen while she dreamed of hundred dollar bills falling on her like rain. Something in her belly clenches like a fist. Who would hand over the keys to a car like that to a complete stranger?

"What if something happens to it?" she asks, slowing the Challenger for the turn that will take them to the dealership.

"Don't borrow trouble, Maya. Nothing's going to happen to the car. You're a solid driver."

"I don't mean an accident. What if it breaks down, or gets stolen?"

"If it breaks down you call AAA. I'll give you a copy of my card. And who even thinks about something like a car getting jacked from a hotel like the Cook?"

"Someone who can't afford sixty thousand dollars if you decide I'm to blame." She glances over at him, hoping she hasn't gone too far.

A fierce smile makes him look predatory for a moment, like maybe he isn't the nice guy he's been pretending to be, and she wonders again if the rumors about him are true. "The car has LoJack installed. I can monitor its location with an app. The instant I think something's amiss—possibly even before *you* know it—I'll be on the phone with the police. LoJack claims most stolen cars take less than thirty minutes to recover. I'd be eager to see if that's the case. Make no mistake, Maya, I'll be keeping an eye on my property. I'm not stupid, and I'm not a sucker."

The ferocity seeps out of his smile and what's left is more the *let's be best friends* variety he showed back at the house. "But nothing's going to happen," he continues. "Everything will be fine, and this time tomorrow you'll have a nice payday to spend."

They're coming up on the dealership, the big blue and white CAPSTONE CLASSICS sign looming over the modern glass building and lot full of vintage hot rods and sports cars. She pulls into one of the spots in front of the showroom. The sales manager is inside, sucking up to a potential customer. She can practically hear his obsequious wheedling from here.

There's one more thing to address with Moretti before she accepts. Before she can be *sure*, because this offer sounds too good to be true. Her father didn't raise a fool. She knows what powerful men are like, how they think.

"Is this on the up and up?" she asks in a low voice. She stares straight ahead, not wanting to make eye contact. Hoping he understands what she's getting at, so she doesn't have to spell it out in crass terms. "Tell me the truth. You're not looking for anything else from me but a delivery?"

"Look at me, Maya."

She turns. Her face is burning, but her jaw is set and she holds his gaze. Her hands squeeze into fists in case he's about to try something.

"I'm old enough to be your father," he says gently. There's no hint of whatever raised that feral grin moments ago. "I don't have an ulterior motive, and I'm not offering so much because I expect some sort of … sexual favor from you. I need this car taken to my son, and I'm trying to make it hard for you to refuse. That's all."

Maya nods once. She puts the Challenger into neutral and engages the parking brake.

She says, "Then I guess you've got yourself a driver."

5

She can't help but laugh when she wheels onto the brick drive for the second time—now in her Miata—and sees the gleaming black '77 Trans Am parked in front of the house. Moretti is leaning against the driver side door, legs out and feet crossed, checking his phone. He's changed into jeans and a polo shirt, and looks like a model from a men's fitness magazine. *Fit After Fifty: How to Look Your Best.* The westering sun hangs low in the dusky sky and paints everything in soft orange, making the gold Screaming Chicken on the hood appear aflame. Moretti waves her under the *porte cochère.*

"Well? What do you think?" he asks as she's getting her travel backpack from the trunk of her car. Like a little boy, seeking approval from a parent.

She whistles. "*Cherry.* But if you expect me to do this, you better not even *consider* calling me the Bandit."

His brown eyes twinkle with amusement. "You continue to surprise, Maya Sanchez. *Smokey and The Bandit* is, what, twenty years older than you are?"

"Classics are timeless." She shrugs. "Thank my father for passing on a love of old movies."

Affecting a mock serious look, he says, "You know, now that I think about it, you *do* have a long way to go ... and a short time to get there."

Maya rolls her eyes. Dads and their jokes are the same everywhere.

He opens the trunk and she stows her backpack, then pulls

the spare out for a closer examination. It's a space saver. Not a full-size tire, but good enough to get her to a service station if she has a flat. The jack is clean and unused. She circles the car, squatting next to each tire to check the tread and rim. The radials look like they just rolled out of the factory. She nods approvingly. "Mind starting it?"

Moretti gets behind the wheel and the Trans Am wakes with a growl. He revs it a couple of times, the aggressive roar echoing back at her from the house. At the front of the car she pops the hood. Everything underneath gleams.

"Nice," she murmurs. All the belts move smoothly, no rubbing or squeals. From the fan comes only the sound of moving air. The distributor and battery wiring harnesses are secure, the radiator cap snug. Each hose is clamped properly and brand new. The hood slams shut with a satisfying *thunk*.

"Thanks," she mouths, and mimics turning a key. Moretti shuts the engine off and gets out, looking pensively at her.

The body of the Trans Am is pristine all the way around, with no dings or scratches she can see, and she runs a hand over one of the quarter panels. There's the slightest difference in color between it and the door next to it, so subtle that only someone who spends her days detailing cars would even notice. She doesn't mention it. No one likes to have the flaws in their work pointed out.

"All good?" he says.

"Almost."

She drops to the bricks and wriggles partway under the chassis for a look at the undercarriage. From the corner of her eye she sees Moretti stepping away from the car, and when she pushes out he's frowning down at her, his arms crossed.

"Looking for something?" he asks, almost sneers.

"Leaks, mainly. Oil, gas, radiator. Anything that might cause me a problem on the road. Is something wrong?"

"Just never seen an examination this detailed." He sniffs, plucks at a piece of lint on his shirt. "Wanted to clear the air."

"What do you think I'm looking for?"

She knows what he's asking, because it's been at the forefront of her thoughts since he dropped her off at Capstone. Only one thing makes sense when a rich stranger offers you five grand to drive a car for a few hours: that there's more to it than what it seems. The job within the job. It's just a matter of finding out what it is. She's already established it isn't sex—so he said—which really only leaves one other option.

"I know the things they call me behind my back, how they say I make my money." Moretti barks a peal of humorless laughter. The air feels about ten degrees warmer all of a sudden. "I've been around the block a time or two. Enough to learn how the *jabronis* talk when someone with an Italian name is successful. I'm not a mafia don, Maya, or mobbed up, or a made man. My life is pretty boring. My grandparents came to America to escape Mussolini's regime when my father was just a baby, and my mother is from Illinois."

Maya wishes the ground would open up and swallow her.

He gives her an apprising look. "Surely you understand people jumping to conclusions about you based on your name or how you look."

In her head, she hears the taunts of the upper class white kids from her suburban high school. Calling her *wetback*, telling her to *go back to Meh-hee-co* … despite the fact that she'd grown up with them all right there in Marietta.

He says, "You've watched too many movies. If I wanted to ship drugs to Louisiana I'd use FedEx as my mule, not you. But I *don't* want to ship drugs, because that's not what I do. I make my money honestly, whether you or anyone believes it or not. Understood?"

Her cheeks feel like they're on fire, but she doesn't look away. "Understood."

"Are we good?"

She nods.

"Alright, then."

They swap keys, and he texts her the addresses for the LSU dorms and the Cook. She enters the hotel into her map.

"Right at eight hours, just like you said." She still stings, still feels awkward from being called out. "Not so bad. I ought to be there no later than two thirty, with the time change. Maybe a little earlier if I hustle and traffic's light. Plenty of time to catch some shuteye."

"Room's reserved in your name, prepaid." He gets his AAA card from his wallet for her to take a picture, and texts both his number and his son's. "Call or text me if you need anything or have any trouble. Whatever the time. Don't worry about waking me."

Maya drops her phone into her purse and gets into the Trans Am. The bucket seat is as soft as an easy chair. Perfect. She starts the engine and checks the tachometer, oil pressure, and temperature gauges. All look good. Wipers and horn, check. She directs him around the car to verify the lights and blinkers function properly. The last thing she wants is to get pulled over in rural Alabama or Mississippi in the middle of the night because of a burned-out taillight. Everyone knows how *those* stories end.

"The paperwork is in the glove box," Moretti says, like he's reading her mind. "A car like this is like a magnet to some cops."

"Thanks," she says. Time to get the show on the road. "That it?"

"I'll move your car around to the back if you don't object," he says. "The garage is safer."

She thinks about the spiked fence surrounding the property and wonders if the garage has armed guards and a battery of guided missiles. "Sure."

He opens his wallet and thumbs through the bills, counting out four fifties. After a moment of thought, he adds two more and hands her the money. "For gas," he says. "She's a drinker. Probably thirteen miles to a gallon on her best day. Whatever's left over is yours. Get something to eat."

She tucks the cash into the side pocket of her handbag, next to the pepper spray.

"You want part of the payment now? For the road?" he asks.

She shakes her head. Too easy for something to happen to it. "I'm good."

"Drive safely, Maya," he says. "And thank you for this. I won't forget it."

"Thanks," she says, "and I'm sorry for the ... misunderstanding. Really."

He slaps the roof and steps back. As she pulls onto the road she raises a hand to wave, but he's already turned to go inside.

6

Maya stifles a yawn, pressing a fist to her mouth. Her eyes burn. The hum of the radials on the pavement is a gentle lullaby, luring her toward sleep. She shakes her head and cracks the window to get some fresh air moving through the car. Wake herself up a little. The swirling breeze carries the tang of salt from the Gulf of Mexico, six or seven miles to the south. She checks her phone. The map says another ninety minutes to the hotel. Somehow it feels like both an instant and an eternity.

By the time she had crossed into Alabama it was fully dark, the velvet sky an indigo twinkling blanket. The parts of the cotton state revealed in the headlights had been a vast void, never-ending fields intermittently interrupted by small towns and burgs. She had taken a break in Auburn, for a fill up and greasy fast food burger. Somewhere in the middle of the nothingness, between Montgomery and Mobile, she had stopped at a travel center for more gas and to squeegee dead bugs—the things were practically a plague through the agricultural belt —off the windshield. Now, as she's approaching the Louisiana border, the boredom and long day are starting to catch up with her. She's ready for a hot shower and soft bed.

Mississippi has been flat and bland, littered with casino and resort signs. The towns have exotic names like Escatawpa and Pascagoula and Picayune. Because the Trans Am's radio is original and therefore has no Bluetooth, she can't listen to her own music or a podcast. All she's been able to find on the dial is country music, holy rollers, and countless talk shows ranting about *the Socialist agenda.* Just as well, she supposes, because there's no USB to plug a charger into and the last thing she wants or needs is to run down the battery on her phone in the middle of nowhere.

Lightning flickers in towering thunderheads out over the dark waters of the Gulf. The storm system has followed her across the state, first faint and distant, now much closer, as though it's tracking her. She's at the western edge of a place called Diamondhead—the name sounds to her like somewhere rich people live—when from the passenger seat her cell sounds off. The series of discordant chimes fills the car and startles her wide awake. Thinking of the lightning, and the numerous tornadoes and hurricanes and derechos that seem to hammer this part of the country year-round, she picks it up for a look at the notification that's popped up. Not a weather warning, but an AMBER alert. She dismisses it.

Civilization has fallen away, and she's virtually alone on the straight road. The land here is low and wet, a sure sign that she's nearing the bayous of Louisiana. A bridge carries the car over a river that winds through the countryside like a black snake, and on the other side the ground is higher, grassy fields again.

She's coming to an exit. The fuel gauge has edged down to just under a quarter of a tank. Not critical, not yet, but she needs to refill soon. Besides, the energy drink from the last pit stop has made its way through her and she needs to pee. There's a blue service sign at the ramp descending to the crossroad, but it only has one logo, for—naturally—another casino and resort, in a place called Bay St. Louis. A dim part of her remembers hearing somewhere that all the casinos in the state have to be on the water, which down here means the Gulf. All the signs make sense. But that's miles out of the way. No thanks. She can stop at the next exit. The map app says there's one more before she crosses into Louisiana. Worst case, Slidell is only another ten miles over the border. It's a large enough city that she's heard of it, which means plenty of options despite the hour. Even with the terrible gas mileage, that shouldn't be a problem.

As the Trans Am advances toward the overpass she notices strobing blue lights on the crossing highway, moving fast. She lets off the gas for a look. Now she hears the wail of the sirens, shrill and hysterical, as a pair of police cars race southbound toward the coast. Probably something to do with the AMBER alert. High excitement for the most rural part of a rural state.

The flashing lights diminish in the rearview mirror, and she's alone again except for a pair of tiny red taillights far ahead. The grass yields to forest, tall pines that edge right up to the shoulder. In the median, smaller trees and heavy undergrowth rise, until the two-lane strip of asphalt is more like a tunnel, magnifying the feeling of isolation. Of the opposing traffic, all that's visible are sporadic glimpses of oncoming headlights through the foliage. She checks the map. Four miles to the final exit, then she'll be in Louisiana.

The headlights reflect off a service sign on the side of the interstate announcing REST AREA NEXT EXIT in stenciled white letters on a utilitarian blue background. Just reading the words seems to increase the pressure on her bladder tenfold, and she depresses the accelerator. A few minutes later there's a second sign. An exit lane peels away to the right. She takes it. Maybe there will be a gas station nearby, too, even though there wasn't any mention on either sign. Just the rest area and several casino restaurants.

At the bottom of the off-ramp another sign directs her to go left, and she passes under the interstate. On the far side, a roadblock has been set up in the northbound lanes, just past the on-ramp to I-10. A short line of cars waits to get through. She hopes the delay isn't long, since she'll have to sit through it on the way back. A quarter-mile past the roadblock is a traffic signal, and a dual-purpose billboard advertising the welcome center and a science museum for kids instructs her to TURN HERE. Diagonally over the science museum logo is the word CLOSED, in bright red letters.

Maya signals and takes the turn.

7

The road follows a sweeping arc through the darkness for more than a quarter mile. She passes the entrance to the science museum, which is blocked by an orange and white barricade bearing a sign about renovations. The pavement curves around to the right until it enters a phalanx of trees so evenly spaced they have to have been planted. According to the map, it continues in a half-mile loop around the welcome center, with parking lots on either side of the building. Sure enough, just ahead the road forks, and the headlights reveal a marker at the split directing buses, trucks, and RVs to the left and cars to keep straight. Underneath, a sign admonishes NO OVERNIGHT PARKING.

She follows the arrow for cars and enters a long empty lot with a row of parking spaces on either side. The building is a low, brick thing, barely discernible through trees and shrubs. Three sodium vapor streetlights do little to dispel the darkness, which clings to the area like a shroud. She pulls to the curb directly underneath one and looks around for signs of life. Nothing. Tension twists her gut. She considers backing out and returning to the interstate. Just nope out of here and haul ass over to Slidell. It's not that far. Then she remembers the roadblock, and the handful of waiting cars. God only knows how long it will take to get through that, and she *really* needs to pee. The place appears empty. She has her pepper spray. What are the chances there's a psycho lurking at an empty rest stop in the boonies of Mississippi at one in the morning?

She grabs her handbag and climbs out of the Trans Am and locks the door. The air is ripe with the sweet scent of magnolia blooms. Crickets and frogs perform a raucous symphony with no conductor, and from somewhere close comes the distinctive clink and clank of a halyard against a flagpole. She jams the keys into her back pocket and carries the pepper spray at the ready, flip-top back, thumb on the depressor. The small canister feels inconsequential in her hand, but it promises to deliver twenty-five shots of liquid hell. Enough for a whole gang of wannabe rapists, should the need arise. The handbag goes over her shoulder to free up her other hand for the phone and quick access to 911. Maya follows the widest of the concrete paths into the trees and bushes, scanning constantly for anything out of the ordinary, anything threatening.

There are actually two buildings, it turns out. The larger one, directly ahead, is the welcome center proper, surrounded by a covered walkway supported by white columns. Small canopy lights along its length weep weak yellow teardrops down the bricks. To the right, at the end of another unlighted path, the second structure is open on either end. Brightly colored vending machines line one wall, and a mural of state attractions covers the other. She frowns. This place has to have been designed by a man. Who else would put so many dark walkways through trees, without a concern for what might lurk among them?

She makes it to the welcome center unscathed and finds the front door locked. A plaque mounted on the bricks informs her the hours are eight to five. Great. Inside is nothing but more darkness, save the soft green glow of an exit sign over the door on the far side. Maybe she should just squat by one of the bushes and let loose, security cameras be damned.

Maya turns to go, and spots a white metal RESTROOMS sign hanging from a pair of chains at the end of the promenade. Perfect. She hurries down, resisting the urge to hold her crotch like a three-year-old about to wet herself, teeth gritted, thinking about how much worse the pressure seems to be the closer you get to the toilet. It feels like she's on a stage, walking through spotlights before an unseen audience.

The ladies' room is clean and well-lighted, with pale blue tile walls and a checkerboard floor. It smells of Lysol and hand soap. An exhaust fan whines and rattles overhead. The steel bolt on the stall door engages with a satisfying *thock* that makes her feel safer, even though the logical part of her knows one well-placed kick would splinter the flimsy panel. She sets the pepper spray on the toilet paper dispenser, which holds two rolls nearly large enough to serve as tires for the Trans Am, and hangs her handbag from a hook on the inside of the stall door. The seat is cold despite the heat of the night.

She catches up on her texts while she does her business. Maybe she should send Moretti a quick message, something along the lines of *hey, just about to cross into LA, everythings good.* Then again, maybe not. It's after two in the morning in Atlanta, and even though he said she could text anytime, the thought of waking him up to basically say *nothing's wrong* doesn't feel like the right thing to do.

The AMBER alert is still showing in the list of notifications, and she brings it back up. It's a string of informational facts, barely composed into sentences. Caucasian girl, 13. Abducted after midnight, Bay St. Louis. Caucasian male assailant, mid-thirties, medium build, no facial hair. Red Jeep Cherokee with Kentucky plates. Call this number if you see anything. Poor kid. Definitely has to be the reason for the roadblock. Probably a family thing. They almost always are. She deletes the notification finishes up.

The industrial-strength toilet flushes with a mighty *whoosh* that sounds like a jet engine, so powerful it creates a cool, moist breeze she feels on her arms. Lovely. She moves her things to the counter by the sinks. Thrusts each arm under the running water up to the elbow to rinse off whatever foulness has misted her, then soaps and washes her hands before splashing her face as a pick-me-up. The automated dispenser on the wall hums and spits out brown paper towels that feel like sandpaper.

When she pulls the door open the hot air is a furnace blast

and she grimaces. Clouds of flying things thump and bump idiotically against the canopy lights, occasionally dive-bombing her. She squeezes the pepper spray so tightly her hand hurts. Back at the front door of the welcome center, her eyes go to the other building. A jolt of caffeine would help. It's not even a hundred feet from here. Still no sign of any other people. The place is deserted. Thirty seconds. That's all she needs.

She crosses the pool of darkness quickly, watching the shadows in case one of them is something more. There are five machines in a row: two Coke, two Pepsi, one snack. She checks over her shoulder to make sure no one's creeping up on her, then sticks her phone into the side pocket of her handbag and roots around for money while she checks her options. One of the Pepsi machines has an energy drink that claims to be even stronger than coffee. Perfect. She finds a dollar and tucks her handbag under her arm to smooth the bill before feeding it into the validator. The act is awkward because there's no way the pepper spray is leaving her hand. She's seen enough movies.

The bill is rejected. Of course.

She flips it around and tries the other end first, only to have it vomited back out.

That's when a man's voice, right behind her, says, "Technology can be a fickle mistress, can't she?"

8

Maya yips in surprise and whirls, raising the hand with the pepper spray automatically. Her heart hammers, about to shatter her ribs. Some winged thing in her belly flits and flaps, banging around like one of the moths under the lights outside. The handbag slips from beneath her arm, bursting open when it hits the concrete. Its contents scatter in every direction.

"What the hell?" she barks.

The man is young, close to her age, with unkempt greasy brown hair and a scraggly beard. Beady blue eyes stare holes through her. Crazy eyes. He looks like that psycho Charles Manson guy from the Tarantino movie. Her thumb wants to depress the trigger, wants to send a jet of liquid fire into those creeper peepers. Maybe two. One for the right, one for the left. That would leave her twenty-three.

"Sorry, dude," he says, lifting his hands in the universal *whoa* gesture. "I didn't mean to scare you."

He steps closer. She recoils, her hip smacking into the convex front of the Pepsi machine, which dimples in and pops back out with a smart *tock*!

"Let me help," he says, and drops to his knees. He begins scraping together the mishmash of makeup, bills, coins, tampons.

"Please don't," she says. Her voice is shaky, and she hates the weakness in it. "I've got it."

His shaggy head tilts up and he gawps up at her. Takes in the canister of pepper spray aimed at his face. Her defensive posture,

27

the terror writ large across her face. Up close, she realizes his eyes aren't so much beady as they are red and squinted, and there's a miasma of skunky weed stank clinging to him. It's amazing she didn't smell him coming. As she tries to steady her breath and calm her racing heartbeat, she can practically see the wheels turning in his smoky mental haze as he susses out the bigger picture.

Then his bloodshot eyes go comically wide and his mouth falls open. He scrabbles backward across the concrete, almost to the entryway. "Oh, shit, man, I don't know what I was thinking, coming up on you like that. I was just trying to make a joke. My name's Brandon. I'm not a bad dude. I'm sorry. *Really*."

"It's okay," she says, but doesn't take her eyes off him. Doesn't lower the pepper spray. Of course he wasn't thinking. He's a man, and men don't have to worry about coming into places like this alone.

Slowly, he stands. "Do you want me to wait in my car until you're finished?"

She shakes her head. The *last* thing she wants is for him to be out there, out of her sight in the dark. "Can you just stay right there?"

"Absolutely. Jesus, I feel like such a shit-for-brains." A grin spreads across his face. "My girlfriend tells me I'm the biggest airhead she's ever known. She's going to give me hell when I tell her about this."

"Don't sweat it." Maya doesn't return the smile. She kneels and scoops things into her open purse one-handed, pepper spray ready. All she wants is to get the hell out of here, away from this guy. She sees nothing else on the floor and rises to her feet. "Do you mind giving me some room to get by?"

"Sure." He steps over to the wall with the mural and leans with his back against it. "Aren't you going to get your drink?"

"I'm good." As if falling asleep at the wheel is still a concern. Keeping to the opposite wall, she scurries out. Acting like a scared little mouse leaves a bad taste in her mouth, but him saying he's *not a bad dude* doesn't mean jack. People lie.

The Trans Am seems to be a half-mile away through nearly tangible darkness. She jogs the walkway, checking over her shoulder every few steps. Before she loses sight of him through the trees and shrubs, Brandon is still standing with his back to the wall, eyes on the floor.

She's running by the time she reaches the parking lot and slaps the purse on the roof of the car. Her hand is shaking so much from the adrenaline that it takes her three tries to get the key into the lock. Finally, it slides home and she flings the door open. All she can think about is him sneaking up from behind again, grabbing her. Doing whatever. She snatches her bag from the T-top and falls into the seat, slams the door and palms the lock knob.

Maya gooses the pedal and the tires bark on the pavement. The car slews out of the parking spot in reverse, catching Brandon the headlights as he leaps and crashes through the shrubbery, sprinting toward her with lips peeled back. Barely twenty feet away, he roars something bestial, but his voice is lost in the scream of the engine when she finds first gear and tromps the gas. The car fishtails, squealing rubber, and throws curling clouds of white smoke.

9

The last she sees of Brandon is his silhouette in the rearview mirror, chasing after the Trans Am but quickly falling behind. What a freak. A giddy half giggle, half sob escapes her, and the eyes looking back at her from the mirror are wide and wild. When the single lane begins to curve to the left she lets off the gas. The car slows to a more reasonable speed. She follows the loop around the welcome center, fearful that at any moment the young man will hurtle out of the darkness like a killer from a horror movie, though logic tells her there's no way anyone could cross the grounds that quickly. Not even an Olympic sprinter.

A minute later, the loop rejoins the entry drive and she breathes a sigh of relief. Her chest hitches. Jitters still shake her hands. She signals a turn at the red light, willing herself calm while she watches the mirrors for any sign of Brandon. The metronomic click of the flasher seems very loud. After an eternity, she gets the green and pulls out onto the highway, where blue lights a quarter-mile ahead remind her there's one last tribulation before she can be back on her way. The gas needle has crept a little lower since the last time she checked. Still not critical, but she'll feel better once she fills up in Slidell.

She rummages in her purse for her phone to check the map for gas stations in case there are any closer … but comes up empty. Hot acid panic bubbles up her throat as she pulls onto the shoulder to search with both hands. It's not there. Not in the main compartment, not in the side pocket. She slides a hand over the seat in vain, growing more frantic. Leans down to search both floorboards. Checks each pocket, patting and rubbing herself like she's trying to put out a fire. It's not in any of them.

It's gone.

There's no way in hell she can finish the delivery without her phone. Not only does it have the map with directions, it has the contact information for Moretti and his son. Without those she's screwed, at least until Capstone opens in the morning and she can call for his number. But that'll be too late to deliver the car on time.

"*Damn* it!" she shouts, pounding the wheel with her fist.

Had she even put the phone in her bag when she was picking her things up? She casts her mind back to the vending area, but it's no use. The autopilot was in control then, blocking out everything except for the need to get away from the strange man.

And now she knows she has to go back.

She roars with unbridled rage, beats her hands on the wheel. Wants to get out of the stupid car and walk away. It's insured. Moretti went out of his way to tell her that again and again. Just mosey herself down to the roadblock and ask the cops to borrow a phone. Call her father. He'd drop everything and come right away for the chance to lecture her like a teenager too stupid to survive on her own because it's the only thing he knows how to do. But giving up isn't in her nature. She got herself into this, she can get herself out. Deep inhale through the nose, slow exhale out the mouth.

A new thought occurs. What if Brandon had seen her phone after she left? Maybe that's why he was chasing after her, trying to be a Good Samaritan and not the psycho she imagined him to be. To live up to his proclamation that he's *not a bad dude*.

Then again, what if he is?

"If you don't go back and look, you're boned," she tells the panicky woman looking back at her from the mirror. "You've got the pepper spray. You can do this."

She checks for traffic and pulls a U-turn across all four lanes.

The parking lot seems somehow darker now, and there are no vehicles or people to be seen. Had Brandon even been in a car? She can't remember seeing one in the lot, but she had been ... distracted. Surely he had. *Surely.* But where had he gone? No one was behind her at the light. She would have seen them, because she was watching. Could he have pulled out while she was looking for her phone?

Sudden tears of fear and frustration burn her eyes.

"Knock that crap off, Sanchez," she says, swiping at them with the back of her hand.

She angles the Trans Am toward the curb, directing the headlights along the pathway where she came out, in case the phone had bounced out of her bag when she was running. It might be laying out there right now, waiting to be found. She engages the high beams and the garden explodes with light. Trees and bushes stand out in sharp relief.

"That's what I'm talking about," she murmurs. Of Brandon there is no sign.

Holding the pepper spray like a pistol before her, she climbs out of the car, wrinkling her nose at the lingering odor of burned rubber. Lightning flashes to the south, followed by a rumble of thunder a few seconds later. Joy.

"Hello? Brandon?"

There's no response.

Maya works her way slowly up the concrete path, looking for the phone and calling his name. The high beams do a remarkable job, bathing the area in clean white light, but she sees neither man nor device. Soon she's back at the pavilion. No sign of either inside, just the smell of marijuana so faint it might be her imagination. She drops onto all fours to check under the vending machines in case it slid under one, and crawls the length of the building, acutely aware of the way her butt is pointed right at the entryway. Like a target for a creep.

Still nothing.

She blinks back fresh tears. How can everything have gone so wrong so fast? All she wanted was to pee and get a drink, and now where is she? Stuck in the middle of nowhere in the dead of night, without knowing how to get where she needs to go and no easy way of reaching out for help. For what? Some money. Suddenly, five thousand dollars doesn't sound like enough to deal with all this. *Fifty* thousand doesn't.

Maya stands and traces her steps back to the Trans Am, in hopes that a second look will turn up the missing phone. The headlights are blinding, and she shields her eyes to search the terrain. But it's all in vain. Her phone is nowhere to be seen, the parking lot still empty. Another rumble of thunder rolls in from the direction of the Gulf. Leaves rustle, stirred by a breeze headed toward the water as though being pulled out to sea.

She has no choice but to keep going. There's no point in sitting here all night, waiting to see if Brandon will return. She doesn't know if he even *saw* the cell, much less has it in his possession. He could be ten miles from here by now, puttering along without a care in the world. Oblivious.

Interstate signs will get her to Baton Rouge. Once there, she can find a phone and start making calls. First to the hotel, for directions. They probably even have contact information for Moretti, since he booked the room in his name.

This can work. It has to.

Maya gets back into the Trans Am.

10

The two officers manning the roadblock look like caricatures, a pair of roided up gym rats with shaved heads and square jaws and tactical gear attached all over their blue uniforms like flair. Tweedledee and Tweedledum. Both are white, with tree trunk necks and arms so thick they poke out like those on a Stretch Armstrong doll. Older than her, maybe a little north of thirty. They watch each approaching vehicle with hooded eyes, standing on either side of the lane they've left open. The gauntlet. It's almost her turn. She fishes her license out of her purse.

While the officer on the left—Tweedledee—bends to talk to the driver of the Toyota ahead, Tweedledum shines a light into the car, aiming the beam at each of the four teen occupants. The driver proffers his license for examination. Tweedledee checks to make sure the driver's face matches the photo. Hands it back and waves them on. The Toyota pulls away. To Maya, he makes a *come here* gesture. She inches forward and lowers the window, tries out a smile. It feels forced. The last few minutes have been too distressing. Her mind threatens to gallop away like a spooked horse.

"Well, *hello* there," Tweedledee says, leaning in so close she can smell the garlic from his last meal. He rests a tanned and waxed arm on the sill of the door and runs his tongue over his teeth. "Where we headed tonight?"

"Baton Rouge," she says, eyes on the taillights as they dwindle to pinpoints. Still on high alert. Her legs jitter with nervous energy. She pulls in a deep breath. Got to hold it together before she finds a couple of bored assholes on her case.

"You a student there?"

"Just visiting." Light from Tweedledum's flashlight crawls across the front of her shirt and drops to her lap, where it pauses for a moment before continuing down her legs. She wishes for a pair of coveralls from work and not the fitted tee and tight jeans she'd worn in hopes of a better tip. Her hand tightens on the wheel.

"Mind showing me your license, registration, and proof of insurance?"

It doesn't escape her notice that he hadn't asked the kid in the last car for so much, but that's to be expected in this part of the country. She won't be surprised if he wants her to produce a green card. This is a block she's been around a time or two before. Handing over her driver license, she says, "The others are in the glove box."

She reaches over in a slow and deliberate *don't shoot me* movement and twists the latch, absurdly picturing in her head a brick of cocaine tumbling out when the door drops open. That would be the perfect end to all this, to discover that Moretti is using her to mule his product despite the agitated assurances of being on the up-and-up. In the movies, the guys who claim to be legitimate businessmen never are, are they? Cuffed in the back of a squad car at the mercy of these two would be a perfect end to this shit show. She can only imagine the things they would suggest she do to resolve her problem.

But of course no drugs fall out. The paperwork is the only thing in the compartment, crisp and new. When she turns to hand it over the officer's eyes have drifted to her chest, where the shirt pulled tight during her twist. Her face grows hot. Why is she embarrassed, when he's the one who should be? As Tweedledee studies the documents, Tweedledum plays his light on the passenger seat, sliding the beam over her bag and down into the foot well before moving to the back.

"This your daddy's car?" Tweedledee says. The breeze is

picking up and the papers rattle between his fingers, trying to fly away.

"No. I'm just driving it to LSU for Mr. Moretti." Another deep breath, nice and slow. "It's a gift for his son."

"I see," he says, not sounding like he does at all.

She wonders if the officers can track down a number for Moretti. Maybe radio to have dispatch look it up while she waits. No. Not after the way the two of them have been eyeballing her, like they're taking a few mental snapshots for the old spank bank. There's only one car behind her. Once it's gone she'll be all alone with these guys. It's far too easy to picture the awful ways *that* scenario could play out. Absolutely not.

"We're out here looking for a missing thirteen-year-old girl named Abby Dunn, Miz Sanchez. Maybe you saw the AMBER alert?"

"I did."

Nodding, he continues. "I can provide a few more details. She was wearing green jean shorts and a yellow t-shirt, and the man that took her had on black jeans and a blue or black pullover. Clean-shaven white male in his mid-thirties, dark hair, and a thirteen-year-old blonde girl," the cop says. "You see anybody like that tonight? Maybe a red Cherokee?"

Spider lightning races across the night sky behind him, forking again and again. It illuminates towering clouds that seethe like boiling water.

"No, sorry," she tells him, shaking her head. "I just pulled off the interstate a few minutes ago for a quick bathroom break at the welcome center."

He nods thoughtfully, and returns the paperwork. Thunder booms like a cannon and he jumps, fumbles and nearly drops his flashlight. Throws a baleful glance over his shoulder like he thinks he can intimidate Mother Nature with a cop look. "Well, thank you for your time, Miz Sanchez. You have a safe drive to Baton Rouge. Keep an eye on the weather. Looks like it's going to get ugly."

His eyes make one last lingering pass over her breasts, then he steps back and waves her on before turning his attention to the next car.

11

Maya turns onto the I-10 westbound on-ramp, feeling naked and alone without a phone to highlight the route. How did people survive before they were invented? She quickly brings the Trans Am up to speed and merges onto the empty road. Maybe she can find a truck stop or travel center in Slidell and buy a cheap handheld GPS. Don't they usually put places like that in the first real town across a state line? At least with a GPS she can get exact directions to the Cook Hotel. Moretti might even offer to reimburse her for it, and if not, the peace of mind will be worth the hit to her credit card. What's a couple of hundred bucks compared to that?

The interstate begins to ascend. The grassy median first narrows, then transitions to a low concrete barrier dividing the opposing pairs of lanes. Guard rails sprout on either side, and the radials *babump* over an expansion joint as the asphalt gives way to elevated concrete. The road becomes a bridge that continues to rise in a gentle swell. Soon the car is twenty feet above the tree tops.

It occurs to Maya then that Tweedledee and Tweedledum could have helped her find her phone, if she'd been thinking, rather than freaking out. Can *still* help her find her phone, if she goes back. All she has to do is give them her phone number and return to the welcome center. They call the number, the phone rings and lights up, and boom. Problem solved. Assuming Brandon didn't pick it up and leave with it, for whatever reason seemed to make sense at the time to his weed-infused brain.

But first, gas.

She checks the fuel level. The needle hovers a hair above an eighth of a tank. Some quick math tells her that's enough for probably thirty more miles. Forty tops. Plenty to reach Slidell.

Still, it looks so *low*. And if the gauge is off, even by a little...

Best not to think about that. There's nothing to do now but push on.

A bolt of lighting turns the night into day, revealing a broad river fifty or sixty feet below, meandering through densely wooded wetlands. A raindrop splats on the windshield, then a couple more, the first volley from the storm. The oncoming headlights of a tractor-trailer show fat droplets streaking to the pavement like meteors before the truck whooshes past. She thumbs the wiper switch on and off, a single swipe to flick the water away. Thunder and wind rock the Trans Am as she reaches the pinnacle, sending her heart into overdrive for an instant. Visions of getting shoved over the side by the storm and plummeting like a stone into the bayou fill her mind. Gators and snakes and bears and who knows what down there, waiting for a tasty morsel to drop like manna from heaven. Thankfully, the road is beginning to return to earth. Swampland rises to greet her. WELCOME TO LOUISIANA, a blue roadside sign proclaims in white letters arcing over a *fleur de lis*.

Rain begins to pepper down, and she switches the wipers to the lowest setting. Thin steam rises from the asphalt, creating phantoms in the headlight beams that get whisked away by the wind an instant after they form. The storm is almost on top of her. On either side of the road, trees rock and sway. Leaves fly like green insects. There's a billboard for a place called PeePaw's Gas and Snaks, big red bubble letters over a cartoon geezer in overalls and a straw hat. The old man's *aw, shucks* grin shows straight white teeth clamped on a corncob pipe. The most important words are at the bottom: NEXT EXIT LEFT.

Thank God! She can fill up the tank, then return to the roadblock to ask for help locating her phone. It's a long shot, for sure, and she doesn't really want either of them to have her number. Not after the way they were looking at her. But if it gets her cell back then she can deal with any fallout. Numbers can be blocked or changed. Best of all, if things go her way and she finds it quickly, the round trip will only set her back a half hour, tops. She can still make it to the hotel with plenty of time to get some rest before she has to—

The Trans Am shudders and the wheel begins to shimmy in her hands. Something in the engine knocks *tat tat tat*. The V-8 sounds suddenly labored, struggling to perform but unable to, and the accelerator goes soft and sluggish. She lifts her foot off the pedal and the car immediately begins to slow.

Biting back the panic that wants to fill her like a black tide, she glances down at the fuel gauge. It still shows an eighth of a tank. The car isn't acting like one that's running out of gas, anyway. There's no hitch, no dying gasp for a sip of gasoline. At least not yet. The oil pressure is normal. Her gaze falls on the temperature dial. The needle is kissing-close to the red line marked 260.

As she looks on, it edges higher.

"Are you freaking kidding me?" she shouts. Can *anything* go right? She turns the air conditioning off and switches the heater on full blast to pull heat away from the engine. Her speed has dropped to sixty miles an hour.

A blue service marker announcing GAS appears in the headlight beams. Below it is a brown sign that tells her she's ENTERING HONEY ISLAND SWAMP.

Fifty miles an hour.

Streamers of steam start to slip from beneath the hood. The needle holds steady, just touching the red line.

Forty.

She can see the exit ahead, splitting away to vanish into the darkness.

Thirty.

A bolt of lightning spears into the forest on her left. An instant later, a cannonade of thunder ruptures the night. The boiling skies open up and torrents of rain begin to fall, drumming on the T-top so hard she can no longer hear the laboring engine. She thumbs the wipers up to high.

"Come on, baby," Maya says, rubbing her hand on the wheel. Sweat beads on her forehead from the hot air blasting in her face. "Just a little more. Get you fixed right up."

Twenty.

Steam billows from under the hood in clouds. Between it and the rain, she can barely see the road. The temperature needle has slipped into the red, kissing the line from the other side. Maya takes the exit and the Trans Am descends into the lowlands. There's a stop sign at the bottom but no traffic in sight, so she downshifts and idles through a wide left turn onto the two-lane road without stopping. The tires send sheets of dirty rainwater into the grass growing up to the edge of the asphalt.

"Please," she murmurs, trying to get more from the vehicle while staying just this side of permanent engine damage.

Lightning and thunder explode directly overhead. She screams in fury. A roiling stream races alongside her, faster than the flagging car. The car passes under the interstate, and for a moment all is quiet within except for her ragged breathing and the rattling engine as it fights to keep them in motion. Coming out the other side, Maya gets her first look at Peepaw's Gas and Snaks through the slapping wipers.

It's cloaked in darkness, closed for the night.

12

She coasts into the small parking lot in front of the old store, bringing the Trans Am to a stop beside a gas pump so outdated it still has numeric rollers for calculating the total, like an odometer. Tears of discouragement sting her eyes. Why did she ever agree to take this godforsaken job?

Neon signs for Budweiser and Natty Light and some brand called Abita she's never heard of glow in the glass windows of the old cinderblock building, casting a dim scatter of color onto the pavement. A fluorescent tube at the rear of the store flickers and blinks. No one is inside the place, of course. Peepaw has probably been in bed since eight o'clock. A scream tears itself loose, harsh and animalistic, so filled with power and fury it makes her throat ache.

But she feels the tiniest bit better.

She can't just sit here and wait, all alone with her thoughts. She has to do *something*, storm or no storm. Inaction will drive her crazy. She isn't wired that way. Maybe she can get the car running again, long enough to get it to a real repair shop. Maybe. If she's lucky. If the problem is something minor and not catastrophic.

Too many maybes, too many ifs.

But a chance is a chance.

Maya blinks back her tears and gets out of the car.

Rain hammers the sheet metal roof of the canopy in a cacophonous roar. The wind is a banshee, whipping the trees and grass into a frenzy and driving spikes of chilly rain into her face. In a few seconds she's soaked. She pops the hood and raises it, grateful that the building is blocking the brunt of the weather, so that it's not ripped off the hinges. It's almost impossible to see anything in the engine compartment.

Her phone has a flashlight. She curses.

The radiator is the obvious first place to check, but it's too hot to touch. Despite the wind she can feel heat baking out at her like an ironworks furnace, smell the reek of burned coolant. The metal clicks and pops, cooling. Leaving the hood up will speed the process.

She walks to the building. The billboard had been right. There's not much inside but a few racks of chips, candy, and other snacks—or *snaks*, according to Peepaw—and coolers filled with beer and soft drinks.

She's willing to bet there's also a phone.

Part of her wants to walk out into the grass and look for a rock. Put it through a window. Force her way in. Call 911 and beg for someone to please come help her out of this mess. But she can't, because the cops in this part of the country don't take too kindly to someone with her complexion breaking into a store, even if she has the noblest of intentions. Not to mention the fact that she's driving a car that doesn't belong to her and doesn't know Moretti's number. They'd lock her up faster than green grass going through a goose, as Peepaw himself might say. And speaking of, even if Peepaw is a nice old gent and doesn't press charges over the breaking and entering, she'd have an arrest record. Future employers don't look too kindly on those, and the plan she's made for her life doesn't involve staying at Capstone, detailing cars forever. She has to figure something else out.

Maya returns to the Trans Am. The engine isn't cool, not by a long shot, but the heat has diminished enough for her to take a closer look. She sticks her head under the hood and waits for Mother Nature to provide some illumination. After a few seconds lightning strobes *pop pop pop,* and in the brilliant flashes she sees exactly what caused the car to overheat.

The radiator cap is gone. Not loose, like she expected. *Gone.*

Could the pressure from the steam have blown it off? Unlikely. The things are designed *not* to blow off, with a pressure relief valve built in to vent steam when a vehicle is close to overheating.

So what happened to it?

When she checked the cap back at Moretti's house, it had been securely in place. She remembers grabbing it, giving it a twist. Hearing the clicks. It was fine. Caps don't just suddenly fall off.

But that doesn't really matter now, does it? What matters now is that it's not here, and she needs to deal with that. A missing cap would most definitely cause an engine to run hot. If she can get some water in the radiator and find something to serve as a makeshift replacement ... she might be able to get out of this hellhole and make it to a real garage. Slidell isn't far. The plan forms even before the echo of the thunderclap has faded.

She looks around contemplatively. At one end of the building there's an aluminum downspout running from the gutter to the ground, where it elbows into knee-high weeds. Rainwater gushes from it in a flood. Maybe not the cleanest supply in the world, but it's running so fast most of the dirt and debris that can harm the engine must have surely washed away already. And there's probably a spigot somewhere around here, too, now that she thinks about it. Around back, most likely. Either way, water isn't a problem.

Somewhere deep inside her, a spark of hope ignites.

There's an aluminum garbage can next to the gas pump. She removes the lid and sets it aside. Drags the receptacle into the spill of light from the store. Rain streams down her face and she wipes it away with her shirt. Once she has the car running she can get her backpack and change into dry clothes, but right now she has something more important to do. Rooting deep in the trash, her hand brushes across smooth plastic. She pulls out a large Burger King soft drink cup.

The spark flares into the tiniest flame, a candle in a dark room.

But she can't find anything suitable to serve as a radiator cap. Most of the garbage is paper or plastic, neither of which is up to the job. Maybe if there was a towel or something, a piece of cloth she could wad and stuff in the hole, that would work. Not perfect by any measure, not even *good*, but all it has to do is hold for a few miles. Just until she can get to Slidell, where there will be—

She remembers her backpack, and the outfit she packed for the next day. There's a pair of black athletic socks in it, nice and thick and able to be rolled into a sphere the size of a tennis ball. And if those aren't enough to make a snug fit, there's a t-shirt, too. She can make this work.

The candle bursts into a raging wildfire of hope. A smile lights up her face. She snatches the keys from the ignition and rushes to the rear of the Trans Am. Jabs the key into the lock and twists it. The lid flies up as something smashes into it from beneath with a loud BANG and Maya recoils, gasping.

A shape bursts from the cramped space.

Lightning strikes nearby and lights up the whole area.

It's a girl, her eyes gone wide and rolling with terror. She wields a tire iron like a baseball bat, and at the sight of Maya snarls and leaps, swinging the weapon with every bit of her strength.

II

FRED ANDERSON

13

The seller squints against the blazing Mississippi sun reflected into his eyes from the white sand and wonders if it's possible for a person to melt. Despite dropping ever closer to the horizon, the thing seems to be losing none of its power. What scant breeze there is feels like a hot wet blanket and smells like dead fish. At least the hat and zinc and sunglasses protect his face from the worst of it. His t-shirt and swimsuit are soaked, and a greasy wet sheen coats every inch of exposed skin. The sunscreen he's reapplied faithfully every hour is no match for the rivers of sweat. Tomorrow he's going to regret spending so much time out here.

But the premium commanded by the product makes even the worst sunburn worth it.

He's sitting on a terrycloth blanket on a strip of molten beach between the Gulf of Mexico and the town of Bay St. Louis. The product is twenty yards away, lying on a wooden lounge chair in the shade of a rented umbrella. There's a whole row of them. He'd love more than anything to rent one for himself and get out of this hell, but that would put him too close to her. Close is risky. Close gets you noticed. So he roasts in the sun like a piece of meat under a broiler, waiting for his opportunity.

The secure message from the buyer had come to his prepaid smartphone yesterday, the same way they had every six weeks or so for the last two years. *Seeking white female, blonde/blue, 12-14. 150+. Can you provide?* Of course he can. A hundred and fifty large—or more—for two days' work and almost no expense?

He'd be a fool *not* to.

Early this morning, he left home in Tallahassee and drove two hours to the airport in Biloxi. His car went into the long-term garage, but he had no intention of catching a flight. He stowed his personal phone in the glove box. Plausible deniability. No way to prove he was anywhere other than the airport. Using the throwaway and a prepaid Visa, he caught a Lyft down to the public beach, dressed like one of the tourists in a garish teal swimsuit and Hard Rock t-shirt. Oakleys and a smear of zinc paste across the bridge of his nose disguised his face well enough, helping him to blend in even more, and a straw outback covered his hair. He walked east along the beach road, flip-flops slapping the pavement, to the Harrah's Casino sign, where he crossed and pushed through glass doors into blessed coolness.

It took less than ten minutes to find the right player, a chubby older man by himself at the dollar slots, feeding coins into a machine and slapping buttons with great difficulty because he was two sheets into the wind. A cloud of whiskey stink cloaked him, and he was barely able to keep his balance on the stool. Resting on the control panel near his drink was a car fob with a Jeep logo and a few keys. Taking it was as simple as dropping a fiver on the floor and nudging the guy. *Hey, buddy, I think you dropped something.* While the drunk man tried to bend over without falling, the seller scooped up the keys and walked away. It would be hours before the guy even noticed they were missing.

Five minutes later he was in the parking garage with the fob held high, pressing the unlock button. It led him to a red Cherokee, two years old. Nice and roomy. Perfect. He drove it out and stopped at the first strip mall he saw, where he used a screwdriver from his go bag to swap plates—Alabama for Kentucky—with a Ford truck parked in the next spot. By noon, he was strolling the beach in Gulfport, on the prowl for a girl who checked all the boxes on the buyer's order.

The product is all alone now. When the seller first arrived, her family had been here—parents and a younger boy he assumes is her brother—but after what appeared to be a heated argument the others left together. She's had eyes for nothing but her phone ever since. Alone and preoccupied is as good as it gets. The less cognizant she is of her surroundings, the less likely she is to notice him.

Motion from the Gulf draws his attention. There's a boy wading out of the surf, tall and gangling with a shock of curly brown hair and very white teeth. He looks about the same age as the product, smiling nervously as he tentatively approaches her and speaks. There are more teenagers out in the water where he came from, far from shore, easily missed. It's so shallow along the coast here he has no doubt they're standing and not treading, even though they're a few hundred feet out.

There had been nothing promising anywhere on the beach in Gulfport. Plenty of girls the right age for his needs, none good enough to warrant the offered price. He knows the kind of quality the buyer expects, and wouldn't waste his time with inferior items. Every girl had been too fat or too thin, too curvy or too tomboyish. This one had greasy pizza cheeks, that one had a face like a horse. Not worth his time.

After a couple of hours, he had returned to the Jeep and moved further along the coast toward New Orleans—where he would make the delivery if he found anything suitable—to a place called Pass Christian. No luck there, either. He only stayed for an hour, beginning to believe the trip was going to be fruitless. But in the next town—Bay St. Louis—he struck gold. As he was looking for a place on the sand to set up shop she walked right by him, close enough to touch.

Enchanting.

Exquisite.

Twelve or thirteen, just starting to show the first budding signs of adolescence. Cornflower blue eyes seemed to catch the sunlight and amplify it, perfectly complementing Cupid's bow lips and a heart-shaped face. Her legs were long and slim and deeply tanned, her blonde ponytail bleached almost white by the sun. A scatter of freckles across her cheeks served as a reminder of her innate childishness, but the swell of her chest under the thin cotton shirt hinted at the woman she will become.

His first thought upon seeing her was to demand more money.

The boy takes a seat on the empty chair by the girl and the two begin a dance as old as time itself. He leans toward her, hanging on her every word. She fidgets with her phone and bites her lip when he's not looking. He holds court, moving his hands theatrically, pointing to his friends out in the water. She twirls a finger in her long blonde hair and cuts her eyes away.

Finally, she stands up and strips down to her one-piece. The seller's breath catches in his throat. She may be the most flawless product he's ever seen. Though he doesn't share the predilections of the buyer's customers, when he looks at her he understands the desire. She is perfection in every way, and as she turns his direction to drop her clothes onto the chair he quickly snaps a picture with his phone and messages it to the buyer. The affirmative response is immediate.

She's worth more, he sends. *250*. A cool quarter of a million dollars. His heart is pounding. He's never tried a counteroffer before. But he's been doing this for two years, and excels at it. He always delivers, and this product is on a whole other level.

The throwaway phone vibrates. *Agreed.*

The boy and girl wade into the murky water. The seller opens the carryall and pushes aside his regular clothes so that he can get to his go bag, from which he withdraws one of the Bluetooth trackers. The black plastic rectangle is the size a pack of matches, with a range up to four hundred feet in perfect conditions. They never work as well as the advertisements claim, but he doesn't need perfection. He just needs good enough, and the device is more than adequate for that.

He rises and saunters to the edge of the parking lot, then stops and turns back as if he's forgotten something. Instead of returning to his towel, he heads straight for the chair where the product was sitting. It has been his experience that if he carries himself with confidence, like he has every right to be wherever he is, doing whatever he's doing, people ignore him. This time is no different. He straddles the lounge and takes a seat, watching the distant pair. They're still going out, facing the open water, up to their chests in the Gulf. Everyone nearby the seller is silent, and none of the other teens out there point in alarm at the interloper. No one pays him any mind at all.

Casually, he picks up the pair of green denim shorts and checks the pockets. Her phone is of no use. It's locked, and the tracker is too big to fit behind it in the case. He ignores it and focuses on a better find: a keychain with a change pouch shaped like a miniature handbag. Both keys on the ring look like housekeys. One has a plastic tag with *Gulf Rentals* stamped on it in gold letters. He can't believe his luck because he'd assumed her family would be staying in a hotel. Rental houses are the easiest places to get into at collection time, because they invariably have cheap contractor-grade locks that are so easy to pick a child could do it.

The purse has a fabric divider to separate paper money and coins, and holds only a few crumpled bills. He drops the tracker into the empty compartment and closes the clasp, then puts the keychain back in the pocket it came from. Now he can keep an eye on her with his phone, from the comfort and shade of the air-conditioned Jeep.

The seller gets up and goes to gather his things, whistling.

14

Abby Dunn waits for the walk signal and crosses the beach road, humming a Taylor Swift song. Her head is in the clouds. She's just spent the most wonderful hour with the *cutest* boy. His name is Liam and he's from Arkansas and he's fourteen and is simply. To. Die. For. Just thinking about his gorgeous face and the way it lights up whenever he smiles makes her feel fluttery in her chest, like a butterfly is loose in there. And those dimples! What she wouldn't give to kiss them! The most slay thing is that he seems to be just as interested in her as she is him. Why couldn't they have met before now? Tomorrow is her last day, and she's been informed that she has to go on some stupid swamp tour over in Louisiana with her stupid parents and her stupid little brother. A family thing. No ifs, ands, or buts.

It isn't fair.

Thank God she had refused to go to the Aquarium with them earlier. How anyone could bear to watch all those sad dolphins and seals in their tiny pools performing tricks for screaming humans is beyond her. Her parents had finally relented and told her she could stay on the beach if she promised not to leave, and to be back to the house where they were staying by eight. She feels bad about arguing with them, because it had gotten ugly. She said some not very nice things about coming to this armpit of a vacation spot, with its smelly brown water and no fun *anywhere*, even though she knows they're only here because they can't afford to go somewhere nicer, like Florida.

But if she hadn't fought, she wouldn't have met Liam.

She reaches the corner of Sycamore Road and turns inland. The sky has gone pink and orange to the west. Long shadows stretch across the street, and the first lightning bugs have started to flash. Their rental house is only a couple of blocks from the water, and so small that when the four of them are in it at the same time they're practically up each other's butts. There's not even enough room for them all to watch TV together. Not that there's anything to watch on basic cable.

Liam's friends had a cooler full of Budweiser on ice and she had drunk two. Her beer cherry popped. The first one tasted so bad she thought she was going to puke every time she took a sip, but she gritted her teeth and forced it down because she didn't want to look like a baby. Then Liam dared her to chug the second one because he said you couldn't really taste it that way, so she had ... until burning foam streamers shot out her nose and everyone laughed. She laughed too, eyes watering, but wanted to die inside from the cringe. Her head is swimming as she walks down the sidewalk toward the rental. She's not sure if it's from the guzzled beer or being near Liam.

Maybe if she apologizes to her parents for being such a b-word earlier they'll let him come with on the swamp tour tomorrow. She's willing to beg if that's what it takes, and if Liam doesn't have the money she'll happily pay his way. It can't be more than twenty dollars, can it? She has more than that left from the money she saved up. Even if it was free it would be too much, as far as she's concerned. The only thing that could make two hours in a boat in a mosquito-infested sauna full of alligators *remotely* bearable is the thought of Liam sitting beside her, so close their legs touch. Holding hands. She feels a flush on her cheeks.

What if he tries to kiss her?

He might, if they get a chance to be alone. And if he does, she might faint dead away. Suddenly the evening feels a lot warmer, the butterfly in her chest much more active.

Just as she reaches the house her phone buzzes. It's a text from Liam. *miss u already lol.*

Abby giggles and runs up the driveway to the front door, oblivious of the red Cherokee turning off the beach road two blocks back.

15

The seller shifts uncomfortably on the seat. His legs feel like they're on fire inside his jeans, but he doesn't have a choice. He needs pockets, because he can't carry his go bag for this part of the trip. Both hands have to be free. The Jeep cruises slowly down Sycamore Road, past the house where the product is staying. The windows are dark, have been dark each of the three times he passed in the last hour. They're all asleep in there, he thinks. The tracking app is picking up a good signal, and his best guess based on the distance it reports is that she's in the rear of the house. Ideal, because there's an alley back there splitting the block.

After doing recon on the neighborhood once the product had gone inside, he used an app on his throwaway to reserve a shower at a travel center in Gulfport, and went to clean up and eat. The beach clothes went into the trash. Dinner was at a sub shop attached to the convenience store, and afterward he parked the Jeep among the big rigs and dozed fitfully for a couple of hours once he had made preparations for the collection. Sleeping was difficult because he was beginning to feel the rush.

A quarter of a million bucks for one girl. And that's just *his* commission. God only knows what she'll go for in the dark web auction. That kind of money can only come from the Middle East. Saudi Arabia, probably. American girls of the Caucasian flavor command a good price there, where an abundance of oil money and a carnal taste for young white flesh create a strong market. The buyer knows how to extract the maximum price from his bidders. Bad for the product, good for him.

The seller circles the block and parks near the mouth of the alley, thinking about how he should have purchased some aloe or lidocaine spray at the travel center. Oh, well. He'll be back home before daylight and can lie in an ice bath all weekend if he wants. Until then, he needs to put on his big boy britches and suck it up.

The streetlamps create puddles of light, but overall the area is pleasingly dark. That's good. Less chance of being seen. He disables the Jeep's interior light before opening the door, and after loading his pockets with things he needs for the collection from his go bag, eases it shut as quietly as possible. His heart rate starts to increase, getting his blood up.

He's never met the buyer in person. They have spoken a handful of times, always through the messaging app, which is Swiss and anonymous, encrypted end to end for safety. The buyer sounds older than him, and German, even though he's based in New Orleans. Sometimes the seller thinks about how many other sellers must work for the buyer, because the children for sale to the highest bidder appear to come from all over the world. New Orleans has one of the largest ports in the country. A prime spot for sending and receiving shipments.

When he discovered the auction site via a *what's the worst website you know?* Reddit thread, he had been immediately intrigued by the possibilities. Not for the products, that's not his thing. For the money. The excitement. The adrenaline rush of making a collection and delivering the product, staying one step ahead of the law. Life is so *boring* otherwise.

No one is in the alley. Not after midnight on a Thursday. People don't come to the Mississippi coast to get their all-night party on, they go to Florida or New Orleans. This is a place for families, and families are in bed early. Pea gravel crunches softly underfoot as he walks, barely audible over the whirr of crickets. Lightning bugs spark all around. He checks the tracker app. Next house on the right. It's a cottage, more deep than wide, like the shotgun houses in New Orleans. Probably five rooms total, not counting bathrooms. Two of the three bedrooms will have bunk beds, so the owner can claim the tiny place sleeps six. Eight if the couch in the living room folds out. The girl will probably be on the bottom bunk in her own room. Boys always want the top.

His process is flawless for maintaining anonymity, the most important part of the transaction. When it's time to collect a new product, he first decides on the hunting grounds, generally along the coast or in a larger city. Birmingham, Nashville, Atlanta. Never in or around Tallahassee. You don't shit where you eat. Next, he locates the airport nearest his destination that's large enough to have paid parking, so he can leave his car. Parking costs ten or fifteen dollars a day, tops, and most jobs are two-day affairs. Bagging a product in his own vehicle would be idiotic.

The postage-stamp yard is surrounded by a cutesy white picket fence. He steps over it to avoid any unwelcome squeals from the gate. There's no garage, just a carport on the side of the house with an older minivan parked beneath. No lights on inside that he can see. The seller checks his phone again, using his hand to shield the screen. Thirty feet from the tracker.

He steps onto the patio, careful not to trip over the cheap plastic chairs the owner set out to advertise the house as having an outdoor entertainment area. In his day job, the seller is a realtor, his face on billboards all around Tallahassee. He knows every trick.

From the airport, he uses a ride-share to go where people congregate, and steals a suitable vehicle for the hunt. It's not always as easy as fooling a drunk old man, but it's never difficult to find transportation if you know where to look and what to do. After that it's just a matter of selecting the right product, establishing a plan for collection, and executing. His go bag contains everything he needs.

Once the product is in his possession, he secures it in the back of the transport for the drive to New Orleans. There, the seller chooses a location at random and parks the stolen vehicle. He messages the GPS coordinates to the buyer and receives payment in a numbered account within the hour. The first time, he had left the car in a Walmart parking lot and stayed nearby to see who showed up. After twenty minutes, a tow truck from a local garage pulled up. The driver winched the car onto the bed and drove away with it. Another layer of separation for protection, the seller believes, not an active participant in the transaction. Let Jethro the grease monkey get arrested if the cops show up. Getting back to his own car after the dropoff is a matter of a bus ride or one-way car rental.

He climbs the steps to the tiny stoop at the back door, unsnapping a holster at his waist. From it, he withdraws a combination tactical flashlight and stun gun, and thumbs on the light to study the deadbolt. Just like he expected, one of the cheapest brands made. Piece of cake. The flashlight casing is squared off to prevent rolling, so he positions it on the stoop railing with the narrow beam directed at the lock. The most dangerous part begins now. Absolute silence is a must, because waking someone can cost him a quarter mil if he has to bail … or the other person their life if he decides not to. The seller pulls a set of lock picks from his pocket. As he's opening the leather case to take out the tension tool, the deadbolt retracts with a soft *thock*, and someone inside the house pulls the door open.

16

Abby is so mad she could spit. Why do her parents have to be so *mean*?

hope i get 2 see u tomorrow, she thumbs. *if my mom isnt being a b.*

Her mother had met her at the front door as soon as she had come through, right in her face, confronting her because she was a lousy ten minutes late. *We have rules for a reason,* she said. Abby tried to apologize, to explain she lost track of the time because she made some new friends—well, one friend in particular, not that she'd mention a boy while getting yelled at—and had lost track of time. But as soon as she opened her mouth to defend herself, her mother's nose wrinkled and her lips turned down, and she said *have you been drinking*?

Things went downhill very fast after that.

Abby had been banished to her room to *think about what you've done.* Told how lucky she was because *the world isn't a nice place for a girl by herself and guardian angels don't exist.* Before she even made it to the hall her mother called her back and demanded her phone, hand out, palm up. *I want you to think about your behavior, not fiddle-fart with this thing,* she said. Through it all, her father sat on the couch and pretended to read his James Patterson novel so he didn't have to get involved. Her little brother lurked in the doorway of his room, smirking like a giant smelly butthole, happy that for once he wasn't the one in trouble. She stuck her tongue out at him.

The reply from Liam is almost instantaneous. *we cld meet*

2nite if u want like romeo and juliet lol.

A knife of anxiety twists in her gut. Liam has already figured out that his hotel is just a few blocks up the beach road from the house. She can only imagine what would happen if she was caught going to meet him. Drinking a beer or two and missing her curfew by a few minutes is one thing, sneaking around a strange town in the middle of the night with a boy is another. That's the kind of thing bad girls do. Her mother might literally shoot her, saying something like *if you want to be dead so much, missy, be my guest* right before she pulls the trigger. As much as she wants to see him, she sends back *better not dont want 2 get in more trouble.* She isn't a bad girl.

Not *that* bad, anyway.

When her mother had knocked softly on the bedroom door at ten to kiss her goodnight, Abby apologized and they had A DISCUSSION about how she was too young to drink, the dangers of peer pressure, and the importance of staying safe by being home when you're told. Abby endured the rebuke in silence, head bowed, and though she felt more than a little contrition for letting her parents down, she also knew she'd do it all over again because meeting Liam had been worth it. She couldn't wait to text him, couldn't wait to *see* him, but when she'd asked for her phone back her mother said *Not tonight, you can have it back tomorrow.*

Abby had burst into tears then and told her about Liam, and begged for permission for him to come on the swamp tour to keep it from being so boring. Her mother—predictably—just about had a cow. *You're being* punished, *Ab,* she said. *It needs to feel like punishment. Besides, we don't even know this boy.* When Abby offered that the swamp tour would be an ideal way to get to know him better, her mother said *I've made my decision, I'm going to bed.*

End of discussion, because the queen b-word had spoken.

Her phone vibrates with the response from Liam. *no prob. what if i come there n we sit out front and talk?*

She thinks about it. That might work. Getting caught while

sitting on the front steps would be bad, but nothing like if she actually left the property. And she'd get to see him again. Just the thought makes her giddy. She sends back *ok lol*.

Abby had waited another hour to ensure her parents were fast asleep before tiptoeing out of her bedroom to look for her phone. Her mother generally trusted her, and it seemed unlikely that she would have taken the phone into their bedroom or hidden it. Sure enough, she found it on the kitchen counter and, with a stab of guilt at violating that trust, picked it up and took it back to her room. She got into bed and pulled the covers over her head to hide the glow if someone got up to go to the bathroom.

miss u 2 she had responded to his first text. The fluttery thing inside her was back, and made her feel happy and scared and nervous and excited all at once. *i got busted 4 the beer mom smelt it.*

thought u ghosted me.

She had told him about being sent to her room, and they discussed how much fun the swamp tour might have been if her mother wasn't such a jerk. The last hour had flown by, so captivated had she been.

Now she throws back the covers and gets out of bed, heart racing. Excited because Liam is on his way over, scared spitless because what if Mom wakes up? Her shorts and t-shirt are hanging off the end of the bed and once dressed, she creeps into the hall and eases the bedroom door shut behind her. At the front door she pauses, considering. The room where her parents are is close, hardly ten feet away. The bedroom door is open. She can hear her father's whistling snores from here. If the deadbolt makes any sound at all there's a very good chance it'll wake one of them.

And that would be a. Very. Bad. Thing.

She returns to the kitchen. The back door is a whole room further away from them, making the odds a million times better any noise won't wake anyone. Matter of fact, she should bring Liam around to the back anyway, just so there's less of a chance her parents will hear their voices. Plus, there are chairs on the patio, and it's darker. *Much* darker. Maybe even dark enough that he'll try to kiss her. The thought a delicious shiver of anticipation through her.

Abby turns the deadbolt as gently as she can. It makes hardly any sound. She pulls the door open, puzzled by a sudden spear of light hitting her arm. Before she can move, before she can scream, someone seizes her and claps a gloved hand over her mouth.

17

The seller's heart nearly stops. Even as the door swings inward he reacts, stuffing the lock picks into his pocket. His hand goes to the butt of the Kimber Micro 9 pistol in the holster at the small of his back, but before he can draw, he realizes it's the product. Panic morphs into elation. It's like she *wants* to come with him.

She can't be allowed to scream. If she does, it's all over. He'll be screwed, not only out of his payment, but possibly out of his freedom. Even his life, if dad comes out guns blazing. This is the deep south. Everyone is armed, and itching to shoot. Hell no. He leaps forward and grabs hold of her shoulder. Spins the girl into his arms and clamps a hand over the lower half of her face.

The product becomes a live wire, thrashing and jerking as if possessed. A little firecracker. Her fingers dig at his hand. She tries to bite his palm. He's grateful for the glove. Whistling breath shoots from her nose in hot, panicky bursts. She raises her leg and smashes her heel back into his sunburned shin. The pain is eye-watering. She's stronger than he expected, but still no match. He weighs easily twice as much, and regular visits to the gym ensure he has the strength necessary to subdue her.

Dragging her onto the stoop, the seller crowds her against the house, using his body to hold her in place. The syringe he removes from his pocket is small, loaded with a heavy dose of lorazepam he'd drawn earlier in the travel center parking lot. Night night juice. He clamps the barrel between his teeth long enough to remove and stow the orange needle cap. Leave no trace. They can pull DNA off anything these days.

"Thank you," the seller whispers, mouth to her ear. Her hair smells of strawberry shampoo.

He jabs the needle into her neck and depresses the plunger with his thumb.

18

Abby fights the man, her mind racing even faster than her heart. She tries to scream, tries to bite him. Kicks back into his leg as hard as she can.

Wants to kill him.

He drags her out of the kitchen and shoves her against the back of the house. His face is right next to hers, hot and sweaty. Rough stubble grates painfully on her cheek. She can hardly move. He says something, inaudible over the roar of blood in her ears. There's a sting in her neck. Not a bee or a spider.

A shot.

Some kind of drug. It has to be. The panic she didn't think could get worse somehow does, surging in her like a black tide. She's seen enough movies, read enough books. It's all over now. One quick stick and you're out like a light in like two seconds. Then he can do anything with you—anything *to* you—he wants. And there's nothing you can do.

Except ... it's been *more* than two seconds, and she's not out. She's not even sleepy. Not yet.

The man shifts, trying to find a better grip, and for an instant there's a gap between her and the bricks. She slams her elbow back into his abdomen with all her might, but it's like hitting another wall and has no effect. Dumb. She needs to find a weak spot, someplace where he'll actually feel *pain*. It might give her a fighting chance.

Like his eyes, right there next to her own.

Or his balls.

She lowers her hands, reaching behind her. One good squeeze. That's all she needs. She wants to rip the nasty things off and celebrate to the music of his screams, but she'll settle for one good squeeze. Just enough to make him let go of her, though she won't be sad if one happens to pop like a plum. The man seems to sense her intentions and twists to the side. All she touches is the denim covering his hip. Not good. He presses her harder against the house, so tight now it's hard to draw a good breath.

His eyes, then.

But she can't raise her hand. She's pinned. And even if she wasn't, his face is suddenly so far away, her arm so heavy. It's as if gravity just tripled, or even quadrupled. The terror drains out of her like water from a bathtub, *glug glug*, and she finds herself relaxing, refilling with a blissful peace. Black roses bloom before her eyes. How lovely they must smell! She longs to gather an armful and bury her face in them, to bathe in the sweet scent.

As she drifts away on a dreamy little cloud, Abby sighs.

19

The seller holds the product against the wall until he's certain she is unconscious, then lowers her carefully to the stoop. She's worth a lot of money and needs to be kept in pristine condition. He caps the needle and returns the syringe to his pocket. He powers off the stun gun light and holsters it, then lifts the girl into a fireman's carry. She's completely limp. As he steps down onto the patio, a stage whisper comes out of the darkness under the carport, just a few feet away.

"Abby? Is that you?" A tall, thin shape detaches from the shadows. "Wassup, girl?"

A boy. Probably the one from earlier. Her new friend, the one who lured her away from the umbrella. His unknowing helper. The boy stops short when he realizes the person he's speaking to isn't Abby. The LED on his phone flares and he shines it at the seller.

"Who are you?" he says. There's panic in his voice, making it quaver. He sounds about six years old. The boy takes a step closer and raises the phone higher for a better view. "What are you doing? Is that Abby?"

The seller considers this new wrinkle. Putting the product down to attack with his hands will be an exercise in futility. There's no doubt the boy can easily get away from him. He's as skinny as a beanpole, and probably fast as greased lightning. Deploying the stun gun is only going make him scream. He'll wake everyone up, bring them out to see what's going on. The kid is about to start screaming anyway. It's plain in his tremulous voice. Which leaves the pistol. He certainly can't draw it and start blasting, unless he wants to wake even more people and trigger ten calls to 911. Not to mention a possible murder charge if he gets caught. But that isn't going to happen, because the Jeep is less than a football field away. His legs are strong, and the product light. It doesn't matter how fast he is. He only needs a few seconds.

The seller turns and bolts for the alley, one arm around the girl's legs to keep her from slipping off his shoulder. He hurdles the picket fence. Stumbles on the landing and careens into a plastic trash bin before correcting himself and sprinting down the alley. The noise sets off a dog in one of the yards. A fusillade of angry barks echoes off the houses.

The boy gives chase, bellowing for help. There's no doubt that between him and the dog, people are starting to wake up in their happy little rentals, but it doesn't matter—the Jeep is just ahead, waiting at the curb. The seller bursts from the alley, panting, and races across the road to the rear of his ride. Right on his heels, the boy alternately screams for help and relays his location and movements to someone on his phone. Probably a 911 operator. The seller yanks the handle. Flings the hatch up. Lights are starting to come on inside nearby houses. Shit. He shoves the product into the cargo area and slams the liftgate.

"I have to hang up now," the boy says. "So I can record him."

As the seller hustles around to the driver side of the Jeep, the kid gets in close with his phone, trying to capture video of his face. He slaps the device away and wrenches the door open, cursing. Wishing now he'd just pulled out his pistol and capped the boy back at the house.

Before he can climb into the Cherokee the kid is back, as irritating as a mosquito, this time tugging on his shoulder to turn him around. The seller spins, reaching for the stun gun. He jams the business end against the kid's chest and triggers it. There's a sharp crackling *pop*, and the kid goes down with a high, gabbling shriek. His phone clatters on the pavement. A fierce smile twists the seller's face.

By the time he shuts the door, the kid is already getting to his feet, phone in hand. He moves to the tail of the Jeep. For an instant the seller thinks the boy is going to try to rescue the product and slaps the button to engage all the locks, but the kid is no hero. He's just recording the license plate to show to the cops. Up and down the block, front porch lights flare. People are out of bed now, shambling out in their sleep clothes to investigate the commotion. A siren pierces the night. Close. *Too* close, like some jackass rookie has been cruising around the small town, looking for people to hassle because he has nothing better to do.

The seller starts the engine, squealing the tires when he stomps the pedal to the floor. The Cherokee peels away from the curb, nearly clipping a minivan parked in front of one of the bungalows. From his earlier recon he knows the next right will get him up to Highway 90, which will carry him all the way into Louisiana. As he makes the turn, flashing blue light fills the Jeep. A wailing police car has turned off the beach road, two blocks back, and screams down the road after him.

20

The Cherokee hurtles down the residential street toward the highway. He yanks the seatbelt across his body and latches it. The Caprice is right on top of him, howling siren so loud he can't hear himself think. It's like an icepick in his ears. Blinding headlights fill the rearview mirror. Houses streak by on either side, strobing blue in flashbulb bursts.

"Hold it together," he murmurs.

At the intersection with Highway 90 he makes a hard left through the red light. The Jeep drifts lazily through the turn, tires screeching. There is no cross traffic, for which he is grateful. The small town shut down for the night hours ago. He fishtails on the straightaway and jogs the wheel to correct. The two vehicles race west toward the Louisiana line, almost twenty miles away. Too far. It might as well be a hundred. The Cherokee is no match for the souped-up Caprice. If he doesn't make something happen—and soon—they're going to put him *under* a Mississippi prison.

The seller digs in his pocket for his phone, opens the map. It's nearly impossible to study it and watch the road at the same time, and he fights just to keep from drifting into the curb. Businesses flash past, grocery stores and strip malls, gas stations and drug stores. All closed for the night. He searches frantically for another route to Louisiana. Something that will increase his chances.

A second cop skids onto the highway behind him and joins the chase. He curses. So much for the odds. The Jeep is fast approaching another car and the seller swerves around it, gaze skittering from the road to the screen and back. There. Something that looks promising: a meandering road through what appears to be fields, forest, or swamp. Any are better than the wide open four-lane highway, where he has no doubt other patrols are converging somewhere ahead to trap him. It's what they do.

If he's going for it, he needs to go *now*. He stamps the brakes and cuts left. The Cherokee jounces over the curb into the median, throwing him forcefully into the door. His head cracks against the window hard enough to make his ears ring. Vaguely he is aware of the product shifting in the cargo hold.

A second later the Jeep has crossed the grassy strip and bumps over another curb, this one sending him into the center console, ribs first. The pain is instant and blinding. He barrels into the parking lot of a dollar store at an angle and floors it, careening out the side exit. The first cop overshoots and has to turn around, but the second is still running hot, right on his ass as he searches for the road he'd seen on the map.

It's so small he almost misses it. For a protracted, terrifying moment he thinks the Jeep is going to roll when he makes the tight turn, but it holds. The pavement is old and crumbling, little more than gravel and barely wider than the vehicle. Trees and undergrowth crowd in on both sides. All good. That means no one can sneak in and spin him out with a PIT maneuver. Only one patrol car followed him in. Also good.

Sporadic driveways break the monotony of the dense green growth, though no house lights are discernible through the foliage. He shoots across an intersection and the road narrows even further, little more than a path now. According to the map, it ends in a neighborhood in another half-mile, a dense grid of streets maybe twenty blocks by ten blocks. Manufactured homes on postage stamp lots. It has to be. The perfect place to lose a tail —or tails.

A wall of trees looms directly ahead where the road he's on tees into another. He tromps the brake pedal hard enough to lock his seatbelt, and takes a hard right. The cop is going too fast and judders across the asphalt, anti-lock brakes hammering. Two tires drop into the shallow ditch on the far side. For a moment he's stuck, engine screaming as he tries to back out.

But a moment is all the seller needs.

At the next intersection he peels right, and again in the same direction at the next. After another block he goes left. The trees are thick, netted with kudzu. It's like driving in a tunnel. Impossible to see through, ideal for his needs. He switches off his lights and slows to a crawl, lowering the windows to listen for the cops and keep his distance. The warm night air smells of blooming honeysuckle. He zigzags through the patchwork of streets, headed generally southwest, toward the bay road. The map says it will eventually lead him back to Highway 90, about two miles from the state line. Several times he sees police cars, crossing in front and behind at full speed in a vain attempt to locate him. He's not sure how many there are. Too many.

Five minutes later he reaches the southern tip of the development, and wheels into the faculty lot of an elementary school. Behind the empty playground, he parks in the shadows to study the map more closely. If he wants to save his skin, he needs to find a fast route back to the highway and Louisiana. As he searches, his pulse begins to return to normal. His breathing loses the harsh rasp of panic. Calm fills him. So he had a hiccup at the house. So what? He's still in the game. The cops don't know where he is, and the product is sleeping peacefully, ready to fatten his bank account. He spots something on the map. A shortcut that will shave couple of miles off the path he already found. Perfect.

Two police cars wheel past the school, stopping at the four-way on the south side of the playground. He shuts off the screen. Both vehicles turn in the direction he needs to go. He'll have to be careful. At least they'll be in front of him. If he can make it to the bridge unnoticed, in fifteen minutes he can be crossing the Pearl River into Louisiana. Out of their jurisdiction. Granted, they may have already alerted the cops on the other side to be on the lookout, but he can't worry about that right now. Right now he has enough problems.

He waits two minutes for the cops to move on, then circles back out to the road. Everywhere is dark, and except for the insects, quiet, as if he's the only person left alive after an apocalypse. At the intersection, he switches his headlights on and makes the turn. One hour to New Orleans and the drop. All he needs is a little luck.

Lightning splits the sky out over the Gulf. A storm is brewing, still far away.

21

The seller breathes a sigh of relief as he pulls onto the asphalt of the bay road. Though on the map the shortcut had appeared to be a road, in reality it was nothing but graded dirt with a scant gravel covering. Narrow, set on a berm with drops into brackish water on either side, it wound through some of the lowest, boggiest land he had ever seen. More than one heart-stopping time he'd felt a tire dip as the ground crumbled away beneath it. Buzzing, chitinous bugs filled the air like fog. He'd had to roll the windows up to keep from choking on them. At one point, some rangy, loping *thing* had crossed in front of him. He has no idea what it might have been. Nothing friendly, that's for sure.

When he relaxes his grip on the wheel, his fingers ache. The trek through that horror show had been the longest two miles of his life. But now he's out, and only three miles from the bridge. This part of the state is desolate, deep in hurricane country, where Mother Nature sees fit to wipe the slate clean every few years. Businesses and homes are few and far between. The seller doesn't understand why anyone would choose to live in such a place.

After a mile, the bay road butts into Highway 90. As he approaches the stop, he realizes too late that there are two police cars parked across the larger road a quarter-mile to the east, light bars blazing. A roadblock. *Damn* it. He wonders how many they've set up, and where. A town the size of Bay St. Louis can't have a very large force. Either there are only a couple or —more likely—they've enlisted the sheriff or nearby towns for assistance.

For a moment he considers dousing his lights, then decides against it. They have to have seen him already, and the act would surely be interpreted as suspicious behavior. All he can do now is the one thing that has worked so well for him in the past: pretend he's supposed to be here, and has every right to take the turn west onto the highway.

So he signals and does just that.

There's no reaction. No sudden whoop of siren, no headlights swinging around his way. Letting out the breath he didn't realize he was holding, he watches the blue lights recede in the mirror as he accelerates away. After a mile he begins to relax. One more to go. He can barely see them now, two tiny twinkling blue stars in an expanse of black. Except ... just a second ago they had looked like only one. Even as the seller watches, eyes jogging between the road ahead and the rearview, the two specks move further apart.

At least one of them is coming after him, maybe both.

He floors it and the Jeep surges, but the cop is still gaining. He swears. Making it to the bridge no longer matters. The Caprice can run him down without even breaking a sweat. And if anything, the section of Louisiana across the river is going to be even more barren, with fewer roads and places to hide. He curses again through gritted teeth. North. That's where he needs to go. Toward the interstate, if he can make it that far. What a pisser. A good half-hour wasted, for what? Not a damn thing. There's no time to get the phone and search for another way. He's got to do something, and soon.

The road ahead sweeps to the right. He remembers the layout from studying the map. One last curve, then a straight shot west over the Pearl and into the swamps of south Louisiana. Thirty-five miles to New Orleans. The perfect route, now spoiled because he can't shake the stupid cops. But when the Jeep rounds that final bend, what he sees first isn't the bridge, it's two more police cars forming a second roadblock a thousand feet ahead, just where the concrete abutments start.

"Oh, you sons of whores," he says, conversationally. It's almost comical the way everything is coming apart. Nearly two dozen collections under his belt, each one perfectly executed, and now this. It's like fate doesn't want him to get a leg up.

Behind him, a siren begins to oscillate.

The headlights pick up the reflective green of a street sign on the right, just past a run-down title loan business. He has no other choice and takes it, hoping beyond hope it's not a dead-end. The police car on his ass skates through the turn, rear sliding. It quickly recovers and begins to gain immediately. The new road is nothing but twists and turns, and the seller white-knuckles the steering wheel trying to stay on it. But it's headed north, and that's good. North is the interstate.

The Caprice makes a move. It swerves into the other lane and leaps forward, engine screaming like a banshee as the officer tries to spin the seller off into the ditch. Time to shit or get off the pot. He slams the brakes hard enough to engage the anti-lock system and the Jeep stutters and judders over the pavement. Before the cop can react, the police car roars up alongside. As it noses ahead, the seller wrenches the wheel to the left and slams the Cherokee into the side of the cruiser. The impact nearly tears the wheel out of his hand, but the other car shoots off the road and is stopped short by a towering cypress.

Score one for the little guy.

The crumpled car first dwindles in the mirror, then vanishes as the pavement curves again. He has to get off this road. There is zero doubt in his mind that at least one—if not all three—of the other police cars are already coming for him. Trying to box him in. A glance at the map shows that in four miles he'll hit Highway 607, and from there it's only a mile to the interstate. But it's no good, because now they know where he is. They're going to *expect* him to go that way. A sudden image of cops converging on him from both front and rear sends a jolt of real fear through him. It's coming down to it now. If they expect him to zig, he needs to zag.

He lets off the gas and slows, zooms the map. Just ahead, a

very thin, very faint line branches off the road he's on, barely more than a shadow. Some kind of farm track, he thinks. But it goes almost all the way to I-10, terminating just yards from the dual thick bands marking the interstate. Freedom. Maybe there's a way through. He knows there is likely a fence, that there must be some law because every interstate he's ever been on has had one, but they're flimsy, usually little more than chain link or welded wire. Easy work for a vehicle the size of the Jeep. Desperate times call for desperate measures.

He drops the phone on the passenger seat, and when he sees the narrow lane splitting away to the left, takes it.

22

The seller sits parked near the end of a dirt road—barely more than a trail this far in—with the windows down and the engine off. Tiny flashes of yellow-green flare all around the Jeep as lightning bugs search for mates. Insects and night birds and frogs fill the air with raucous song. The only other sounds are those of the occasional vehicles that pass by on the interstate, close enough that he could hit one with a rock if his aim was true. His sunburned legs feel like they've been dipped in gasoline and set alight, and a long scratch down his inner arm where the product had apparently scratched him during their struggle has gotten sweat in it and stings like hell.

A big rig grumbles eastward on I-10, bound for destinations unknown. He watches its lights flicker through the foliage as it passes and wishes he were riding in the cab, headed away from this hell in which he finds himself. Just beyond the nose of the Cherokee, several downed trees block the track at the point where the woods give way to grass. It looks like a microburst or small tornado came through recently, because although wilted, the leaves haven't dried up and blown away. A straight shot to freedom, ruined by another damn random thing, like some agent of chaos has been one step ahead of him all night.

He wants to scream, wants to punch something.

Part of him wants to cry.

Maybe he should abandon the product and take a walk out through the grass to the shoulder. Stick a thumb out and hope for the best. His car waits for him at the Biloxi airport. He could hitch a ride to the correct exit. Catch a Lyft if one is available at this hour, or get a room for the night in one of the hotels he remembers seeing on the way in this morning. A lifetime ago.

But giving up is not in his nature.

The seller picks up his phone and returns to the map. There has to be something else, however small. Some other way to get the product out. Pinching the screen for a wider view, he realizes the cops have very likely penned him in. He sees four strategic spots—two of which he's already been up close and personal with, just minutes ago—where roadblocks could block every path out. And it's a distressingly *small* area, maybe seven square miles, with few roads. Most of it is forest and bayou, places no vehicle can go. The belt of tension around his chest seems to ratchet a little tighter. Trapped, like a rat.

The phone suddenly comes to life in his fingers, vibrating and trilling an alarm, and he startles. A notification bubble pops up. An AMBER alert. *His* AMBER alert. He skims the text. Almost no details about him. The description is generic enough that there are probably a thousand men in the tail of Mississippi right this minute who meet it. Thank God for small favors and stupid boys.

But the Jeep is another story. They know everything about it, including the Kentucky tag number. If he's going to get out of this, he needs a new ride. That's what he should have been doing all along instead of trying to make it across the border. He could've stopped in that blessed quiet period and grabbed another car.

Woulda coulda shoulda.

The question is: what can he do *now*?

He dismisses the alert and returns to the map, zooming in on his location. A little more than a half-mile due east of him there's some kind of children's science museum, and next to it a Mississippi welcome center. Two large parking lots. Parking lots mean cars—especially at the museum, because there's a good chance it will have some sort of facility van or employee vehicle, waiting to be liberated if it's old enough to hotwire. The welcome center is more iffy. That place surely gets an unwelcome amount of traffic, even in the middle of the night, because it's at the first exit coming in from Louisiana.

Ah, the exit. Highway 607. *Right* there. The way the road is laid out in a big loop around the welcome center, it looks like he could simply veer off it and drive through the trees and grass to the off-ramp. From there he could wrong-way it up to the interstate and be on his way east. He'd need to turn around at the first available spot, but he'd be free.

Except ... he's almost certain there will be a roadblock down on the highway to prevent anyone, and him in particular, from leaving the area. It's one of the four entrapment points he'd noticed. But it doesn't matter. There's no way over to the museum and welcome center from here. Not unless he goes all the way back to the road—which is surely crawling with Johnny Law now because of the accident—and drives to the very highway where he's positive the checkpoint awaits. Certain doom.

He zooms in further, hoping to locate another farm track like the one he's on. Something to get him closer. What he finds might even be better. There appears to be a series of walking trails through the woods, extending outward from the museum grounds. It's easy to imagine foot tours, with khaki-clad guides pointing out trees and flowers and birds to groups of bored children. The terrain view shows the paths as gray when he zooms all the way in. Gray like gravel, to keep all those kids from getting muddy on their walks. Maybe even wide enough for the Cherokee. Two of the trails intersect the track he's on, one just to the south, the other a couple of hundred yards beyond. He had missed both on the way in because he was driving with the headlights off, in case the police had called in air support to search for him. Just trying to stay on the ribbon of dirt had been hard enough.

The seller starts the engine and reverses slowly through the darkness until he spots a pale strip of ground running out through the trees. He stops and gets out. The flashlight reveals a fine, wide gravel path. Nice and straight. Plenty wide enough for the Jeep. It's blocked off by a pair of knee-high gates rigged to work like saloon doors. A padlocked chain holds them closed.

Finally, some luck.

It takes him no more than a minute to pick the lock and open the creaking gates. Before continuing to the museum, the seller goes to the rear of the Jeep and opens the liftgate. When he plays the beam over the product, there's no reaction. Still out. Good. The lorazepam does a great job, but he never knows how long its effects will last because he intentionally underdoses. Any harm the drug does to a product can affect his bottom line. Better safe than sorry, but caution makes it less reliable. Sometimes it lasts about an hour, sometimes closer to two. Never as many as three. No two products are the same. Now that he has a moment, he needs to secure the girl before the drug wears off, something he normally would have done as soon as he put her in the back.

He retrieves his go bag from the passenger seat and takes out a couple of heavy-duty zip ties. One he uses to bind her wrists behind her, the other goes around her ankles. Taut, but not so tight as to inflict pain. He isn't a monster. A quick check of her pockets to ensure she doesn't have a phone, broadcasting her location to the world. All good. Nothing but the keys he'd found at the beach. He leaves them where they are, just in case. The tracker is still in place. One never knows what the future holds, especially on a night like this when everything has gone to hell.

He stuffs a wadded handkerchief in her mouth. Several turns of self-adhesive medical bandage around her head ensure she won't be able to spit it out. Duct tape would be better, but duct tape can damage skin. Damage costs money. Now she can't scream, can't run away. Even if she's awake when he finds a new car and makes the transfer, she won't be able to do anything.

When he finds a car, not *if*. He likes the unconscious change in his thinking. A little can-do attitude never hurt anybody.

The low reverberation of thunder rolls toward him from the Gulf, and he looks up at the sky. Clouds are moving in, and the breeze that rustles the leaves smells of ozone. He needs to get going before the weather gets bad. The seller closes the hatch and gets behind the wheel. Easing along barely over idle speed, the Cherokee creeps up the lightless walking path toward the science museum.

23

He feels the last of his hope dissipate like smoke from a burned match. At the science museum, the sprawling parking lot had been completely empty, except for two pieces of heavy earth-moving equipment and numerous pallets stacked high with construction materials. Scaffolding covered the two-story building like an exoskeleton. When he continued on to the entrance, he discovered a large orange and white barricade blocking the drive, weighted down by sandbags. The sign hanging from it read CLOSED FOR RENOVATIONS. He'd had to get out of the Jeep and drag all of it aside just to get past.

Then, as he entered the loop around the welcome center, he had spotted the police roadblock out on the highway through the evenly spaced trees, just a couple of hundred yards away. Right where he thought it would be. For once, he wouldn't have minded being wrong. Things continued to get worse. There were no vehicles in either the brightly lit lot for cars, or the smaller truck and RV lot on the back side of the loop.

After making a complete circuit he'd reentered the car lot and gone off-road in the darkness, angling through the sparse trees toward the exit ramp. He took care to use the emergency brake when needed, so his taillights didn't draw the attention of the cops manning the checkpoint. Fifty feet from the ramp he had encountered a run-off ditch, with sides too steep for the Jeep to navigate. Now he waits morosely among the trees in the shadows, fuming, not sure what to do next. Abandon hope, all ye who enter here.

The cops can't camp out there forever. Maybe he can wait them out. Yeah, right. Who is he kidding? Daylight is four hours away and as soon as there's even a hint of the coming dawn he becomes a sitting duck. The trees aren't thick enough to camouflage the Jeep. And he can't leave through the main entrance, because they'll spot him right away. The roadblock isn't more than a quarter-mile from that intersection.

What if he goes back to the farm track? Pop the product with another dose of trank, catch a little sleep, then try to slink out in a few hours and blend into the morning traffic. Won't work. Traffic out here is going to be nearly non-existent, even during rush hour. Hardly anyone lives this far from town, and over in Louisiana it's nothing but swamp for miles. He'll blend like oil in water.

His gaze is drawn to movement, headlights sweeping across the trees down the lot as a vehicle approaches the curve leading in. Whatever it is, it's loud, preceded by the heavy rumble of its engine.

A muscle car, one of the old ones.

It rounds the bend and parks not far from him, under one of the bright sodium vapor lights. Black or dark blue, he can't tell. Maybe a Camaro or Trans Am. He doesn't know or care. Cars aren't his thing. The driver side door swings wide and a young Latina woman gets out. She's small and very pretty, with short black hair that shines in the lamplight. The kind of woman he might want to know better if he wasn't on the job. A spitfire in bed. But right now, she's tense—not that he can blame her, given the surroundings—looking every which way for potential threats, holding something up like an amulet to ward off evil as she vanishes onto one of the dark walkways.

He turns his attention to the car, more relevant to his needs than the woman. It's old. Vintage automobiles have no modern theft deterrents, no ignition immobilizer systems or push-button starts or proximity fobs. With his skills he can literally be ... gone in sixty seconds. The mental wordplay pleases him. If he were to pop the trunk and transfer the product to it, he could hotwire the car and use it to get through the roadblock and on to his destination. Crisis averted. But he already sees a big problem with the plan. Namely, the woman. As soon as she sees it missing she'll call the police, who he suspects are very likely on high alert for stolen vehicle reports right now. *Especially* in the triangular area he thinks of as his cage. Could he make it through the checkpoint before word of the theft makes it to those guys? Probably.

Not good enough.

He has more lorazepam. Why not use it on her when she comes out? Can't call 911 if you're asleep. And by the time she wakes up, the product will have been dropped off and the buyer alerted to the pickup location. Now *that* sounds like a plan. He'll need to hide the woman once she's unconscious, lest someone of lesser character find her, helpless and vulnerable, and do … unsavory things with her. Plenty of men are animals and wouldn't hesitate if given such an opportunity. The Jeep will be safe, out of sight in the trees. A perfect spot for a nice long nap, with the insects and frogs singing a summer lullaby.

This could work. Could truly, actually work.

As he draws up a load of trank into the syringe, he considers how to move the product. She's light enough to be easily carried, but a horrifying vision of headlights spearing him midway across the lot with a bound and gagged girl cradled in his arms nixes that idea. No thanks. He knows the odds of that happening are slim, but playing the odds are how you lose everything.

And he's no loser.

The seller eases the Jeep out of the trees and over the curb, pulling into the spot beside the antique car he now realizes is a Trans Am, like the one from that old Burt Reynolds movie. He leaves the engine idling. There's no danger of her hearing it over the ambient chirps, cheeps, and buzzes.

It takes him no more than fifteen seconds to open the trunk with his lock picks. Much of the available space is taken up by a backpack and a spare tire. There isn't enough room for the product. Fleetingly, he considers stashing her in the back seat, but that's no good. The cops at the checkpoint would spot her in a heartbeat. Better to make room. He lifts out the tire and sets it on the pavement, puts the backpack atop it. The woman has been gone almost two minutes. Nervous energy tickles his gut. He needs to get a move on.

Opening the Jeep's hatch, he risks the flashlight to look the product over again. Is she awake? He can't tell. A light slap on her bandaged cheek yields no reaction, no cringe or whimper or flutter of the eyelashes. Nothing. But she could be faking. It's happened before. That's okay. He has another way to test her, one guaranteed to work even if he finds it distasteful, the kind of thing an immoral man would do.

24

Abby lies on her side, willing herself to full wakefulness. She can't move. Her hands are rendered immobile behind her back, bound at the wrists. Some gross, slimy thing fills her mouth and makes her want to gag. A tight band holds her legs together at the ankles. Terror rises in her like a bubble as she tests each restraint.

Hazy memories begin to come back, slowly, as she becomes more alert. A man at the back door of the vacation house, pressing her hard against the bricks. The bee sting of a shot in her neck. Something about the smell of flowers, but it won't coalesce into anything solid.

She stands on a precipice, one tiny step from a plunge into full-blown panic. Her throat begins to close. Tears threaten. Can't cry. If she cries, her nose is going to start running and stuff up. She envisions herself choking to death slowly on her own snot, unable to draw a breath because of the foul thing in her mouth.

Must. Calm. Down.

Where is she? More importantly, where is *he*? Abby opens her eyes a crack. It's so dark here. Cramped. The top of her head is touching a wall, as are her feet. She can't straighten her legs. Rough carpet rubs her arm when she tries to move, and something underneath her presses painfully into her hip. Keys. She remembers putting them in that pocket after she grabbed them to meet Liam.

Liam.

Did he have anything to do with this? She remembers their conversation, his suggestion first that they meet, then that he come to her when she nixed that idea. Insistent, almost. She thought it was because he liked her, but ... does he know the man who attacked her?

No. He was nice. Better, he was *sweet*. He wouldn't do something like this.

She thinks.

As Abby shifts to ease the pressure on her hip, there comes the sudden sound of an engine turning over, and a rumbling vibration through the floor.

She's in the trunk of a car.

No, wait. If she turns her head up, she can make out the outline of a large window. Trunks don't have windows. She's in the back of a van or SUV. Not as bad as a trunk. Still bad.

Where is the man? Is he the one who started the engine? What did he do to her?

What does he *plan* to do to her?

New terror takes hold. She pushes it down. Freaking out will get her nowhere.

The vehicle starts to roll, jostling her. Like they're driving over bumpy ground instead of on a road. Her hands. She has to get her hands free if she wants any chance at getting out of this. Focus on doing, not worrying.

Abby brings her knees toward her chin, curling into a ball. Tries to force her hands around her butt and feet, to get them in front of her. There's a bump, then another, and the ride becomes smooth. The engine is barely making any noise. They can't be going any faster than walking speed.

What is he doing?

Just as she thinks her hands are going to slide over the bulge of her butt, the vehicle comes to a stop. She hears the door open. Instinct takes over. He mustn't know she's awake.

Not until she can fight back.

Abby is barely able to get herself back into position before the hatch is raised. The night sounds become much louder. She senses the man looking down at her, then a hand cups her chin, turns her head skyward. How can he not hear her heart pounding, see the pulse throbbing at her temple?

She has to stay calm, and can't give him any sign that she's awake. When he slaps her cheek gently she nearly thrashes in revulsion, but clenches her hands into fists and lets the pain of her nails biting into her palms calm her. The man lets go of her chin and she allows her head to loll.

But just when she thinks that she's fooled him, that she's safe for the moment, a hand snakes between her legs, touching her *there*. Cupping her. Pressing against her with a finger. His face is close. She hears each breath, feels the weight of his gaze.

Must. Not. React.

It's a test. That's all. Just a test.

Every part of her wants to scream, wants to gouge out his eyes, wants to *kill* him for what he's done to her. For everything he intends to do to her. Somehow she doesn't. She lays there and focuses on keeping each breath deep and even and controlled, like she's sleeping. Wishing him dead.

After an eternity the hand is withdrawn and he scoops her into his arms. The smell of his flopsweat is pungent, stomach-turning. She remains limp, letting her head roll loosely. With it thrown back he can't see her face, so she opens her eyes. They're in a darkened parking lot, with no houses to be seen. No smell of the Gulf, or sounds of people or traffic. Just an old car with its trunk lid raised. Where has he brought her?

Bright lights play over trees at the end of the pavement. Another vehicle is coming. She hears the man's breath catch and squeezes her eyes shut as he quickly steps to the car and lowers her into the waiting trunk. She senses rather than sees the lid closing over her, sealing her in blackness.

25

The seller lowers the lid and uses his body weight to quietly latch the trunk before the incoming vehicle gets far enough around the curve to light him up. By the time an aging Mustang enters the lot and takes a spot a few spaces down from the Trans Am, he's busily loading the spare tire and backpack into the cargo hold of the Jeep.

A kid in his early twenties emerges in a cloud of pungent smoke. He looks like an updated version of Shaggy from the Scooby-Doo cartoons the seller watched as a kid, mangy beard and all. The seller glances toward the welcome center, certain the woman is going to be coming back any second. She's by herself at a closed rest stop in the dead of night. She won't dawdle. He mentally urges the kid to get his ass in gear, before things go any more south than his appearance has made them.

As he passes on the sidewalk, Shaggy tips his head at the seller. "Sup?"

The seller nods and grunts a reply.

Once the other man has vanished into the darkness, he climbs into the Jeep and returns it to the protection of the trees. Everything has just gotten a thousand times more complicated, but maybe it can still work. The woman has been in there for a solid five minutes. The kid for only a few seconds. She should be back well before him, theoretically giving the seller time to subdue her. *Theoretically*. If the timing works in his favor and she doesn't spend an eternity.

Just as he reaches the curb, on his way back to hide behind

the Trans Am and wait, the woman bursts from one of the shadowed walkways, running full speed for the car. She tosses her purse on the roof and fumbles at the door, trying to unlock it, casting terrified glances back. The seller hears the thunk of the lock, and she flings the door open just long enough to snatch her bag and fall into the seat. A second later, the engine roars. Reverse lights flare and the Trans Am sweeps out of the parking lot in a tight arc. Shaggy bolts out of the darkness, straight at the retreating vehicle.

What the hell? Did he try something untoward with her, knowing full well the seller was right outside?

The woman gets the Trans Am into gear and hits the gas so hard the tires spin. Shaggy yells something the seller can't make out, trying to get her attention. White smoke boils up around the rear of the car, then it swerves around the stoner and hauls ass out of the lot, slewing into the curve. The seller watches her go, and with her, the product, silently cursing the agent of chaos that seems to have it in for him.

"You forgot your phone, dude!" Shaggy yells into night air, like he thinks she can hear him.

Well now. This changes *everything.*

A new plan starts to come together even as the night swallows the words. The seller doesn't know what happened between the two of them, but what he does know is this: she'll be back for that phone as soon as she realizes it's missing. Who wouldn't? Not only are the things expensive as hell, they're essential in every facet of life now. He doesn't know how anyone could get along without one.

And if she comes back, he's not out of the fight.

The Trans Am had a temporary Georgia tag. She's not from here, is likely a traveler on her way to or from home base. There's a near certain chance she came here from the interstate and will be returning to it.

Which means she can be his courier. Let her carry the product through the roadblock, without him anywhere near. Tag her Trans Am with the GPS unit and follow at a safe distance. If the cops search her car and find the product, it's not his problem. He can go back to the airport for his car and home to Tallahassee. Ask the buyer to give him another shot in a day or two. But if they don't …

He needs to get busy.

Shaggy hears him approaching from behind and turns.

"What's going on?" the seller says with a smile. He reaches to his hip and casually unsnaps the holster.

"I didn't mean to scare her but I did. She dropped all her sh —stuff. But she missed this," Shaggy tells him, holding up a cell phone in a yellow case. The younger man reeks of pot smoke. So nasty. He blinks at the seller a couple of times, like he's trying to solve a particularly difficult math problem, then looks around and says, "Where'd your car go, man?"

"Right over there, *man*," the seller says.

He points at the Mustang, and when Shaggy turns to look, jams the stun gun into the young man's side and holds down the button. Crackling pops fill the air. Shaggy stiffens and falls hard, screaming. The forgotten cell phone clatters to the pavement. The seller drops to his knees and pulls the syringe out of his pocket. Taking the disabled man by the wrist, he locates a steady pulse beneath the thin flesh. There's no reaction when he slides the hypodermic into the vein and thumbs the plunger. The effect is immediate and Shaggy's eyes roll back. *Much* better when you can get a vein.

"Zoinks, Scoob!" he says, his tone mocking. "What're we gonna do *now*?"

The seller collects the lost phone and shoves it into his back pocket. After tonight is over, he might like to call on the woman socially, to see if she's as interesting as he imagines.

But first he has work to do.

26

Abby stares at one of the glowing red taillights as she concentrates on curling her legs as tightly against her chest as possible. The trunk is like a coffin, closing her in. Stealing her breath. Heat bakes up through the metal underneath the carpet, and sweat pours off her. The air is thick with the stench of exhaust. It feels like she has a coating of gasoline on her throat, and part of her worries that she's going to choke to death in this awful place. The muffler is as loud as a freight train, and the vibrations make her teeth rattle.

But it could be worse. She could be up front with *him*. Close enough for him to touch her again. A shudder wracks her. He had started the car only a few moments before, revving the engine almost to the point of deafening her before slinging her all around as he spun out. Just a thief stealing a car, the same way he stole her and who knows what else.

Abby closes her eyes, takes a deep breath and lets it out slowly, then refocuses on the taillight. If she lets him stay in her head, he wins. She throws her shoulders back and works her bound hands against her butt, trying to get them down and around it the way she almost had before. It's a lot harder in the smaller space, but as she wriggles and twists, she's able to get them around her hips ... only to find them caught behind her feet.

The car slows to a stop, idling.

What is he doing up there? The panic that hasn't gone too far threatens to return. She *needs* to get free if she wants even the slightest hope for escape. Needs to focus. Blowing out all her breath, she curls her legs even tighter, until her knees touch her chin. It works. Her hands slide over her shoes. There's a sharp searing pain in one elbow, but they're in front of her now. She rips the bandage off her head and spits out the slimy wad of cloth, taking great gulps of the hot, stinky air.

The engine revs and the car begins to move. Gentle force pulls her toward the right side of the trunk. He's turning—but almost right away they begin to slow. A shimmy runs through the vehicle as the tires move onto rough ground, and the vehicle once again comes to a halt.

What's going on now?

"Stop it, Ab," she whispers. "Quit worrying about him."

There are more pressing things, like her hands, which are still tied. In the weak red glow she can make out the thick zip tie around her wrists. There's no way she can break it. Crap. Reaching for her ankles, she finds another down there. Double crap.

Suddenly, someone in the front of the car shouts, "*Damn* it!"

Abby freezes. It was a woman. Not him.

What the heck is going on?

After a few seconds she hears the woman scream—but not a scream of terror, like the man is hurting or killing her. One of anger. Curious. She cocks her head, listening to see if she can figure out what's happening. The car roars and Abby slides to the right side, this time with more force.

They're turning around.

27

"Up you go, big boy," the seller says to the unconscious man.

He takes a deep breath and catches Shaggy under the arms, heaves him into the Jeep's cargo hold with a grunt. Something in his lower back registers a complaint. After tonight is over he needs to book a long session with a masseuse. And sleep, lots and lots of sleep. Before he closes the liftgate, he searches the man's pockets for the keys to the Mustang and grabs the backpack he took from the woman's trunk. Running to the car, he keeps a wary eye out for the Trans Am, in case she comes back before he's ready. That wouldn't do. Wouldn't do at all.

The sporty car oozes the stink of pot smoke, and he wrinkles his nose. How can anyone live with that? Lightning flashes, and several seconds later thunder follows. Definitely closer. He starts the engine and backs the car over the curb, parking it out of sight next to the Jeep. Fifteen minutes. That's what she gets. If she's not back by one-thirty, to hell with it. It's too dangerous to sit here and wait any longer. Abandoning the product—if it comes to that—will suck, but sometimes you have to cut your losses. In all likelihood there's a girl even *more* exquisite over in Florida, anyway. A wider selection, for sure.

Putting the windows down for some clean air, he pulls the woman's phone from his pocket and tries to wake it. Locked. Oh, well. Worth a shot. He powers it down in case she has a second phone or laptop she can use to locate it. The way his luck has been tonight, the thing would rat him out and lead her right to him, ruining his surprise. He sticks it in the glove box for later, when he has more time to study it, and rummages through his go bag for his GPS tracker. Old faithful. The unit is smaller than a deck of cards, with a magnet on one side so it can be easily affixed to a car. He must have used it more than a dozen times to track products when tagging them with one of the Bluetooth devices was infeasible.

Headlights appear at the end of the lot, and the Trans Am motors around the curve. The seller smiles. Not even five minutes. She must be jonesing *hard* for that phone. Tough titty, little kitty, it's gone gone gone. The car parks at an angle with the curb, lights pointed in the direction of the smaller building where he had seen the colorful lights of vending machines earlier. Probably the place she had come running from. Pretty smart.

"Now put those brights on, sister," he murmurs. "They'll help you see even better."

And they'll blind her to everything he needs to get done.

As though she heard him, the dual cones of harsh halogen white seem to intensify fivefold, casting the trees and bushes in sharp relief. Shadows cloaking the walkway are driven into hiding. Excellent. The woman starts tentatively toward the distant building, careful to keep in the light. She calls the young man's name, which is apparently Brandon. How boring. *Shaggy* is so much better. It fits the kid. Like, to a tee, Scoob. Better than *Brandon*, for sure.

It's time.

The seller slips out of the Mustang and darts across the parking lot, staying low even though he knows there's no way she can see him through the headlight beams. Still too much of a risk, the way things have gone tonight. He crouches at the back bumper of the Trans Am, warm exhaust painfully bathing his sunburned shins through the jeans, and feels underneath for a suitable spot on the frame to attach the GPS device. It snaps to the steel with a quiet, solid *clack*. Now for the most important —and most difficult—part. If anything goes wrong here it's all over. That or he'll have to take the woman down. He isn't sure if he has enough trank for another dose, and he *really* doesn't want to have to subdue her physically, like some common thug. He's better than that.

Peeking over the fender, he sees the woman far into the gardenscaping, nearly to the building. Her back is to him, her head down to study the ground. The seller moves to the other side of the Trans Am to keep the car between them and creeps to the curb, where he drops to his belly on the asphalt. It still holds a remnant of the day's heat. He wriggles to the space between the headlights, taking great care to stay below them lest he throw a shadow across the woman and alert her to his presence. She never looks back.

Standing, he locates the hood release and pulls it gently, holding the hood down with his other hand to prevent it from popping. Silence is the name of this game. He raises it slowly, in case the hinges have something to say. They don't. She's taken care of the car, that much is obvious. A glance back shows her nowhere in sight. Probably inside. Better hurry.

Heat radiates from the engine compartment, making his blistered arms burn. Is it hot enough that he's about to get a geyser of steam and boiling antifreeze to his face? He doesn't know. But he has to do this, or the plan won't work. Occasionally, you *do* have to play the odds if you want to win.

Using his shirt to provide at least minimal protection to his palm and fingers, he gives the radiator cap a quarter turn. There's a tiny *pfft* as the pressure equalizes, but no sudden blast, no explosion of pain. Three more twists and it comes off in his hand. Triumph flickers like lightning across his face. Without the cap, it shouldn't take long at all for the car to overheat once she reaches interstate speeds. He lowers the hood and latches it slowly. The sound does not carry.

When he checks for the woman again, she's already more than halfway back to the parking lot, eyes down. Heart stuttering, he hits the deck and worms under the halogens and around to the side of the car before she walks out of the cone of light and spots him. The safety of the trees seems a mile away as he crouch-runs back, diving into a pool of shadows just as she reaches the car and gets in.

The Trans Am reverses away from the curb and leaves at a much more sedate pace than it had the last time. The seller watches it go, then takes out his phone and brings up the map once he's sure she won't be able to see the glow. A new green dot has appeared on the screen, arcing around the loop on the far side of the welcome center.

Perfect.

28

Abby lies on her side in the trunk, her mind racing. The car has stopped again, and once more sits idling. A moment ago, she had heard a noise from up front that she's pretty sure was the car door opening, then a slight shift, like someone had gotten out. Shortly after, the woman's voice came to her, close by. She was calling out *hello*—but as a question, the way people in the movies do when they're sneaking into someplace they're not supposed to be—and then *Brandon*, or maybe *Brendan*. Something like that. Is it the man's name? Maybe he's not in the car with her after all.

Or maybe there's a third person.

She hopes not. Assuming she gets the chance, it's going to be hard enough to escape from the woman. Even harder if the man is out there, too. But three people? No way. She's fast, but not *that* fast. Not to mention the whole *just a kid* thing.

She needs to stop thinking like that. If she allows the fear and doubt take over, there's no way she'll be able to get away, no matter how many of them there are. Hands and feet. That's what needs her focus right now. Unless she can free them, she's not going anywhere and might as well give up. She tests the bond around her arms again. The skin where the zip tie binds her feels raw, because the unforgiving plastic had bitten into her flesh earlier during the struggle to bring her hands to the front. It's not possible for her to break it. Not only is the band too thick, she lacks both strength and leverage in the position she's in. Maybe if she was out of the trunk, on her feet, she could figure something out. Maybe. But not here, not like this.

The only real option is to try to pull one of her hands through the loop. When she worked them over her butt and feet, her lower arms had rotated, turning her wrists inward. Now they face each other. The change in orientation has made the zip tie the tiniest bit looser. She lowers her head to the carpeted trunk floor. Sweat beads her face, and she shrugs a shoulder to wipe it away before it gets in her eyes. It's like a sauna in here, one that smells like a gas station.

Abby extends her hands, palms touching like she's praying, and brings her elbows together to maximize the free space between her wrists and the zip tie. Summoning a mental picture of it slipping out of the loop, she begins to slowly inch the left downward, working it back and forth as the plastic pulls tight. After a moment she stops. It hurts like a mother, and she isn't making any real headway. What she needs is something slippery, like the suntan lotion she had slathered on her shoulders and legs earlier today, or some soap. What she wouldn't give for a bit of either. Just enough to get the ball rolling. Would sweat work? There's plenty of that. But sweat isn't really slick, just wet. Plus, her arms are already dripping and it's not really making a difference.

An idea springs to mind. A little gross ... but it just might work. What about spit? It's slippery. There's a reason her mom says things are *slicker than spit*. Even better if she can produce a little—ew, yuck—snot to go with it. It's worth a try. Right now, just about anything is. She presses her wrists to her lips and tries to work up some saliva. If this doesn't work, she doesn't know—

clack

Abby freezes. The sound, tiny as it had been, had come from right in front of her. Something metallic had hit the body of the car, no more than a foot from her head. Who's out there? Are they about to open the trunk? Her stomach twists and rolls. She feels so helpless! But she doesn't dare move. Better that whoever it is continues thinking she's asleep. It's safer that way.

A moment later she hears a second noise, a muted *thunk*

from the front end. Had the person gotten into the car? She doesn't think so. There was no movement, no shift like weight had been added. She squeezes her eyes shut and tries not to let fear of the unknown take hold. It's hard. There's something indescribably creepy about the sounds, something furtive. Like whoever is out there is hiding. Is it him? Is it her? Maybe it's Brandon-or-Brendan. She cocks her head, listening. Nothing. *What are you* doing? she wants to scream. Let out some of the pressure that's building toward a panic attack. But of course she doesn't. She lays there with her eyes squeezed shut and wishes them away.

Seconds pass, then the car rocks and there comes the instantly recognizable sound of a door shutting. The car begins to back up, and Abby relaxes a bit. Putting her wrists to her lips, she tries to produce some spit, but finds the terror has dried her mouth. She's never going to get free! The tears she'd successfully banished earlier return with a vengeance, filling her eyes. This time she welcomes them.

Why did this have to happen to *her*? It isn't fair! She should be sitting in one of the rickety plastic chairs on the patio with Liam, talking and holding hands and

Maybe. Even. Kissing.

Not kidnapped and crammed in the trunk of a loud hot smelly car with no idea what was going to happen next. But of course she *does* have an idea of what is going to happen, and it's not good. The sex thing. She's not dumb. That's what people do when they steal kids, especially girls. They hurt them and rape them, and then they kill them.

Her breath hitches and she begins to cry. She didn't do anything to deserve this. Sobs wrack her. She's so *scared*! And she knows down deep that she won't be able to get away, because little girls almost never do. They end up on HAVE YOU SEEN THIS CHILD posters and in shared Facebook posts from kindly old grandmothers and on true crime podcasts.

The car swings through a curve and begins to accelerate. Abby takes a deep, shuddering breath and wills herself to stop crying. Save the pity. Right now there's work to do. And, she realizes, a nose now overflowing with some of the slipperiest stuff in the world to help with that work. Her little brother should be here to see this next part. He'd love the grossness of it. The thought makes her giggle, halfheartedly.

Using her middle fingers to close off first one nostril, then the other, she blasts a pair of snot rockets into the gap between her wrists. It's sick and nasty and gooey, but oh so slick. *Slick as snot*, as her mom might say. Maybe it's the thing that's *slicker than spit*. She rubs her wrists together, twisting them to spread the mucus around as the car once more begins to slow.

As it comes to a stop, Abby tries to pull her left hand free. It hangs on the zip tie, skin bunching up like fabric against the bond ... but it's *almost* there, almost pulling through. She gives one final pull, the hardest yet. Her thumb feels like it's coming out of the socket, but her hand slips free of the loop of plastic. Yes! It takes all her effort not to cheer from the exultation.

Voices come to her. First a man, then the woman. She can't make out the words. It doesn't matter what they're saying, anyway. What matters is that she's one huge step closer to being free. She quickly shucks the zip tie off her right hand and wipes her wrists on the piece of cloth that had been her gag. Next comes the tie around her legs.

But first ... first she needs to look for a weapon.

29

The seller waits in the Mustang under the cover of the trees. He checks his phone again. The green dot marking the Trans Am is stopped a quarter-mile to the northeast, at the roadblock. Moment of truth time. If he gets out of the car and walks thirty yards toward the interstate, he can watch to see if they check her trunk, but he doesn't. They won't. She's a pretty girl. They'll let her breeze right through. Him? He might be a different story. Before he takes his shot he needs to make sure Shaggy doesn't have anything in the car that might land him in hot water. It's unlikely the cops will find a reason to search it, but you can never be too safe. If they're feeling pissy, for whatever reason, all bets are off. He knows how they are, itchy with the desire to hassle people. This is the Bible belt, and the Mustang reeks of pot. That might be reason enough. Getting so far tonight only to be arrested for possession would be the cherry on top of the shit sundae. So he'll search Shaggy's car and give himself a little protection, and the Trans Am a little distance. There's no need to ride her ass. She'll break down soon enough.

He does a quick sweep of the passenger compartment with the flashlight. There's a pill bottle stuffed with marijuana buds and a baggie of gummies stashed in one of the cupholders in the center console. Both go out the window. Maybe Shaggy will find them when he wakes up. Improve his night a little. In addition to the pretty woman's phone and an automobile registration slip in the name of Brandon Hayes, the glove box holds a revolver. The only thing a strange gun can bring is trouble. He discards it.

Good thing Shaggy hadn't thought to bring it when he left the car, or things might have gone differently.

Satisfied the interior is clean—from a crime perspective, anyway—he turns his attention to his go bag. The mostly empty bottle of trank, hypodermic, and remaining zip ties are wiped clean with his shirt and deposited in three different bushes. No fingerprints to worry about, he's worn gloves the entire time. Any DNA left by happenstance after the wipedown will be taken care of by the rain. All good. When he pops the trunk, there's nothing of note inside. The spare tire, jumper cables, a set of bungee tie downs. His go bag looks right at home among them. Nothing incriminating here, officer.

After a moment of debate, he decides to keep his pistol in its holster, tucked in his waistband at the small of his back. It might become necessary, should the woman feel froggy. There's little chance the police will pat him down, he thinks, and if they do, he has a permit to carry. It's a risk he's willing to take. Never trust another man's gun, and never give up your own.

He gets back behind the wheel and checks the map. She's just leaving the on-ramp to I-10, headed west. Perfect. He'll be that much closer to New Orleans when he catches up with her. But first, the checkpoint. The cops are going to want to see the registration. He retrieves it from the glove box. Brandon Hayes. He commits the name to memory. It's not the name on his fake ID. He doesn't like inconsistency. Will the difference make the cops suspicious? Under normal circumstances, probably not, but tonight? Tonight he thinks it just might. He needs a cover story. Something to explain why he's driving the car of yon Mr. Hayes, Shaggy to his friends.

Gusty wind buffets the Mustang. Over the last several minutes the lightning has become almost constant, flashing like strobes at a rave. Thunder booms like artillery fire. It's going to rain any minute. He can smell it. Satisfied with what he plans to tell the police, the seller starts the engine and puts the windows up.

Time to get this show on the road.

30

After all the talking and sitting and doing nothing, the car is finally moving again, picking up real speed. The engine thrums, and Abby feels safe to roll over and search the rest of the trunk. Blindly, she runs her hands over the rough carpet, looking for anything she can use to protect herself. A gun or a knife, preferably. Yeah, right. She'll be lucky to find a screwdriver, and if she does, it'll probably be one of the tiny ones, like her mom uses to fix her reading glasses. But, if worse comes to worst, she has her keys. Positioned between her fingers, one could take out an eye. If she's lucky.

She touches cool metal. Some kind of rod, with evenly spaced notches all along the length of it. Midway down, a second piece encloses the shaft. It's rectangular, heavy. A thin tab juts from it, which she's able to wiggle. When she pushes down on the tab firmly, there's a click and the rod moves just a bit. The motion is familiar. It's for changing tires, she thinks. To lift the car. She can't remember what it's called. Doesn't matter. That thick chunk of metal adds too much weight. One swing, and it would sail out of her hands like Thor's hammer, only instead of smashing a bad guy it would leave her defenseless. Or worse, she'd manage to hold onto only to have it come around and brain her in the back of the head. Both options suck.

She continues the search. A clap of thunder rattles the car, making her heart leap. Jeez! Her fingers skitter over a bump in the carpet. Abby pauses. There's something underneath. She locates the edge of the mat in the back corner and works at it, trying to catch hold with her fingertips. When the carpet pulls loose, she peels it back and slides her hand under. Another metal rod. Because the engine is so loud now—it feels like they're going *really* fast—she doesn't worry about the low scrape as she pulls it out. The sound is nearly inaudible to her, and she's only about a foot away.

It's a tool of some kind, about two feet long. Solid. Weighty, but not overly so. There's a bend in it, making it the shape of the letter L. The base has a bulge at the tip, a thicker section of metal that's hollowed out in the middle, like a heavy-duty cookie cutter. It feels like it could bash a skull in. She likes that. But the other end. The. Other. End. It's flat, with a sharp edge. A *very* sharp edge, like a knife. One that would poke right into someone's guts with a solid jab. Once she watched her father take up a section of baseboard in their house because it needed to be replaced, and he used something called a pry bar. The feel of the flat, bladed end on this thing makes her think of that.

Rain begins to spatter on the lid trunk lid and the car shimmies. Wind. A sudden thought makes her pulse race. Her breath catches. The thing in her hands is like a knife! Quickly, she flips the tool around. Presses the bladed edge against the zip tie binding her ankles and begins to saw at the thick loop of plastic. It's awkward and oh so slow, but the edge is sharp enough to do the job. When the steel finally parts the tie, she's nearly giddy. Free! Despite the bleakness of her situation, she allows herself to feel a little hope.

What next? Abby rolls to face the rear of the trunk. She clutches her tool to her chest, eyeing one of the glowing taillights. If she pokes it hard enough with the blade, both the bulb and colored plastic will break. She had once read a book where a kidnapped girl was in this same situation and managed to knock out one of the lights. Forcing a hand through the hole, the girl waved it around until another driver noticed and called the police. But Abby doesn't think she can do that. Break things, sure. No problem. It's just that the mounting frame is like a cage. It surrounds the whole assembly, and her hand is too large to fit through any of the spaces. All she'd do is alert everyone in the car to her wakefulness, forfeiting any advantage brought by the element of surprise when they open—

The smooth hum of the engine gives way to a knocking sputter. It begins to wheeze like a sickly old person. The car hitches, starting to lose speed. Something is wrong. Abby takes a deep, calming breath. Dries her sweaty palms on her shirt to ensure her grip on the metal bar is good, and won't let it slip loose when her life depends on it. Things are about to get real.

Rain and wind pummel the vehicle, louder even than the failing engine. Centrifugal force tugs at her. They're turning, jerkily. It feels like the car is barely moving, a dying gasp as the engine fights to stay alive. Another turn, and the hammering rain suddenly diminishes, as if someone hit the volume button. She can still hear the storm raging, but it's like they've pulled into a garage or under an overpass.

The engine dies with a final rattle.

A sudden scream—a shriek, really—turns Abby's blood to ice. What's going on out there? Did something happen to the woman? Is *he* here? She hears the easily recognizable sound of a car door opening. The car rocks a little as someone gets out.

For an eternity the only sounds are those of the furious storm. She holds the metal bar in a death grip, wiping her hands on her shirt every few seconds to keep them dry. The air is heavy and wet, wrapping her like a hot blanket.

A metallic click and a sharp *whang* shake the car. The hood, for sure. She knows the sound. Someone just flung it up, angry. Likely checking the engine to see what's wrong. A stink seeps into the trunk, stronger even than her own body odor. Like burned chemicals. Blech. She tries breathing through her mouth, but then she can taste it, somehow both acrid and sweet at the same time. What she wouldn't give for a few breaths of the wind that keeps slamming the car hard enough to rock it on the springs!

There's a new sound, a long ragged scrape, like something being dragged. She wishes she could see what was going on.

Being blind like this sucks worse than homework. The taillights go bright red, *pop pop pop*, as lightning flashes. Thunder explodes and she jumps. Her weapon whacks the trunk lid. She freezes, listening. Certain she's given herself away, Abby squeezes the bar hard enough to make the cords in her neck stand out.

Suddenly, there's a noise right next to her head. A key, sliding into the lock. She readies herself, trembling from the consuming terror and adrenaline rush. Fight or flight. That's something she learned about in science last year. The memory of sitting in the bright classroom, listening to Mrs. Samuels explain what she called an *acute stress response* comes to her as clear as day.

As the trunk lid unlatches with a click and someone starts to raise it, Abby chooses fight.

III

FRED ANDERSON

31

Maya spins away from the attacking girl, throwing a defensive hand up to protect her head, and instead of cracking her skull the tire iron bashes her left shoulder. The tidal wave of pain is immediate and immense, staggering her. She stumbles out from under the canopy, left arm hanging limp and useless, and belly flops into a dirty puddle. Even as she scrambles to regain her footing the girl is on the move, coming for her through the pelting rain with the weapon held high.

"Wait!" Maya screams, raising the hand that still works. Her shoulder is a throbbing agony.

The girl skitters closer, brandishing the tire iron. She draws it back and roars, teeth bared.

"*Please*," Maya says. "I'm not your enemy."

"You're not my friend, either." But miraculously, she stops, watching Maya through wide panicky eyes that dart in every direction. Her breath comes in short harsh gasps. "Who are you?"

Maya's mind races, trying to make sense of the situation. Surely the girl didn't break into her trunk to hitch a ride. She can't be more than, what, twelve or thirteen? Unless she's a runaway. But how? When? Every thought just leads to more questions.

"My name is Maya Sanchez. Why were you hiding in my trunk?"

"I wasn't *hiding*," the girl snaps. "He put me in there."

Moretti. That son of a bitch. It has to be. All that concern about being used to mule drugs, and she had never once considered the man might be into trafficking something a thousand times worse. But … the line of thinking doesn't add up. She had opened the trunk at his house to check the spare and stash her backpack, and there was definitely no little girl inside. Just the tire and jack. Then it comes to her, all the pieces of the puzzle snapping into place at once. The AMBER alert, and her pit stop at the empty welcome center.

Brandon.

She recalls trying to remember his car, and how she couldn't. Because she hadn't seen it. He had hidden it somewhere—maybe in the truck lot or out in the trees—because he knew she might recognize the red Cherokee from the alert and call the police. Then he had come looking for her, to kill her and steal the Trans Am. New wheels. The police were looking for a Jeep, not an old sports car. It all makes sense now.

And somehow, she'd managed to get away from him.

Terror grips her as she realizes how close she'd come to dying. But she's alive, and so is the girl. That's what matters.

"You're her, aren't you?" she murmurs. "Abby?"

"Where are we? Are you meeting him here?"

They're talking past each other, too scared to think straight. She needs to do something to get the girl calmed down. Otherwise, she's liable to attack again … or worse, run away into the storm to God only knows what. She thinks of the sign at the exit. ENTERING HONEY ISLAND SWAMP. Jesus. Rolling her injured shoulder to test the range of motion—the pain has already begun to diminish—she tries to think of the right thing to say.

"Let's share information," Maya says. "First me, then you. Then we'll have a better understanding of what's going on. Agreed?"

The girl considers. "Okay."

Maya says, gesturing, "I was hired to deliver this car from Atlanta to Baton Rouge. Half an hour ago, I stopped at a rest area for a potty break. There was a man there—he said his name was Brandon—acting strange. I think he put you in my trunk and was planning to steal the car because the police are looking for a Jeep." She doesn't mention the part that feels so obvious now, that Brandon was planning to kill her. The girl is already terrified enough. "He scared me and I drove away, but not even five minutes after I got back on the road the car started to overheat. I barely made it here, and didn't expect it to be closed. The radiator cap is gone, but I know it was there in Atlanta because I checked it. I think he took it." She slicks wet hair from her forehead. "Now you."

"Tell me how you know my name first."

"I saw an AMBER alert for a girl about your age, blonde. Abby something. I figure that's you."

The girl nods. "Dunn. I met a boy on the beach today. Liam. He wanted to come over to our house—the house where we're staying, I mean, on vacation—to hang out and talk. When I opened the back door to sneak out, there was a man waiting." Her breath catches, and one hand unconsciously rubs her neck. "He grabbed me and gave me a shot of a drug or something. I tried to fight back, but it knocked me out. When I woke, I was in the back of … maybe it was a Jeep. Not a car. I was tied up. We weren't driving, just sitting in the dark. He got out and came around to where I was, so I pretended to be asleep."

Abby shivers.

"Are you okay?" Maya asks. She can't tell if the reaction is from the chill in the rain and wind or some memory. A sudden thought horrifies her. "Did he … do anything to you?"

"He touched me in my privates," Abby says, her voice small and scared. "But I think he was trying to see if I was awake. Not, you know, *that*."

As Maya registers what the girl is telling her, the horror gives way first to anger, then fury. Of *course* he touched her, the sick bastard, because that's what men like him do. It's practically a rite of passage for girls all over the world.

"He picked me up and carried me to your car," Abby continues. "We were in a parking lot, with lots of trees around. As soon as he shut the trunk I started trying to get loose." Her voice cracks and she bursts into tears. "I just want to go *home!*"

Maya feels like her heart is going to break. God only knows what Brandon had planned for the poor girl. She longs to reach out, to hug her and tell her everything will be okay. That she's safe now. But none of that is true, because a terrifying thought has begun to peck at the back of her brain, like a robin trying to uncover a half-buried worm. If Brandon planned to kill Maya and steal the Trans Am, why had he taken the radiator cap? He *wanted* the car to break down. Her gaze turns to the road, where she half expects to see him, sprinting through the storm like something from a nightmare.

Abby isn't safe at all. Neither of them are.

"We need to call the police, right now," Maya says. "I lost my phone when I ran away from him. Do you have one?"

She's not surprised when the response is negative. If the girl had a phone, she would have called 911 the instant she freed herself. Her gaze turns to the convenience store. There has to be one inside. She's certain of it. All she needs to do is smash a window and find it. Funny, because not even ten minutes ago she had considered doing just that, but decided against it because she knew she would be arrested. Now? Now she might get a medal instead of jail.

She points toward the building. "I'm going to break one of those windows and look for a phone in the store. May I use your tire iron?"

Abby clutches the weapon to her chest and backs away, shaking her head.

"No problem," Maya says, placatingly. "I'm a stranger. No reason for you to trust me yet. I'll look for something else. Just"—she tries a smile she hopes looks honest and principled —"please don't hit me again."

32

"What brings you to Mississippi tonight, Mr. Foster?" the cop says, nearly blinding the seller with his flashlight. He leans over, so his face is only inches from the cracked window.

"Blackjack," the seller says with a toothy grin that belies the tension in his belly. A second beam plays over interior as the other cop circles the car, checking it out. Showtime. Get in front of any suspicions with a story to demonstrate openness and sincerity. "Came over this evening with my buddy Brandon to see if Lady Luck might grace us with her smile. I lost my ass—er, shirt pretty quickly, but he hit a streak and decided to keep going while the cards are hot. I'm headed home, coming back to get him Sunday unless things go south and he wants me sooner. Treasure Bay comped him a room. Me, not so much, and sharing a bed with him isn't my thing, if you get my drift."

The cop at the window focuses his light on the Louisiana license—a fake in the name of Aaron Foster, purchased off the dark web for five hundred well-spent bucks—in his hand, then double-checks the registration. "I see. And home is New Orleans?"

"Yes, sir."

"That's where Mr. Hayes lives, too?"

Ah, a test. So he *has* made the cop suspicious. Thank God he took a minute to study the details on the registration, or he'd be fumbling right now and making things worse. "No, officer, he lives in Lafayette."

"Mmm hmm," the cop says. "And what about your arm? How'd you get that?"

The light leaps from the papers to the six-inch stripe of fresh scab on the seller's inner arm, where the product had scratched him. In the bright glow, the angry flesh looks bleached. Shit. A flash in the rearview mirror catches his eye as the second cop circles around the back of the car. He feels a trickle of sweat running down his scalp, mercifully out of sight, and turns his arm like he's trying to get a better look at his injury.

"Raked it on the corner of the car door earlier," he says. His words sound far off, nearly lost in white noise that seems to fill his ears. "Wasn't paying attention to what I was doing. Hurt like hell, believe you me."

There's a *whumpwhump* from the rear of the car as the second cop bangs his fist on the trunk lid.

"Mind opening that up, Mr. Foster?"

"What's this all about?" the seller asks. "Have I done something wrong?"

"That's what we're trying to determine."

The seller debates pushing back. Refusing, even. Put on a show, feign a little outrage to throw them off. Tell them to get a warrant, which he doubts very much they can do. There's no probable cause here. They're fishing, either because they're bored, or something about him has set their spidey senses tingling. Maybe the scratch on his arm. Maybe the stupid shit-eating grin when he told his cover story. Who knows? It's a way to find out more. But putting on a show is going to waste time he doesn't have. Not when every passing minute separates him more from the product. From his money. There's no telling when the Trans Am is going to blow. He wants to be close when it does. The more time the woman has with a broken-down car, the greater the chances of her discovering her payload.

"Look, Mr. Foster, I can smell the marijuana," the cop says, his face smoothing, suddenly friendly. "I don't care about that. Smoke 'em if you got 'em, that's my motto. I don't care where you've been or what you've been doing, unless you know something about a little girl that's been taken away from her momma and daddy. We just need to make sure she's not with you, because the man that has her is about your age, and you're driving a car that doesn't belong to you. Letting us take a quick peek in the back is a lot faster than being detained while we track down Mr. Hayes at the casino and verify your story, or wake up a judge to procure a search warrant. What do you say?"

"Be my guest," the seller says. He presses the button to release the latch. A gust of wind rocks the Mustang hard enough to make the springs creak. Several drops of rain splatter on the windshield.

"It's clear," the second cop says.

The officer at the window pushes the pair of documents through the gap. "See how easy that was?"

"I hope you catch whoever took that girl," the seller says. "There's nothing lower than a person who would prey on a child."

The cop nods. "Drive safe, Mr. Foster."

As the seller closes the window, another burst of rain tattoos the car. Lightning rips the sky, follows closely by a boom of thunder that hurts his ears. He puts the Mustang into drive and pulls away from the roadblock. Freedom! A howling wind drives sheets of rain through the headlight beams as he brakes in the turn lane for the on-ramp to I-10. The storm is upon him. He'll need to take it slow for a bit, until things ease up. Not a problem. The woman will be forced to do the same.

But when he checks his phone, the GPS marker on the map is stationary, as if the Trans Am has already bitten the dust. Perfect. His worries about losing time at the roadblock were baseless. She isn't even five miles away. He zooms in. It looks like she left the interstate and stopped at a gas station in a great big swath of nothing. Better, a *closed* gas station, assuming the information provided by the app is up-to-date. How could he possibly ask for anything better?

The seller makes the turn, accelerating up the on-ramp. His product is waiting.

33

Abby watches the petite lady lift the trashcan over her head like the Hulk and toss it at the large window at the front of the store. The flimsy container bounces off the thick glass and crashes to the concrete with a hollow *bong*, scattering napkins and wrappers and plastic soft drink bottles everywhere. A flush of heat burns her cheeks. She knows she should have let Maya use the weapon she found, but can't bear the thought of relinquishing it. Not until she knows for sure she can trust her.

"Oh, *nice*, Maya," the woman snaps. She slicks her short hair back furiously and stalks to the end of the building, where the grass is thigh-high, thick and lush all the way to the edge of the woods. Squinting into the darkness, she says, "I would kill for a flashlight right now."

Abby waits to see what the plan is, but the woman simply stands there, staring intently at the ground. Curious. Then a bolt of lightning banishes the night for an instant, and Maya crows. She takes a giant step into the grass. Stoops. Rises with a chunk of dried concrete clutched triumphantly in one small hand. When she returns to the front of the store and hurls it at the window, the concrete punches a basketball-sized hole through and smashes into a rack of candy, clattering to the tile floor. The second time Maya throws the trashcan, the glass shatters with a raucous crash. Crystalline shards fall like deadly rain, exploding on impact, and fragments spray across the parking lot in cheery clinks and tinkles.

"There now," Maya says. She swipes her hair back again. "Are you okay? Did anything hit you?"

"All good." Abby hates the way her voice still sounds shaky

and childish, like she's about to start bawling like a little baby all over.

Maya uses her foot to break away the jagged pieces left in the bottom of the frame. She steps over the low cinderblock wall into the store and turns back, reaching out. "Need a hand?"

"I've got it." No way is she going to let the woman touch her, even for—supposedly—help. Not yet.

"Suit yourself." Maya beelines for the cashier station, glass crunching underfoot.

Abby waits until she's moved far enough away before entering. The only light in the building comes from beer signs over the cooler and a flickering tube in a nook at the back. There's a door there, marked *Employees Only*. It's hard to see anything. She moves toward the end of the store where Maya went, keeping her distance. Her stomach rumbles. Dinner had been a lifetime ago, and she's been through heck since then. "Is it okay if I get a candy bar?"

"Go ahead," Maya says. She's behind the counter, stooping to search the shelves beneath. "Do me a favor and turn on the lights? I'm flying blind back here."

Abby selects a Snickers and tears the wrapper away from one end for a huge bite. Heaven. As she chews, she looks for a switch. There's one next to the front door and she flips it. Cold white light floods the tiny store.

"Thanks," Maya says. All that can be seen of her is the crown of her wet head, peeking over the counter between the cash register and a rack of lip balm. "There's got to be a—holy cow, I didn't even know phones like this still existed!"

She rises like a specter, grinning. Abby likes her smile. It makes her look nice, someone who might not be a kidnapper after all. Maya is holding up a boxy thing made of molded beige plastic like it's a championship trophy. There are two pieces connected by a thick, coiled cord, with a series of numbered buttons on the larger. When Maya plops it on the counter it lands with a solid thud. Something inside it emits a sharp metallic *ting*.

"What is that?" Abby says through a mouthful of candy bar. She gulps the last bite and balls up the wrapper. Pockets it.

"A telephone. One of the ancient ones that uses wires. We had one like it when I was a little kid. Like, first grade little. Figures a place called Peepaw's would have a remnant of the Stone Age."

Maya lifts the smaller piece and presses it to the side of her head. Frowns. She mashes a few of the numbers, shaking her head, then pecks at a button on the top with a staccato series of taps. "Crap."

"What?" Abby asks.

"It's dead. No dial tone."

Abby isn't sure what she's talking about, but *dead* doesn't sound very good.

"Maybe the storm knocked it out," Maya says. "Or maybe it's just a relic and hasn't worked for years. *Shit.* Sorry."

"My dad says worse than that all the time." The thought of her parents jolts her, makes her sad again. She wants more than anything to see her family, right now. Even her stupid brother.

And Liam. *Especially* him.

"I'm going to check in the back," Maya says. "Maybe there's an office, and a working phone."

She rounds the end of the counter and crosses to the cubby between the beer and soft drink coolers. The *Employees Only* door squeals when she pushes it open. Beyond is nothing but blackness. Maya vanishes, and a moment later lights come on. Abby follows, into a storeroom that runs the length of the building. The hum of the coolers is very loud back here, the temperature at least ten degrees cooler. Stacks of beer cases line the cinderblock rear wall. At one end of the space is a tiny bathroom, and at the other, an office that's little more than a closet. Maya turns on the light in there, looks around, turns it back off.

"So much for that idea," she says. "Time for plan B."

34

Maya wants to put her fist through the flimsy office door. All they're doing is wasting time. They need to be on the move, not standing around this godforsaken place. Brandon is coming. She understands this now, and is pissed that it took her so long to realize it. He sabotaged the Trans Am for one reason: so he would be able to find her—or more specifically, Abby—again. Her original thought, that he'd wanted to kill her back at the rest stop, was laughably wrong. He was trying to *scare* her, so she'd run like a bat out of hell. Why? Because he needed her to get Abby past the checkpoint. It's obvious. The police were on the lookout for him, and she showed up just in time to save his skin.

Nothing but a damn mule after all, just not for Moretti.

He's a heck of an actor, she has to give him that. The addled stoner persona, Mr. *I'm not a bad dude*, had been pretty convincing. Enough to change her mind initially, anyway. She should have trusted her gut, instead of falling for his performance. It was all in the eyes, small and close-set. Serial killer eyes. She'd let him mislead her into believing it was just the weed while all along he was scheming, planning his second act. The stolen radiator cap would ensure she had to stop, making it simple for him to swoop in and reclaim his prize. He could be out there in the darkness right this minute, waiting for them. She harbors no doubts about the value of her life now that she's served her purpose. The goosebumps she feels when she rubs her arms aren't from the chill of the storeroom.

"What's plan B?" Abby says, snapping her out of her thoughts.

"The Trans Am should still drive. It only overheated because the man at the welcome center—Brandon—took the radiator cap. All it needs is some water. I think, anyway." Maya speaks slowly, choosing her words. There's no need to tip the girl off to her thoughts. That would terrify her even more than she already is. "Before I found you, I was going to refill the radiator with rainwater and try to make it to Slidell. It's a real town, about ten miles from here. There will be people, and a police station."

"Plan B sounds good to me," Abby says. The tremors have left her voice, but not the trepidation. An improvement.

"Let's use water from the bathroom sink instead," Maya says. "It's cleaner. I saw a rack of t-shirts just inside the front door. We can plug the filler hole with one. It ought to make it ten miles, as long as we don't push it too hard. Let's get going. We can be on the road in no time."

She hopes.

Exiting the storeroom, the lights in the sales area seem a hundred times brighter than before, and Maya again has the unsettled feeling of being on a stage, watched by an unseen audience. She shields her eyes with a hand and scans the parking lot for new vehicles. The Trans Am stands alone. Unless he's hidden in the shadows, Brandon isn't here yet. Maybe they have time. Or even better, what if she's lost him? He might have been identified at the checkpoint and arrested, or had some other problem and is now cruising the interstate, searching for them. Fine. Let him look until the cows come home.

"Maya," Abby says. She points at the bottom shelf of the steel rack facing the beer cooler, where a tiny section of space is devoted to a dusty smattering of automotive supplies: quarts of oil, waxy emergency road flares, washer fluid, an open box of smiley face air fresheners in yellowing cellophane … and, wonder of wonders, a pair of bright blue one-gallon containers of antifreeze.

Maya wants to pick the girl up and spin her around. "Outstanding! Way to go, Miss Eagle Eyes." she says. She reaches for a jug of coolant, pleased to see a shy smile—a *real* smile—flicker across Abby's face. "This stuff is even better than water."

After a moment's thought, she grabs a couple of the road flares and jams them into her pocket. If the car breaks down again before they make it to Slidell (a worry she will not be sharing with Abby; for the girl it's all game face, all the time) they might come in handy for flagging someone down to help them. She refuses to entertain the idea that the someone might be Brandon. Not right now. These supplies are a sign that things are turning around. They have to be.

"Let's go," she says. At the window, she nods at the rack of souvenir Honey Island Swamp t-shirts. "Grab a couple of those, would you?"

She feels guilty about having broken into the store, then stealing from poor old Peepaw and running off, but there's no time to leave a note with some money. Better to make amends once they've reached safety. Surely the owner will understand. She'll make him whole, even if she has to pay for the broken window herself. It's the right thing to do. She steps out over the window frame.

The squall has passed, leaving behind only the scent of fecund earth and a gentle rain that sizzles on the oily pavement. Maya goes to the Trans Am, twisting the lid off one of the gallon containers. The mouth of the spout is covered with foil, so she gets the keys from the ignition to tear it away. Standing over the engine, she's pleased to find it's cooled enough that she can hold her hand against the radiator without discomfort. Perfect. She steadies the jug and begins to pour, trying not to waste any of the precious orange liquid.

"Someone's coming," Abby says.

Maya's heart stutters, and she freezes for an instant. Peers around the hood in the direction Abby is looking. A pair of headlights made fuzzy by the rising ground mist emerge from the shadows of the overpass, twin circles that hide the approaching vehicle. Think. She sets the container on the ground and slams the hood, then lunges around to the driver side door. The pepper spray isn't much, but it's better than nothing.

"It's him, isn't it?" Abby says. The tremor is back. "Coming to take me again."

"We don't know who it is." But she *does* know, deep in her gut. The girl is right. Brandon has found them. Her hand locates the canister and she seizes it. She straightens and stands beside Abby to face whatever approaches, keeping the pepper spray out of sight at her hip. "Maybe it's someone who saw the sign or lights and thinks the store is open."

She wishes she believes it.

"Here, take this."

When Maya turns, Abby holds out the tire iron.

35

She accepts the weapon, holding it loosely at her side so she doesn't look deranged and threatening, in case whoever is coming isn't Brandon. The steel bar provides a certain comforting heft. It speaks of the ability to do some real damage up close and personal, should the need arise. She watches as the car slows and wheels into the parking lot, squinting when the bright lights sweep across the two of them. Anxiety roils her stomach into twisted knots. She inches closer to Abby, stepping a little in front to shield her.

"It's going to be okay," she murmurs, not sure which of them she's trying to comfort.

Abby says nothing. Her breath comes in quick, short gasps as the car draws near. It coasts to a stop about twenty feet from them, out in the drizzle. Despite the action of the wipers to flick the falling rain away, from where Maya stands the windshield appears opaque. The engine dies and the headlights fade. She can make out the shape of the driver, but can't see enough to determine sex or age. It's nothing more than a human-shaped shadow cloaked in darkness.

Behind her, Abby whimpers. The car door opens and someone clambers out. Maya feels like she's been sucker punched in the gut. It's not Brandon. The man standing before them appears to be older by ten years or more. The gloom makes it hard to tell for sure. He's too far from the light coming through the store windows. Maybe six feet tall and well-built, with broad shoulders and a narrow waist. White—she thinks— with dark hair. It's impossible to discern any specific features. Maya considers the description from the AMBER alert. This guy matches it a lot more closely than Brandon did.

"Is it him?" she whispers out of the corner of her mouth, keeping her eyes on the stranger in case he makes a move. Her body thrums with tension.

"I don't *know!*" Abby's voice is raw, filled with anguish. "I never saw him!"

"Mister," Maya calls, "can we use your phone?"

"First, you want to tell me what you ladies have done to my store?"

Maya feels like she's been whacked with a goofy stick. "To *your* store?"

The man scoffs. "Did you expect an old man with a corncob pipe? Peepaw is what my little boy calls his grandfather. It's an homage." He glances up at the sky and adds, "Look, I'm getting soaked out here. I'm coming under."

Two cautious steps in their direction bring him into the shelter of the canopy, where the light is better. Her first impression had been correct. He's the right age. Maya feels Abby's hand nervously grab a fistful of t-shirt at her back, and thumbs open the flip top on the pepper spray. One more step and they'll find out if the stuff is as accurate at twelve feet as the label claims, no matter who he is. This isn't the time or the place for a stranger to walk up on her. Better to apologize for spraying an innocent person than die because of indecision.

"Now," the man says, "explain what you're up to before I call the police."

The most beautiful words Maya has heard all night. She says, "Please, call them. We only broke into your store—and I'm truly sorry for that—because we needed to call the police."

"I see," the man says. He puts his hands on his hips, looking past them to the front of the building. "So why didn't you?"

"The phone doesn't work."

For an instant it looks like he's fighting not to smile. "Did your car break down? The cops won't help you with that, not around here. You need a tow truck."

"We'll get a tow truck," she says evenly. Something is wrong here. Why is he asking so many questions? For all he knows the two of them are common thieves he's caught in the act. "But first, we need the police. Will you call them, please?"

"What's your name?" he asks.

"You don't need my name," Maya says. "You just need to call 911. I'll tell *them* my name."

Alarm bells clamor in her head. He's stalling, and there's only one reason for him to do that. This isn't his store. She doesn't know if he's the man who kidnapped Abby or just some random creeper who spotted the two of them all alone in an isolated location and wants to … make the most of his good fortune. The world is filled with such men, she knows.

"What say you, princess?" the man says. He leans to one side and peers around Maya, at Abby. "You want to tell me this lady's name?"

"No," Abby says quietly. She takes a hitching breath. "I want you to call 911, like she says."

"Why won't you just do it? You caught us red-handed. Send us to jail," Maya demands, stepping to the right to block Abby from his view. There's something *hungry* in the way he's looking at the girl. Fear washes over her in an icy bath, and her grip tightens on the tire iron. Let him have the old one-two if he makes a move she doesn't like. One to blind him, two to drop him. A heart-stopping thought suddenly forces itself to the forefront of her mind. "How did you even know we were here?"

He points at the building. "You triggered the alarm when you broke in, and it called my house. Scared the hell out of me. I was dead asleep."

She hears the pulsing *whoom whoom whoom* of blood rushing in her ears. That's a bald-faced lie, because—

"Aw, shit," the man says ruefully, and this time he loses the fight with the grin. "You said the phone doesn't work, didn't you? Isn't *my* face red." He shrugs. "Oh well. Win some, lose some. I'll be taking the girl now. You weren't even supposed to know about her. What the hell happened?"

When Maya doesn't respond, he continues. "Why don't you

lose the tire iron and walk away? It'll be best for you if you do."

"That isn't going to happen," Maya says. She takes a step toward him, then another, brandishing the steel bar. He watches her warily, definitely within reach of a good swing now. "You want her, you have to get through me first."

"Not a problem," the man says, reaching for something behind his back.

Maya doesn't wait to see what it is. She whips up the hand with the pepper spray and unleashes a stream into his face. The effect of the fiery liquid is galvanizing. He shrieks a litany of profanity and spins away, pawing at his eyes. She leaps for him, raising the tire iron overhead to crack his skull, but before she can use it, the thunderclap of gunfire under the metal awning nearly deafens her. A blast of air passes close enough for her to feel the warmth and she shies away.

BOOM!

Another blast, the muzzle flash revealing a face twisted with pain and fury. The door of the convenience store explodes in a shower of tempered glass pebbles she barely hears over the ringing.

"Let's go, sister!" the man bellows.

Maya lunges for Abby, who stands frozen in shock or terror. Tries to turn her around.

"*Run!*" she screams, and pushes her toward the weedy growth at the end of the building.

Together, woman and child flee for the safety of the trees.

36

The seller angrily jams the pistol into its holster and stumbles toward the lights—a distorted kaleidoscope is all he can make out—using the front of his shirt to wipe away as much of the burning spray as he can. God, the *pain*! His streaming eyes and the tender flesh around them feel like they're engulfed in flames. Snot runners dangle from each nostril, and his tongue and throat are sandpaper raw. He noisily hawks up a mouthful of reddish brown foulness and spits twice, then steps over the low wall into the convenience store. His ears ache from the gunfire. The damnable woman had been like a magician, keeping his attention focused on the tire iron while she pulled a *much* worse rabbit out of her hat.

Eyes no wider than slits, hands out, he feels his way to the coolers. Milk is supposed to be good for cutting the heat of peppers. Something about the fat in it. He doesn't know if it works the same for pepper spray, but anything has to be better than this. At the very end of the soft drink cooler are the non-carbonated beverages, and there he finds several pints of whole milk. When he cracks one open and pours the cold liquid over his face, the relief is immediate. The seller tugs his shirt off and uses a clean spot like a washcloth to gently remove the pepper spray. The pain fades to a bearable shadow of what it had been. He reaches for another pint.

When he had turned into the parking lot and seen the woman standing in the glare of the headlights, his first reaction had been one of arousal. She was soaked from the storm, t-shirt and jeans clinging to all the right places, short black hair swept back. Magnificent, and in her own way just as exquisite as the girl. Then he had spotted the product and his mood plummeted. Interest had quickly given way to the sobering realization that his chances of getting her back easily were now close to nil. Unless he could talk his way out of it, the only way would be by killing the woman. He doesn't know if he's capable of such brutality unless his life or freedom is on the line. Selling is one thing, murder is another.

There's a door marked *Employees Only*. Beyond it, he finds a tiny bathroom. He spins a handful of paper towels from the roll on the back of the toilet and honks his nose several times. Before continuing, he turns on the water and soaps up his gloves, scrubbing any residual pepper spray residue off. Once he has dried them, he uses the second pint of milk and more paper towels to properly clean his face. After a couple of minutes he begins to feel human again. The pungent stink no longer fills his nostrils, and much of his anger at being bested has drained away. Sometimes the dice come up seven and the house wins. He rolls the damp tissues in his shirt to take back to the car.

On the way out, he stops at a rack of souvenir tees and chooses a black one with a grinning cartoon alligator showing about a hundred sharp teeth. Underneath it says SWAMP PEOPLE in a drippy, running font. He pulls it on and steps out through the window. At the end of the building, where the woman and girl had disappeared, he shines his flashlight into the blackness. From here, the trees—no more than fifty feet away through the weeds—appear to be an impenetrable tangle. He checks his phone. The red marker shows that the product is more than a hundred feet from him. Much further than he expected. He assumed they would be right at the edge, perhaps even crouching in the tall grass, waiting to see what he would do. But they're at least fifty feet in. Does the woman have any idea where she is?

The seller pinches the screen to zoom out. Nothing but shades of green and blue for miles. The store borders the Honey Island Swamp, a place no sane person would want to go in the dead of night without serious weaponry. Certainly more than a tire iron and a little can of pepper spray. Hell, he has the Kimber and six remaining Hydra Shok hollow points, and can't imagine trekking through alligator-infested Louisiana wetlands. Not even for a quarter of a million bucks. He's taken his best shot —a damn good one, in his not-so-humble opinion—but now it's time to let the product go. Take the loss. It's the first failure out of almost two dozen collections, and he's learned enough from tonight's mistakes to make sure there will never be a second. Hell, he can almost respect the woman with her pepper spray. Outplayed is outplayed. If he leaves now, he can be in bed in Tallahassee before sunup.

"You win, sister!" he calls, one hand cupped to his mouth. "I wish we could have met under better circumstances."

On the way back to the car he notices the open gallon of antifreeze sitting on the pavement in front of the Trans Am and nearly grins. Good on her, figuring out the reason for the breakdown out so quickly. Maybe there's some truth in the old adage about the deceptive nature of appearances, because the woman certainly doesn't appear as resourceful as she apparently is. He tosses the rolled-up shirt into the passenger seat of the Mustang and starts the engine. The windshield has fogged over. He reaches for the defroster switch.

And his gaze falls on the blood-crusted scratch running down the inside of his arm.

"Son of a *bitch*," the seller says. His skin is under the product's nails. His DNA. And that won't do, because his DNA is also in Uncle Sam's database, thanks to a brief stint in the Army right out of high school, a few years after 9/11. He had signed up with grand visions of fighting the ragheads in Iraq, but instead found himself stationed at Fort Rucker. The hardest four months of his life was spent in south Alabama during the hottest part of the year, learning aviation maintenance in a stifling hangar until they drummed him out under Chapter 11. His discharge papers called it an *inability to adapt to military life*. Inability to put up with the crap they shoveled at him around the clock was more like it. Of course, they don't call the garrison

Fort Rucker anymore, not in today's politically correct climate. Old Colonel Rucker fought for the Confederacy under Nathan Bedford Forrest back in the day, a muckety muck in the Klan and big-time slave trader. One of the OG sellers, you might say. The mental quip raises the ghost of a smile.

They had collected the sample when he reported to boot camp. No one said what it was for, but he knew. At the end of a battle, sometimes DNA is the only way to identify the pieces. Taking some from every new grunt ensures those pieces make it back to the right loved ones. When they find his (and oh yes, they'll find it, because they can find that shit *anywhere*) under the girl's fingernails they'll be on him quicker than a jackrabbit on a hot griddle. He has a life back in Tallahassee. A *public* life, where people know him and like him and have no idea about his … fundraising activities.

So no, he can't walk away after all.

As he plays out the options in his head a deep melancholy settles over him. Without any trank to subdue her, there's no way he can carry the product out. In Bay St. Louis, getting her from the house to the Jeep as dead weight had been trouble enough, but awake and fighting back in the middle of a swamp? No thanks. And that's without even considering the woman. It's clear she won't let him near the girl without a fight, and she fights dirty. There's no real choice he can see. The best thing he can do now is track them down and end them cleanly with the pistol. Remove the product's DNA-crusted hands for proper disposal, leave the rest for the animals. The line of predators waiting for a taste will be a mile long. Not what he wants, but does he have a choice? Not if he values his freedom.

The seller shuts off the engine and drops the keys in the center console cupholder. He picks up the damp t-shirt. There's nothing else in the Mustang that can be tied to him except— maybe—the trackers in his go bag. Easy enough to stow all of it in the swamp. Mark the spot with a waypoint to pick up on the way back. Then, if he hasn't returned before Peepaw shows up in the morning to open the store, no big deal if he finds the car.

There are other ways to get home.

But he'll make it back in time. A tire iron and a little can of pepper spray are no match for a pistol and stun gun. Not to mention the tracker hidden in the product's pocket, ready to lead him right to them. He climbs out of the car and retrieves the go bag from the trunk. As he crosses beneath the canopy, he checks the location of the tracker on the map—the product hasn't moved—then enables the bread crumbs feature. Before putting the phone away, he halves the brightness. No need to announce himself.

Gun in hand, the seller steps into the tall grass.

37

Abby stoops beside a pine tree with her hands on her knees, trying to get her breath under control. Not from bolting into the woods, which had not been far at all, but from the terror of everything that had happened only moments before. The man had shown up at the store like something out of a bad dream. How had he even known where they were?

She thinks back to the fury in his eyes as he reached for the gun, the curses that chased them through the grass when they ran. Pulling a long breath in through her nose, she lets it out slowly through her mouth. Mosquitoes tickle at her ears, the eye-watering hum like insanity itself gibbering at her, even louder than the chorus of cheeps and peeps from multitudes of serenading frogs. Between the cloud cover and thick canopy of branches, it's nearly impossible to see. Which could be *good*, all things considered. If the hordes of creepy-crawlies and critters she imagines are around them were visible, she might scream.

Beside her, Maya is nothing but a vague shape facing back the way they came. Keeping watch. Abby wants to throw her arms around the woman, to apologize and thank her for standing up to him. For not handing her over when he demanded it—and for actually charging in like a superhero, ready to beat the snot out of him with the steel bar if he hadn't pulled a gun. A *gun*! He. Shot. At. Them. The thought makes her knees go weak, and she sags against the tree trunk.

Light dances through the greenery. A flashlight, by the store. The beam sweeps from side to side as the man searches. Something spidery dances down her leg and Abby sucks in a quick breath, swiping skittishly at it. Just a trickle of water. The grass they ran through had been up to her waist, dripping with rain. Her legs and sneakers were soaked before they made it even halfway to the treeline. A nervous giggle bubbles up and she swallows it.

"Don't worry," Maya whispers, misunderstanding the gasp. "He's too far away, he can't see us."

The light goes off, and the man calls out something she can't make out over the frogs. Maybe the word *sister* is in it. She can't be sure. A moment later, headlights bloom and there comes the faint sound of a car starting. Maya reaches out and squeezes her arm. Dapples of muted white play across the woman's face.

"Is he leaving?" Abby asks hopefully.

"Not sure. Stay right here, I'm going for a closer look."

Before Abby can argue, she slips away into the darkness, leaving the girl alone with the wildlife and her fears.

38

Maya creeps toward the back of the store, keeping to one side of the scattered light that filters through the undergrowth. She stays low, watching for any sign of movement indicating the presence of the kidnapper as she moves from trunk to trunk. Nothing. Soon she reaches the border where the forest ends and the weeds begin. The rain has slowed to little more than a fine mist that swirls and dances in the headlight beams. A path emerges from the trees here, a ribbon of dark earth through the grass in what appears to be a straight line to the building. Interesting. Too bad they hadn't seen it when they were running. A trail would have been a lot easier to navigate than the clutching brambles and vines and saplings. Thin scratches cover both her arms, and she thinks she probably ruined her jeans on the splintered end of a broken branch.

But she's alive, as is the girl.

She turns her attention to the parking lot, where the oblique angle affords her a view of him in his car. The man is just sitting there, the gray blob of his face barely evident in the glow coming from the store. What the hell is he doing?

After a moment, the engine shuts off. The headlights fade. He throws the door open and strides to the rear of the car. Pops the trunk and roots around for something. A duffel bag, it looks like. When he slams the lid and starts in her direction her stomach flutters, but he's walking more slowly now, fiddling with his phone. The wan bluish light from the screen makes him look like a corpse. And somehow she *knows* exactly what he's doing: marking his location, so he'll know how to get back, because—

The phone goes dark and the man vanishes in the shadows, but not before she sees him stalking for the grass at the edge of the parking lot. *Damn* it. She turns and sprints down the trail, hoping whoever created it did a good job of clearing the path, because she's going far too fast for the conditions. If she falls it's going to be painful. Her sudden activity silences the singing frogs, and over the thudding of her heart she hears the crackle of twigs and rustling leaves as the man breaches the treeline.

"Abby," she stage whispers, slowing to a walk. Rainwater drips from the leaves, pattering all around her. The girl can't be more than ten or twenty feet away if she'd stayed put. "*Abby!*"

"Here," comes the soft reply.

The man is getting closer, stumbling through the vegetation, loud as a bull in a china shop. Almost like he *wants* them to hear him. Like he gets off on it. The thought chills her.

"Come toward my voice," she says. "*Hurry.*"

A beam spears the gloom fifty feet away, sweeping back and forth in their direction in a quick search. Maya sees a flash of blonde, a glimpse of wide panicked eyes, and then the light is gone again, leaving a harsh red blob that floats in the middle of her field of vision. She grips the tire iron hard enough to make her hand hurt.

"Over here," she whispers. She blinks her eyes rapidly, trying to get rid of the afterimage. There is a ripple in the leaves, a sudden sense of presence. A hand touches her elbow. She grabs hold and pulls Abby close, puts her mouth to the girl's ear. "There's a trail. We have to run."

Her eyes are readjusting to the darkness. She races deeper into the woods, Abby following close behind. The ground soon softens. Mud slurps at their shoes. In her head, a vision of the sign on the exit ramp. They're running headlong into a swamp, and the further in they go the worse it's going to get. But what choice do they have? The man chasing them has only the worst intentions. Of this she has no doubt. At least in here they can hide, wait him out. He won't search forever. Like all cockroaches, he'll scurry for cover at first light before anyone discovers him.

More than anything, she wants to take one of the emergency flares and use it to light the way, to reveal the trip hazards and lead them to the perfect hiding spot. But that would be like painting a target on their backs. The less he sees of them the better. If luck is on their side he'll stumble blindly past once they find somewhere to hide, and they can double back to the car. Get out of this hellscape before he knows what happened.

Maya reaches what she first thinks is a clearing, but almost immediately realizes isn't. She stops short, teetering at the edge of a large, stagnant pool. A mat of floating foliage mostly hides the surface. God only knows what's swimming around underneath. An instant later, Abby crashes into her. She pitches forward, arms flailing. The word *ALLIGATOR* flashes behind her eyes in gigantic blood-red letters, and a terrified yelp slips out. The tire iron leaps from her hand and goes flying. Just before she plunges through the carpet of rustling leaves into the dank sludge she hears it splash several feet away.

Brackish water floods her mouth and nose and she gags. Her hands sink past the wrists into the muck at the bottom. The pool is shallow, only a couple of feet deep. She rips free of the sucking goop and struggles through twisted leafy tendrils to the bank, spitting filth. Her nostrils are filled with the stink of rotting vegetation. Some wriggling thing—*leech*, her mind whispers with sick glee—twists and turns on her cheek. She brushes it away, shuddering. Abby offers a hand and helps her back onto solid ground.

"Sorry," the girl whispers.

A hundred feet away, the flashlight comes on for another two-second sweep. Their pursuer isn't using the path. Good. It'll slow him down.

"Don't worry about it," Maya murmurs. "Let's keep moving."

She takes a few steps back in the direction they'd come from, studying forest floor. The trail wouldn't lead directly into water. Either it ended or she missed a turn. There. The strip of bare earth takes a sharp leftward bend. She had been so lost in her thoughts she never even noticed.

"Come on."

They start along the path, this time at a fast walk so they don't lose it again. It winds through trees that grow closer and closer together. Jagged wooden knobs erupt like rotted teeth from the soft ground all around the thick trunks. Dangling streamers of Spanish moss feel like spiderwebs across her face. Fireflies flash in the darkness, and an owl high overhead questions their presence in its home. As they travel further and further, Maya tries to mentally keep track of the general direction of the store. Eventually they'll come back out, and they may or may not have the path to rely on. Despite the feeling that they've traveled a tremendous distance because of the adrenaline, she doesn't think it's more than a few hundred yards away. And even if they miss Peepaw's on the way back, if she gets the direction right, they'll at least hit the road. That's almost as good.

She sees a flash of light ahead and freezes.

"Tell me you saw that," she whispers.

"I saw it."

How had he gotten past them without making a sound? She listens intently, head cocked, trying to hear anything over the frogs. Nothing. It doesn't make any sense. There's no way he could have gotten ahead of them without them knowing. Even if he'd found his own trail, he would have needed his flashlight to move so quickly, and one of them would have seen it. Would have heard something, at the very least. She turns to face behind them, watching and listening. After a moment she sees it: a faint flicker through the trees, far back. Him. Still coming.

So who's in front, she wonders. A hunter? Surely not. Not at this hour, on the tail end of a pretty strong storm. Only a fool would be out here now. She takes a few steps down the path until there's a gap in the branches, and gets a direct look at the source.

It's a streetlight, shining like a welcoming beacon. An excited smile splits her face, because streetlights mean society, and society means people.

Maya grabs Abby's arm, and they run for the light.

39

A moment later, when the path terminates in a cleared area roughly thirty feet across, she realizes her mistake. On the far side, someone has erected a tall creosote post, and mounted atop it is a buzzing bucket light identical to the ones she grew up playing under on hot summer nights in Marietta. Swarms of insects flit and dart through the cone of white, bumping mindlessly against the dirty refractor. The only thing that keeps her from screaming in frustration is the sight of a cabin beneath it, poking out of the dense undergrowth at the edge of the clearing.

Constructed of rough-cut logs and topped with a corrugated metal roof, the tiny building is about as wide as one of the detail bays at Capstone. The only discernible window, next to the front door, is completely dark. Despite her near certainty that no one lives here because of the remote location, it's hard for Maya to contain her excitement. Working electricity implies that the cabin isn't abandoned, that someone still uses it. The cleared area is *clear*, with no encroaching ground cover. It's been taken care of, clipped and trimmed and maintained in the not so distant past. This time of year, vegetation grows far too quickly for it not to have been. That means there might be something useful inside, like a working phone ... or a weapon. Ever since she lost the tire iron she's felt exposed, vulnerable.

"Let's check it out," she says.

They climb the two steps onto the narrow plank porch. A neat stack of split firewood and old wooden rocking chair reinforce the idea that the cabin gets regular use. Just as Maya is about to knock in case someone *does* live here—perhaps an old Cajun man or woman subsisting on whatever bounties the swamp provides—she sees the heavy-duty padlock dangling from a hasp just above the knob. Damn. She picks up a piece of firewood. It's about eighteen inches long and a little thicker than a billy club. Not as nice as the tire iron, but plenty good to crack a skull.

Abby cups her hands around her eyes and presses her face to the window. "I can't see anything. Too dark."

Maya looks back the way they came. There's no sign of the kidnapper, not yet. It's almost supernatural the way he's been following them, despite their near invisibility and efforts to stay quiet. Maybe he's a tracker, like she's seen in so many movies, able to trace their steps by examining snapped twigs and footprints in the soft ground. Whatever it is, she doesn't like it. In the end, one of two things is going to happen. Either he's going to catch up with them or they're going to get lost, no matter how hard she tries to remember the way back. And both of those options sound pretty crappy with nothing but a glorified stick to defend them, whether it's from a human predator or animal.

"Stand back," she says. "I'm breaking the window."

"But he'll *hear!*"

"What if he does? He's coming, regardless. You've seen him back there. Somehow he just *knows.*" She holds up the piece of wood. "We might as well look for something better than this to use as a weapon. Maybe there's a gun inside."

Abby steps aside, hugging herself nervously as she watches for the man. Maya shields her eyes and swings the firewood into one of the corner panes. One more crime, one more person she'll have to apologize to when this is over. The sound of the shattering glass silences the nightlife for a moment. She runs the stick around the mullions to break out the rest of the pane. Reaching through the hole, she twists the latch and raises the sash. Her mouth is dry. He's going to be drawn to the bucket light the same way they were, and the instant she turns on even more lights inside he won't need broken branches or footprints to know exactly where they are. But she has to. The only way she's going to be able to search the cabin is if she can see.

"We need to be fast and thorough," she says. "Maybe we can be gone by the time he gets here."

Maya hoists one leg over the sill and shoves flimsy curtains aside to clamber through the window. As she turns to assist Abby, she looks out across the clearing in time to see another flare of the flashlight beam, closer than she expected.

40

The seller stops and reholsters the Kimber. Taking out the flashlight, he shields the bulb with his hand and thumbs the switch, letting the muted beam play over the ground immediately ahead. The swamp is full of knobby cypress knees, poking up through the soft earth like the arthritic fingers of some ancient giant. He tripped over one and faceplanted in the mud earlier, when he tried to check the product's location on the map and navigate the underbrush at the same time. The screwup had almost cost him his phone. Pure luck that he'd managed to find the thing again after it cartwheeled into the darkness, and wouldn't *that* have just been the perfect ending for this shitstorm of a night? Now he's more careful, taking his time, even if it means a slower pace. The go bag is stashed among the gnarled roots of a massive bald cypress and marked with a waypoint. There's nothing linking him to the Mustang anymore. He can take as long as he needs to reach them.

But he doesn't think it will be more than an hour, because they've slowed down in the last several minutes. They're tired. When he first entered the trees, they were hauling ass and quickly left him behind. For a time he had been concerned the red marker was going to vanish from the map. Now he's within two hundred feet. Their adrenaline has run out. Exhaustion is catching up. The sucking mud and tangled undergrowth are a constant drag, and sap strength in no time flat. He knows, because even with the kind of shape he's in, it's already begun to wear on him. The woman is good, but she could learn a thing or two about conserving her energy. Maybe he'll explain it to her before putting one of the hollow points between her eyes.

The product, on the other hand … he's starting to have second thoughts about her. It would be foolish to end her. She's a walking sack of cash, and even if getting her back to the car—assuming he reaches them before long and doesn't have to ditch his ride—strains a few more muscles, isn't the payoff worth it? Sure, he doesn't have any trank, but he still has the stun gun to drop her, and a good crack on the noggin with the butt of the pistol ought to put her right to sleep. Make her a lot easier to deal with. It will likely mean a little less money because she won't be in pristine condition, but two hundred grand is better than zero grand, isn't it? Better to come away with something than nothing. Money makes the world go round.

He can do this, if he really wants it.

Somewhere in the dark, a small animal squeals in pain. Leaves rustle as some beast lumbers past. The seller shuts off the light and returns it to its holster. Listens and waits, one hand on the pistol even though he's doubtful of its efficacy against something like a wild boar or alligator. The Kimber is more likely to piss one of those off than stop it, even with the hollow points. Not unless he manages a perfect shot, unlikely in these conditions. When nothing happens, he relaxes a little and reaches for the phone. Checks the dim screen. Forty feet closer now. It looks like they've stopped. Like they're hiding. Excellent. Let them think he can't find them.

At this rate he'll have this wrapped up in no time.

41

Maya runs a shaky hand over the wall just inside the door and flips the switch she finds there. A light hanging from the ridge beam blazes to life, and it takes her vision several precious seconds to adjust. First things first. Security. If she can keep him out for a few minutes, she can better search. At a glance, the cabin looks promising. It's cozy, a single room about the size of the den in her dad's house, unfinished timbers with red clay chinking. Round log rafters span the length of the dull metal roof.

The back door is constructed of the same thick planed boards as the front. Solid. Steel brackets bolted to either jamb hold in place a length of two-by-four, barring the inswing. Anyone wanting through that way would need a battering ram. Perfect. There is a similar setup for the front, but the section of board leans against the wall. Quickly, she steps over and seats it in the brackets. Even though the padlock on the other side should keep the kidnapper at bay, to have the bar lock and not use it would be monumentally stupid. Doors, check.

Now the windows. Hurry.

Her gaze skitters around the room. There had been a small second window by the back door once upon a time, but now an air conditioning unit fills it, held in place by a metal skirt screwed to the logs. The walls to either side are solid. If they can block the broken window, not only will it buy them some time to search, it might mean they can stop running. Make a stand. Maya doesn't know what kind of pistol he has, but it was small. Maybe not powerful enough to shoot through all that wood and clay. She inventories the contents of the cabin with her eyes, looking for anything that might help them.

Against the left wall is a twin bed with a plain gray comforter. Folded neatly at the foot is a colorful afghan, and on the logs above the mattress hang a number of pictures featuring a chubby old bearded man in camouflage coveralls, standing alongside dead alligators and fish of varying sizes. Given the path leading from the back of the store to this place, she wonders if this is the real Peepaw, whose life she has spent the last hour turning upside down. An outdoorsman. She hopes he's a hunter. Hunters *love* weapons.

"Check under the bed for a rifle, or bow," she tells Abby. "Anything that might help us. As fast as you can."

Across the back are a tiny potbelly stove that squats in one corner like a toad, a square table and lone chair beneath the air conditioner, and a mini fridge on the far side of the door. There's a coffee maker sitting on the fridge, and a tall scoop net propped in the corner behind it. A trio of stuffed alligator heads, mouths open to display discolored conical teeth, are arranged by size along a high shelf spanning half the length of the wall. The largest is as long as her arm. Its black eyes glitter in the light as though it's watching them, amused by their plight. Nothing useful.

The right wall reveals that her assumption about the owner was correct. A pair of fishing rod holders have been mounted to the timbers, and more than a dozen rods of various styles hang horizontally in clips that run almost to the roof. Next to it stands a tall, ancient walnut wardrobe. She yanks open the door to find not hanging clothes, but a series of shelves loaded with what at first glance appear to be more fishing gear.

"I found this," Abby says from behind her. She's on her knees next to the bed, holding a shiny black pole about five feet long, similar to a handle for a shovel or broom. One end is rounded, the other has some sort of brass cylindrical attachment. There's a braided cord crimped to a ring on the handle, a cotter pin attached to the other end. Strange. For an instant Maya thinks it's a harpoon and her heart leaps, but a closer look shows her that instead of coming to a deadly point, the tip is more like a straw, hollow and cut flat. Is it supposed to hold a spike or a dart? She doesn't know. What she *does* know is that in its current state it's not a weapon, and next to useless. The pole is likely hollow and not heavy enough to do any real damage. Her pulse is gathering speed. They need more time.

"No good," she says, and nods at the wardrobe. "Help me move this."

"Aren't we leaving?" The girl's voice is going quavery again, and she looks askance at the black eye of the window as she lays the pole on the comforter.

"Not until we've searched everywhere."

Together, they slide the cabinet across the floor. Maya closes and latches the window, and the two position the piece of furniture in front of it. She stretches and grabs the top of the wardrobe. Pulls, trying to tip it over. It remains steady, but the man outside is a lot stronger than she is, and he's going to have the advantage of pushing rather than pulling. Not enough. It won't stop him, will barely slow him. Think.

The bed. If they align it lengthwise in front of the cabinet, it might make a wedge of sorts, so that if he pushes, it butts up against the back wall and—

She shakes her head. Too short. He'll just shove both things out of the way. Easy enough to do on the plank floor. Maybe they need to take the pole Abby found and haul ass out the back. The end is small. It would hurt if jabbed in a belly or throat or eye.

No, dammit. Not yet. There has to be *something*. One more minute.

"Stay low," she tells Abby. "Keep away from the doors."

She opens the wardrobe and peers inside it again, more closely. Tries not to think about how a bullet fired from the porch would punch first through the thin paneled back, then through her skull. Tackle boxes, reels, pliers and snippers and crimpers. A weighty LED lantern. On the lowest shelf is an intriguing collection, things she had first thought were more fishing gear but now realizes aren't. Not unless old Peepaw has been fishing for Moby Dick in the swamp waters. *This* stuff looks useful.

Several barbed treble hooks at least ten inches tall stand like soldiers in formation, each attached to a coil of nylon clothesline. Alongside them is a collection of gleaming steel implements with varying spikes, tridents, and barbs of different size. They look evil. Useful. All have a threaded coupler. Interesting. They must be attachments for ... something. At work, Maya uses a set of brushes that function the same way to clean hard-to-reach places on cars, allowing her to swap out heads for different tasks. An image fills her head: her among the cypress trees, sneaking up behind the kidnapper holding the pole Abby found—now tipped with a barbed trident—in both hands, and spearing it into one of his kidneys.

Of *course*.

She darts to the bed and grabs the handle, lips peeled back in a ferocious panicky grin.

42

Abby watches as Maya strains to twist the piece off the end of the pole, cords standing out on her neck. After a couple of seconds she curses and hurls it back to the mattress. When her gaze lands on Abby, the girl cringes from the sheer fury she sees contained in the dark eyes.

"It's welded on," Maya says through gritted teeth. She hooks a thumb at the big cabinet they'd pushed to the window. "I found some things in there that would make good weapons. They look like attachments for that handle."

"Maybe they're for something else." Abby looks around the room for another pole but doesn't see one.

"Maybe." Maya's forehead is furrowed and her eyes dart in every direction. "I'm going to keep looking. Pull the bed out and make sure you didn't miss anything. Check under the pillow for a gun. The mattress, too."

Dust bunnies roll like tumbleweeds over the plank flooring when Abby drags the steel frame away from the wall. She flips the pillow, then raises the mattress by a corner to look underneath, holding the pole she found in one hand to keep it from rolling off. Nothing at all. Her stomach twists with nervous energy. The longer they stay in the cabin, the closer he gets. If he puts his hands on her again... She shivers. Just the thought stirs her guts and makes her feel like she's going to soil her shorts.

The metal handle is cool in her hand. Something about the pole is eating at her, has been since she first pulled it out from under the bed. A tantalizing memory, just out of reach. The thing is somehow *familiar*, like she's seen it before. But the harder she searches, the more elusive the memory is.

"*Yes!*" Maya cries, halfway into the wardrobe. She backs out, holding up a small green and yellow box triumphantly. On it in white letters is the word REMINGTON, with 357 MAGNUM just below.

"What's that?" Abby says.

"Bullets. There *has* to be a gun here somewhere." Her eyes flash with excitement, and she sets the box aside. "Keep looking!"

Where? Abby wants to ask. The only place besides the wardrobe that might hold a gun is the fridge in the corner, and that's just silly. Who ever heard of hiding a gun in a refrigerator? Still, she pulls the door open. Nothing but a six-pack of beer. Her stomach heaves. If she never tastes beer again it will be too soon.

A heavy thump behind her causes her to jump. It's just Maya, dragging a tackle box out onto the floor to go through it. Abby's gaze passes over the scoop net leaning against the wall in the corner. A second later, returns to it. She sets the pole on the table and picks it up. Something about it is ... off. The handle is bright and shiny, like tin foil, but the net ring is the dull gray of an old nickel. A closer look where the pieces join reveals a thin seam. When she twists them in opposite directions, the ring loosens and begins to turn.

"I found it!" she calls excitedly, unscrewing the ring from the threaded shank.

"*Again* with those eyes," Maya says, and rushes over for a quick hug that makes Abby's face flush with pride. "You should come work with me cleaning cars. You'd never miss a spot."

She selects an attachment with three barbed spikes and in seconds has transformed the handle into a formidable spear, jabbing the air with it like she's goring an enemy. "Now we're talking! It might not be as good as—"

Her voice fades away as her attention is drawn to a metal collar just beneath the attachment point. She loosens it, then takes hold of the spikes and pulls. A second, smaller pole telescopes out.

"Oh, *hell* yes!" she cries, and extends the handle to its full length before tightening the collar.

"Won't that make it harder to use?"

"Watch out." Maya turns carefully—the makeshift spear now stretches most of the way across the cabin—and wedges it between the top of the wardrobe and the base of the opposing wall. When she pulls on the cabinet, trying to move it away from the window, it won't budge. "Let's see that asshole push his way in *now*."

She smiles fiercely at the girl before grabbing the top of the cabinet and giving it a good hard tug. It doesn't move.

"No more running?" Abby says.

"No more running. We stay and wait him out. He can't shoot through the walls, and now he can't get in through the window. He'll be gone by daybreak, I'm sure of it. Cockroaches like him don't like the light. And it's a thousand times safer in here than out there."

Before Abby can respond, heavy footfalls ascend the steps to the front porch.

43

Even as the seller tries to turn the doorknob, he notices the padlock and moves to the window. Something is in front of it, butted up against the sill. Something big. Wan light spills into the half-inch gap between the barricade and the interior wall, providing enough illumination for him to see it's made of wood. A piece of furniture, most likely. Just like in the movies. He reaches through the broken pane and pushes against it, testing. A tiny bit of give, but then it holds fast. Clever. He puts the flashlight down and tries again. Harder this time, putting his weight behind it. Whatever it is, it isn't her. There's no pushback the way there would be if she was leaned into it, struggling to hold it in place. It just *stops*, as if it's set in concrete. Not worth breaking the rest of the panes and popping out the mullions to get at it. Not yet.

He examines the doorknob more closely. It's cheap. Contractor grade, no lock. One good kick ought to snap the assembly and get him in. The sturdy padlock and steel latch above it is another ball of wax. Fortunately, he has something better than his foot for that. He pats pockets until he locates his set of picks. Padlocks are about the easiest things to subvert, and this one takes less than a minute, even without light. He lets the heavy brass clatter to the planks. The hasp squeals when he pulls it open.

"Hear that, sister?" he calls. "That was your protection. In fifteen seconds I'm going to be in there."

He puts his ear to the door, but there's only silence from within.

"The trick with the pepper spray, that was a good one.

Caught me completely off guard. You've got spunk. I like that. Tell you what. I'll give you one more chance. Open the door right now—save me the trouble of breaking it down—and let me have what's mine, I'll take her and go. No harm, no foul. What do you say?"

He waits, counting off seconds. There's no response. When he reaches ten, he takes a step back.

"Suit yourself," the seller says, and drives his heel into the doorknob.

44

Maya snatches one of the giant treble hooks and scoots away from the wardrobe when the man starts shouting through the door at them. She crabs across the cabin to Abby, who is hunkered on the floor at the end of the bed with her knees drawn up to her chin, arms wrapped around them to make herself as small as possible. She takes one of the girl's hands and squeezes it.

"He can't get in," she whispers. "The bar across the door is thick. It'll hold."

She hopes.

It isn't the strength of the two-by-four that concerns her, it's the length of the screws holding the brackets to the jambs. If they strip out of the wood, it's over. He'll pick her off like a fish in a barrel. Abby won't be so lucky. Part of her wants to yank the back door open and flee into the darkness while he tries to get through the front.

"It *will* hold," she insists, more for her own benefit than Abby's.

The man says one last thing and falls silent, but the blood is pounding too hard in her ears for her to catch it.

"Get under the bed," she tells Abby.

She positions herself next to the wardrobe—hook in one hand, pepper spray in the other—in case the bar or brackets fail. Despite her assurances to the girl, it's always better to be safe than sorry. She wills her hands to stop shaking and concentrates on her weapons.

Something smashes into the door.

45

The seller stumbles back, a bolt of pure agony racing up his leg to an explosion in his hip. One wildly swinging hand cracks against the support column at the top of the stairs, and he grabs it frantically before he pitches backward over the edge. He bites off the cry of pain so sharply his teeth clack together. Damned if he'll give her the satisfaction. What the *hell*? It had been like kicking a brick wall, or solid concrete.

The doorknob, which snapped off exactly as expected, tumbles and rolls down the porch until it pitches over the end. In a fit of sudden fury, he yanks the pistol out of its holster and snaps off two quick shots at the broken neck collar where the knob had been attached. The door does not magically swing open to reveal his prize. It's still just as tightly latched. A closer inspection with the flashlight shows him the hollow points hadn't even penetrated the thick wood.

He curses. Four shots wasted, all because he can't keep his cool. He needs to knock it off. There are only four left. If he runs out of bullets he'll have to use his bare hands.

Not that he would mind so much at the moment.

The seller limps down the steps, trying to walk it off. Despite the pain that pounds in time with his racing heart, he doesn't think the ankle is broken, or even sprained. Just pissed off at him for being such a fool. He can relate. His eyes are wet and he wipes them angrily. The front door is obviously a no-go. Maybe there's another one at the rear, or more windows. As he rounds the corner an unsettling thought occurs to him. What if they're not even inside? They could have slipped out the back, snuck past him. Hell, they might be halfway back to the store by now.

Where he had left the keys to the Mustang sitting in the cupholder.

That's probably why he hadn't gotten a response out of either of them when made his second offer. He stops in a sudden panic. Grabs for his phone. When the distance to the red marker shows places the product less than ten feet away, his relief is palpable. He has a sudden urge to rap the butt of the pistol against the side of the cabin. She's so close she might even be against the wall. Scare her the way she had just scared him. But he doesn't. Better to stay silent, just like they are. Keep them wondering where he is, what he's doing. Fear of the unknown is the worst fear. Everyone knows that.

Most of the cabin is hidden in a thicket of shrubs, brambles, and saplings, as if whoever cleared the area in the front had gotten overwhelmed and given up. Despite appearing nearly impenetrable in the shine from the flashlight, it's easy enough to push through. Just a couple of steps in, however, both the undergrowth and the land come to a sudden end, and the swamp proper stretches away into the gloom. He pans the light slowly across the muddy water, playing it over towering cypress trees, rotting stumps, floating mats of greenery. And eyes. So many gleaming red eyes at the surface, shining back at him through the rising wisps of mist. Gators. *Much* closer than he'd like.

The rear of the cabin extends out over the water by three or four feet. It rests on algae coated stilts that vanish into the murk. From where he stands he can see a portion of the back porch, a mirror of the front. But there's no way to get onto it without wading into the swamp. *Hell* no. So many nightmares besides the alligators call the dirty water home he hardly knows where to start. Cottonmouths. Leeches. Snapping turtles. Catfish large enough to swallow a man whole. His imagination is the limit, one he doesn't want to test. Maybe he can reach the back porch from the other side.

As he walks around the front, he reflects on his earlier notion that the woman and girl had escaped out the back. It's almost laughable, now that he's seen what's out there. Not only would he have heard them splashing—and very likely screaming as they became dinner for the hungry critters—but they'd be foolish to even consider going that way. From what little he's seen of the woman, she's anything but foolish. He hopes she got a look at the swamp, though, and realizes just how bad her situation is. They're not getting out unless it's through him, and he has all the time in the world to wait if need be.

On the far side of the cabin he discovers a lean-to, about five feet long and two feet deep. It's constructed from weathered planks and attached directly to the logs. The narrow door on the front is secured with another padlock. An outhouse? Possibly, but why lock something like that? And why put it so close, where smells and germs and pests can invade? Besides, this is nature. A place to shit or piss is only as far as the next tree. Likely it's for storage … but it might also be another way in.

The door is fully exposed to the elements and riddled with dry rot, making the lock picks unnecessary. A solid jerk on the tarnished knob causes the screws holding the latch to pull free. Inside the shed is an array of items to keep the aggressive plant life under control. For ground management, rakes and hoes and even a pitchfork lean in one corner. A sagging shelf holds containers of chemical defoliants and weed killers. Across the back are the tools for bushes and trees, hanging from nails driven into the logs. Handsaws, cutters, clippers. A hatchet and an axe. He lifts the axe off the pair of nails and gives it a test swing. Oh, yes. This would make short work of that front door. For that matter, it would make short work of the woman, too.

Or would, if he were that kind of man.

The remaining wall is bare, except for a metal box mounted at chest height. It has its own door, which he opens. Inside is an electrical panel with two columns of spaces for circuit breakers. Almost all are unused. The main switch is at the top. It makes a loud *clack* when he casually flips it. The big streetlight goes off, and darkness wraps its arms around the clearing. He can't imagine anything worse than being trapped in a cabin, sightless, while someone hacks through the front door with an axe. Let them learn a lesson about running from him.

A flash of color in the castoff from the flashlight catches his eye as he turns to go. On the floor of the little shed is a red one-gallon gas can, and next to it a bright orange case grimy with oil and sawdust. The seller considers these, then hangs the axe back on its nails.

As it turns out, he *can* imagine something worse.

46

When the overhead light goes out, the cabin is plunged into darkness so complete that for a moment Maya wonders if she's been stricken blind in her terror. She can't make out her hand when she waves it in front of her eyes. Not even the outline of the door is discernible. It's like being in a cave, deep in the bowels of the earth. What is he doing out there? She struggles to catch her breath.

Across the room, Abby mewls like a kicked kitten. It sounds like she's on the verge of tears.

"Stay where you are," Maya whispers. "I'm coming to you."

She pictures the room in her head, and where Abby is relative to her position, then jams the pepper spray into her pocket and slides along the wall until her foot bumps the wardrobe. Inching around it, she sweeps an arm up and down, searching for the gig pole. When it makes contact with the brace, she ducks under. How do blind people do this? The room seems enormous now, stretching away forever in every direction. More like a gymnasium than a twelve-by. She shuffles like a toddler, treble hook held behind her so she doesn't accidentally stick either one of them, until her knees make contact with the mattress. Down to the floor. Hook on the bed. She crawls the last bit, one questing hand outstretched. It brushes a shoe. Abby gasps and pulls her leg away.

"It's me," Maya whispers.

There's a quick, scrabbling sound. Abby first collides with her, then grabs her around the neck in a panicked bear hug. She's trembling so hard her teeth chatter. The hot bursts of breath on Maya's shoulder is shallow, frantic.

"Hey, hey," she says, soothing. She strokes the girl's long hair and rocks gently, wishing she knew the right thing to do or say to reassure her. Wishing she'd had experience with calming a frightened younger sibling growing up. "He can't get in. He's just trying to scare us."

"Please promise you won't let him get me," Abby says, and now the tears come. Her sobs, made even stronger because she is trying to keep quiet, shake them both. "I'd rather be dead!"

"He's not taking you," Maya tells her. "I promise."

She hopes she'll be able to keep it.

Her mind is a whirlwind as she tries to determine the best course of action. Hadn't there been some kind of light in the cabinet, with all the fishing supplies? She runs through a mental tally of the inventory, cataloging each item. Yes! On the shelf with the pliers and crimpers and cutters. She sees it perfectly in her mind's eye. It resembles a camping lantern, but she's almost certain that instead of fuel and a wick it has an LED because it isn't enclosed to prevent burns and fires. A heavy base, full of batteries. If they still have some juice, she and Abby are in business.

If.

"There's a light in the wardrobe," she whispers. "I'm going to get it."

Abby's grip tightens. "Please don't leave me!"

"It's only a few feet." When the hold doesn't loosen, she adds, "You can come with me, but you have to let go."

The low snuffling snort of an animal on the front porch freezes her in place.

"What was that?" There's new fear in the girl's voice.

It comes again, just on the other side of the door.

"I don't know." A boar? A *bear*? Do they have bears in Louisiana? She has no idea. If they do and this is one, she hopes it just mauled the kidnapper.

A third snort, as if the beast has caught their scent, but this time something connects and instead of dying the sound *changes*, first to a rumbling snore, then the angry buzz of a small engine. It revs higher, higher still, instantly recognizable. She squeezes her eyes shut, shakes her head. Moans. Why won't he give up? The pitch of the chainsaw drops as the blade makes contact with the door. It begins to chew its way through, vibrating the floor under her hands and knees.

"Let go *now*, Abby!" she says, prying at the arms around her neck. "Stay here."

"What's happening?" Panic laces the words.

Maya shrugs free and scrabbles across the planks, hands seeking the wardrobe. Climbs her way up it to the handle and yanks the door open, half-expecting him to be there, coming through the back like Leatherface himself, but of course he isn't. The whine of the chainsaw is like a swarm of hornets. Desperately she feels for the lantern, fingers dancing over tools and reels and tackle. A fishhook sinks into the soft pad of one thumb and she hisses. Continues. The barb wiggles in her flesh as the hook thumps and bumps over things. Her fingers first brush, then wrap around the heavy cylinder. She seizes hold and locates a switch on the side.

Light—beautiful, blessed light—floods the wardrobe.

The air seems to reek of burning oil and hot wood, but that might be in her head. She pinches the hook just behind the barb and jerks it out of her thumb with a grunt, teeth gritted. Swipes the welling blood on her jeans. A weapon. Now. Her gaze passes regretfully over the box of bullets, landing on one of the gig heads, a four-pronged steel thing that looks like a tool Satan himself might use to prod the damned. Despite its appearance, its *solidness*, it seems inconsequential against a chainsaw. But what choice does she have? She snatches it and crabs backward to the center of the room, holding the light high. Crazy shadows dance and flicker, waxing and waning on the cabin walls.

The bar of the chainsaw bursts through the door just above the knob and the high scream of the engine fills the room. Yellow sawdust thrown by the whirling teeth falls like new snow. The tiny blades carve an arc around the knob as thin wisps of smoke twist and curl in the still air.

Abby shrieks and grabs hold of her from behind.

47

Maya watches helplessly as the chainsaw sweeps down the door, inexorable. It parts the wood with ease, advancing toward the two-by-four. He's going to get in, she realizes. Despite everything they've done, as soon as he severs the bar, one solid kick is going to blow the door wide open.

"Stop it stop it STOP IT!" Abby shouts. Her voice is shrill, piercing. She grabs fistfuls of Maya's shirt in blind panic, pulling until the fabric stretches and the neckline digs into the soft flesh of her throat.

"Let me up," Maya croaks, and miraculously, Abby releases her. She scrambles to her feet.

They can run. Slip away while he's busy with the front door, flank him and be almost to the store and the Trans Am before he even realizes they're gone. Yes!

"Out the back!" she commands. The lantern. Take it or leave it? She desperately wants to keep it, to help them find their way back, but of course she can't. He'll see. Even if she turns it off now to use later, in the woods, he's going to know. Surely his eyes are right now on the thin curve of light shining through the ever-lengthening channel carved by the chain. If it suddenly goes out, he might become suspicious. No, *will* become suspicious. He's smart—crazy smart—in the way he's been able to follow them, like he knows what they're doing before they do it.

She sets the lantern on the floor and darts to the rear door. Throws aside the piece of wood in the brackets. Yanks the door open, lunges out … and finds herself not facing the woods, but on a narrow porch overhanging water that stretches as far as she can see in the gloom. She throws out an arm to stop Abby from running straight over the edge. Wants to scream in frustration. Would they even last a minute in that?

Abby gapes up at her, wide-eyed, nostrils flaring. Full of trust because she's the grownup and grownups always know what to do.

Except she doesn't.

She casts her gaze around, mind going ninety. A boat. There has to be a boat. What kind of outdoorsy man like the one from all those pictures hanging over the bed would have a cabin on the water and *not* have one? With a boat they have a chance, however small. But she doesn't see one anywhere. It makes no sense. Just bushes and trees on either side, drooping over the dark water. Not even the shoreline is discernible.

"Think, Maya," she tells herself.

She puts the gig head aside and drops to her belly on the planks, hanging her head and shoulders out over the water to peer underneath the porch. Behind them, the pitch of the chainsaw drops as it makes contact with the two-by-four. The buzzing engine slows, strives to keep up.

There's a wooden canoe moored to one of the porch supports, bobbing gently in the ripples caused by their running footsteps. She thrills at the sight, but it's so *small*, barely longer than she herself is. The boat is clearly built for one person, not two. Her imagination serves up an image of her and Abby drifting through the swamp in the tiny thing, arms and legs dangling over the sides because both of them won't fit, and she shudders.

But beggars can't be choosers when faced with death, can they?

As she reaches for the carabiner that lashes the mooring line to the piling, a new thought pushes itself to the foreground, triggered subliminally by that tonal shift of the chainsaw. The machine is fighting to cut through the increased load. Maybe the chain is dull or loose, or the man doesn't know what he's doing. But there's something not quite right.

Would it be possible to stop the thing altogether?

Her fingers work to undo the clip, which she can barely reach. The old man must have ape arms, or just hops down into the water to unlash the boat. After what feels like an eternity she gets a grip and pinches the clip to free the rope. Think. What can't a chainsaw cut?

"*Hurry!*" Abby whispers.

And it comes to her

Maya looks up into her panicked face and says, "Metal."

She thrusts the rope at Abby. Shoves to her feet and races into the cabin. He's sawn halfway through the two-by-four now. Plenty bad. Not nearly as bad as it could be. If she can stop him from getting any further, she can spin the bar around, or swap it with the one from the back door. Either would prevent him from kicking his way in, and he can't get through both at the same time. They'll always have a way out, but if she kills the saw, they can stay inside. Safe. Protected.

Her gaze darts here, there, lands on the bed. *Yes!* She rushes over and flips the mattress away. Stepping into the middle of the steel frame, Maya knocks the slats aside and lifts the head rail. She hobble-drags the structure across the room, ducking under the wardrobe brace, and slams it against the door. It fits between the wall and wardrobe only barely The whirring chain is *right there*, flinging sawdust into her eyes and up her nose. She feels its heat, smells burning oil and woodsmoke. Stooping—grateful her hair is too short to catch in the spinning teeth—she grabs the rail underhanded, like a weightlifter, and jerks the frame upward with all her strength, directly into the chainsaw bar.

There's a loud *brrrwhang*. The frame judders with sudden violence in her hands. Teeth catch metal, and the rail is yanked fiercely into the door, smashing her fingers. She screams. Vibrations thrum up her arm, making her whole head ache. A hot spray of sparks tattoos her face and the chain first pops, then snaps. It flies free, whipping a hot welt across her forearm before whickering past her ear. The engine, no longer bound, revs to the screech of a banshee for a moment before dying, and the bar is wrestled out through the cut.

"Oh, you silly, stupid bitch," the man says from the other side. His tone is calm, nearly conversational, and something about it terrifies her even more than if he'd bellowed in rage, the way he had in the store parking lot. "You'll pay for that."

Maya drops the bed frame and sags against the door, panting.

48

The cabin falls silent, which to Abby is somehow worse than when the chainsaw was going, because now they don't know what the bad man outside is doing. And she's just *standing* here idiotically holding the boat rope, watching Maya through the thin bluish haze of smoke as she flexes her hands like an old woman with arthritis, grimacing. He could be halfway around back by now, gun in hand. Coming for her, a nightmare on two feet.

The thought is a dash of icy water. She wraps the rope around the porch support and tucks it, then darts through the door and slams it shut. Lunges for the piece of wood lying on the floor where Maya had tossed it. Picks it up, drops it into the brackets. Just the sight of it makes her feel better. As long as the chainsaw is busted, the thick door might as well be a brick wall. He'd already proven that when he tried to batter his way through the front.

Across the room, Maya flips the bar on the front door so that the cut part is close to the hinges. After a second's consideration, she bends and lifts one end of the bed frame and wedges it as far down into the steel brackets on either side of the door as she can.

"I don't know if that helps," she says, "but it makes me feel better."

The broken chain is lying on the table near Abby, curled into a jagged smile full of shiny pointed teeth. It looks mindlessly evil, like it still wants to bite her. She sweeps it to the floor and sends it skittering under the potbelly stove with her foot. Better. Her gaze falls on the strange pole she had put on the table earlier, when she first saw the net, and she picks it up.

The same sense of familiarity as before washes over her. Where has she seen something like this? It's so *close*. There's a guy in her hazy memory, tall and handsome and bronzed, standing in bright sunlight next to sparkling water covered in lilypads, and he's holding something almost, but not quite, just like this. Talking about why he has it, what it's for. But it won't coalesce into a cogent thought, and it makes her feel crazy. Whatever it is, some part of her knows it's important, that it could mean the difference be—

Something smashes into the front door with a thunderous *whunk* that fills the cabin and shakes the frame. Abby startles, dropping the pole. Maya is already backing away, hands raised as if to ward off whatever's out there.

WHUNK

"What's happening?" Abby cries. The terror that had lessened the tiniest bit now claws through her like a rabid beast. "What is that?"

WHUNK

The wood over the doorknob cracks. A small, dark triangle pops through the surface like a shark's fin, before submerging into the wood as quickly as it appeared.

"*MAYA!*" she screams.

Maya presses the heels of her palms to her temples and bellows wordlessly at the door, teeth bared in fury.

WHUNK

This time the shark fin is larger, two inches peeking in before slipping away with a harsh, wrenching squeal, but that's enough for Abby to recognize what it is.

An axehead.

49

White-hot rage courses through Maya, so savage that for a moment all she can do is roar at the door as the man outside methodically chops through it. She's not even scared anymore—fear has fled in the face of her wrath. More than anything she wants to fling it wide and confront the asshole directly. Is he *that* freaking bent that he'll go through all this just to get his skeevy hands on a little girl? At that moment, her greatest desire is to wrestle the axe away, to stamp one foot on his throat and sink the blade into his face.

But of course she can't do that.

He's bigger and stronger, and with the gun has the upper hand, no matter how prodigious her fury. Her little canister of pepper spray and her glorified fishhooks are no match. Still, if he wants Abby, she's going to do her damnedest to extract a few pounds of flesh first, using anything and everything at her disposal.

WHUNK

The wood cracks and splinters. A scatter of shards fall to the floor. The screech of the axe pulling free is like nails on a chalkboard. Part of the channel originally carved out by the chainsaw has widened. If she were to put an eye to it, most of the porch would be in view. Which means, she realizes, he can do the same. Can look in on them if he gets a notion, could see how unprotected they really are. She stoops for the lantern.

WHUNcrack

The door is starting to come apart now, unable to withstand the onslaught. A few more blows and there's going to be a proper hole. The end of the line ... and all she can think is how tired she is of running. She's *sick* of running. First from Brandon, now from him. All she wanted to do was deliver a car, make a little money, and he's turned her life—their lives, she thinks, glancing at the girl—into a living hell. For what?

"What are we going to do?" Abby asks. Hysteria tinges the words.

Maya motions her over, cups a hand to her ear. Leans close.

WHUNcrack

"Get in the boat and go straight out, away from here," she whispers. "I'm going to stop him."

If I can, she thinks.

Abby recoils. "By myself? I can't—"

"*Listen to me*. It's not big enough for two people. You saw it."

WHUNcrack

There's a terrible groaning, rending sound when he wrenches the axehead out, and left behind is a jagged hole in the wood that's even wider, longer. Close now. Maya flips the switch on the lantern and blackness descends. She drops it and reaches for the girl, finds her shoulders.

"But—" Abby tries.

"I know you're scared. I'm scared, too. But he's going to keep coming. I have to try, while there's still a chance. *Me*, not us. Now go!"

She guides Abby to the back door and—

WHUNCRACK

—the sound resonates, louder because the barrier has been breached. The door rattles in its frame. A panicky look over her shoulder shows an opening shaped like a teardrop, through which shines a thread of light that cuts through the smoky haze like a white laser. It paints one of the stuffed alligator heads, glittering the eye with faux life. She feels for the bar and lifts it out of the brackets, gets the door open and pushes Abby through.

"You can do this!" she whispers. "Remember: straight out. I'll call your name when it's over. If you don't hear me, stay put and wait for daylight. He'd be a fool to come after you."

Her mind goes back to the way he followed them before,

so effortlessly, and everything he's done since to get Abby. Obviously he's a fool, that much is apparent. But she doesn't think he's enough of one to brave the water and all the things that reside in it. She pushes the thoughts away. What choice do they have? At least this way Abby has a chance to live.

"Please don't make me," Abby says, nearly wails.

She pulls the girl close in a tight hug. "Listen for my voice."

Sudden tears burn her eyes as she steers Abby onto the porch and closes the door behind her. Bars it. Turns to face her fate.

WHUNCRACK

The blow comes at an angle, chopping the hole bigger. An elongated baseball now. The thread of light becomes a cone, and the room takes on a dim twilight. She ducks under the bracing pole and goes to the spot where the bed had been. When she flung the mattress aside, the treble hook had fallen over the end, between the wardrobe and the corner. She searches for it, nearing panic.

WHUNCRACK

A clatter as a chunk of wood larger than her fist hits the floor. The room grows brighter for an instant, and she hears the heavy thump of the axe thudding on the porch. The hook! She stoops and grabs it, spins in time to see an arm snake through the hole, now as large as a football. It reaches for the knob but finds the bar instead. Takes hold, trying to raise it out of the brackets but fumbling because of the angle.

Maya ducks the brace and leaps for the door, bringing the hook around in a sweeping overhand arc. She sinks one of the thick barbs into the meatiest part of his forearm, which transforms into a frantic, flailing live wire. The sweet sound of the man's scream of pain splits the night. She rotates her wrist and yanks back with all her strength, absurdly thinking of trying to bait the hook with the world's largest worm. A bulge swells obscenely three inches from the entry point, sharpens to a peak, and the barb erupts. She feels the slight tearing *pop* of the parting flesh, transferred to her hand via the shank. The arm jerks back through the hole but the hook catches, too big to fit through.

When the scream becomes a shriek, a fearsome smile splits her face.

50

Abby looks nervously across the still, dark water as she unwraps the mooring rope from the porch support beam. How can Maya send her out into that, all alone? Didn't she even *see* the pictures of the dead alligators on the wall, or those creepy heads lined up on the shelf like the three blind mice? Where does she think those came from?

thunk

The sound of the axe, made smaller and somehow less threatening by the distance and walls, fills her with fresh anguish because it reminds her that Maya is still inside, about to come face to face with evil. For her. So that she might survive. And all she's been doing is feeling sorry for herself, like a super b-word.

A sharp tug on the rope brings the canoe gliding silently out from under the porch. She squats. Sits on the planks, hanging her legs over the edge so she can catch it with her foot and pull it into position. Scooting forward, she lowers her weight into the tippy little boat, trying not to fall overboard. Once settled on the bench, she looks around for a paddle but instead finds a long pole. Which makes sense—the swamp is likely shallow, and pushing off the bottom faster than paddling.

And with an almost audible click, the elusive memory comes to her all at once.

The next *thunk* of the axe goes unnoticed because her mind is in another place, where the sun shines brightly in a pristine blue sky. There's water everywhere, with reeds and lilypads and stumps out the wazoo. She's in a boat, a flat-bottomed aluminum craft the handsome smiling man sitting across from her says is a *jon boat* as he poles it through the marsh.

The Everglades. That's where they are. In Florida. The Sunshine State.

It feels like she's drifting through the marsh with him, even though she's never been. His TikTok videos are so engaging, so *there*, that it doesn't matter that you're looking at them on a phone screen. He makes you part of his story, talking like you're his passenger—his best friend—as he guides you through this incredible wetland brimming with beauty … and with danger.

Distantly, she is aware of a sound like a man screaming. Or maybe he's laughing. It doesn't matter right now. This is more important.

Alligators are everywhere in the Everglades. Big ones, slicing through the water like ships, all snout and teeth and tail, so he carries something for protection. She can see it clearly in the mental movie now: the metal pole with its welded brass attachment that separates into two pieces; the braided cord connecting them, crimped around a clip that looks like a hairpin, stuck through a hole in the base of the attachment to hold it steady, so the spring inside won't compress.

The safety.

That's what he says the clip is. It's a safety, to keep the bullet inside the piece that looks like a fat straw from firing accidentally, because the flimsy-looking pole is a tool powerful enough to kill the biggest gators in Florida.

Abby's eyes clear and she snaps back to the moment.

"A *bangstick*," she says, parroting the word that follows her out of the memory.

Maya has a gun and she doesn't even know it.

51

The seller sags against the door, moaning. His arm feels shredded, like it's been split from elbow to wrist. *Agony.* Hot blood flows freely, and in his feverish imagination he hears it pattering like rain on the cabin floor. DNA, sprinkled everywhere. Sweat trickles into his still-sensitive eyes, burning and stinging. Vaguely he is aware of a pounding, and isn't sure if it's his heart or something else.

That Mexican bitch stabbed him!

He is going to gut her. Rape the corpse. Absolutely. She'll die screaming for what she did to him.

But later.

Right now, he has to free himself, before she does something even worse to his poor arm. Not even the Kimber can help him while he's tethered to the door.

Clamping the flashlight between his teeth so he's able to see what he's doing, he tries rotating from the shoulder and in order to withdraw the gaffed appendage slowly, expecting at any second for her to attack. Maybe to chop his hand off this time. When the thing piercing him catches on the edge of the hole, he hisses, almost loses the light. He uses the fingers of his other hand to work it through, and gingerly manages to extract himself inch by inch. Each time it—Jesus Christ, is it a *grappling hook?*—bumps against the door, fresh jolts of pain course through him.

Finally, he's free, able to examine himself with the flashlight. The three-hooked apparatus dangling from his arm looks like something Batman would use to scale a building. It even has a swinging coil of clothesline tied through the eye in a hangman's noose. The bend that curves through his forearm is streaked with gore, with a barbed tip to inflict maximum damage upon any attempt to back it out. Except, he realizes, maybe he won't have to do that. Holding the implement immobile, he curls the injured arm to his chest and returns to the toolshed. There, he selects a handheld pair of pruning shears hanging from a nail. The blades are clean and sharp and shine bright in the light … but will something designed for branches cut through metal?

Only one way to find out.

The seller grips the handles in his sweaty hand and positions the blades just behind the barb. The *stinger*. Takes a deep breath. Squeezes hard and fast. Dull pain flares at the base of his thumb as he bears down harder and harder. Then, a metallic *shhhhink* of the shears coming together, the sharp *tick* of the metal parting, and the severed tip falls away. He sighs with relief, drops the shears. The sensation of the cool bend sliding through flesh and muscle as he draws out the hook makes his stomach lurch. Rivulets of blood stream from both pencil-sized holes.

Oh, yes, that bitch is going to pay.

And there's just the thing to get the party started waiting for him on the shed floor. It'll even take care of all that DNA.

52

Maya crouches between the wardrobe and the corner of the cabin, out of any possible line of fire. She peers around the front, a fresh treble hook clutched in one hand, but the man isn't interested in shooting at her. All he cares about is extricating his arm. Shadows and shapes thrown by the twitching light that pours through the hole dance on the floor as he twists and turns, occasionally mewling in his efforts to get free. Now is the time to strike, while he's preoccupied. A second hook through his arm will make it impossible for him to escape. No part of her has reservations about hooking him while he's unable to fight back. She's seen enough movies to know how things end when you don't finish off the bad guy when you have the chance. She readies herself to spring.

Something hits the back door *bangbangbang* and she nearly climbs the side of the wardrobe. What the...?

Abby.

Heart racing, eyes on the activities at the front, she scuttles across the cabin, keeping low. Wanting to curse the little girl for not following directions and putting herself back in danger. Doesn't she realize she's the one the man is after?

"I know what the bullets are for," Abby says breathlessly as the door swings wide. She rushes in and her eyes dart to the table, back to Maya. "It's that pole. The weird one from under the bed. Where is it?"

"Get over there," Maya says, pointing to the safest corner. "Stay down."

She slams the door and bars it. Pans the room with her gaze. Light. They need light. What's coming through around the man's arm isn't enough to see clearly. The mattress is a gray rectangle slumped against the potbelly stove. It won't stop a bullet, but it'll stop a pair of eyeballs. As she stoops to lift it the cabin goes dark and she spins, raising the treble hook.

He's free.

The hole in the door is clear, an oblong purple blob of night in the near blackness. Footfalls clomp down the steps, and there's a flash of light quick as a snapshot when he moves past, going around the side. If he's headed for the back, good. Maybe all that blood will lure an alligator to Captain Hook him.

But if he's returning to whatever treasure trove provided him with the chainsaw and axe...

She doesn't want to think about that.

Maya props the mattress on the front door, blocking the view. One push will knock it over, but there's nothing left to hold it in place. Both the refrigerator and the table are easily displaced, and they're all out of gig poles to serve as braces. As soon as she picks up the lantern and turns it on, Abby scurries to retrieve the metal pole from under the table.

"It's a bangstick," the girl tells her. "A gun. Sort of."

"Back to the corner," Maya says. "Tell me from there."

Giving Abby the protected spot at the side of the wardrobe, she squats with her back to the wall to keep an eye on her and the doors at the same time.

"It's for killing alligators. You put a bullet in here," Abby says, pointing at the end that looks like a straw. "When you poke something with it, it fires."

She grips the very tip and turns it easily, opening a seam above where Maya was holding when she tried. The braided cord is crimped on a ring that spins freely around the tip as Abby keeps twisting until the pieces separate. A fat bullet slides out and tumbles to the floor.

"Holy shit," Maya says, wonderingly. "How did you even know about this?"

A pleased expression flickers across the girl's face, there and gone. "TikTok. This guy in the Everglades had one."

"Can I see it?"

Abby taps a finger on the cotter pin through the base of the attachment before handing over the bangstick. "It won't fire until you take this out."

Maya examines the weapon. Inside the threaded tube where the tip had been attached, she sees what is obviously a firing pin. She removes the cotter pin and presses down on the attachment. It compresses on a spring until the firing pin is flush with the end. With the other piece attached and a bullet between the two, one quick jab and...

"Bang," she whispers, unable to contain a smile, or the sudden rush of joy that fills her. It might not be on equal footing with his pistol, but it's a hell of a lot better than the treble hooks. As she reinserts the cotter pin safety, she adds, "You've got some serious big brain energy, girl."

Abby ducks her head, color rising in her cheeks.

Maya picks up the bullet and is reassembling the bangstick when they hear heavy steps on the porch. A new sound, but not at the door. From the window, right beside them. The wardrobe trembles. Flexes away from the sill. The gap between the wall widens by a half inch. He's trying to bull his way in. She tightens the barrel of the bangstick and stands. Removes the safety.

But the next sound isn't one of violence, of the kidnapper trying to break through the back of the wardrobe. It's a slosh. A thin scraping on the paneling, like a cat begging to be let in. Glugging liquid pours down the paneled back, splatters on the plank floor. The thick aroma of gasoline boils up around them in an eye-watering cloud, and a reddish stream flows out of the gap, forming a puddle on the cabin floor.

"Grab the ammo and the light!" Maya says frantically. "Go out the back. To the boat."

"Both of us?"

"Both of us."

Abby scrambles for the door.

Maya moves in front of the open cabinet door and readies the bangstick.

53

The seller pours most of the remaining mix in the gas can through the broken pane, then backs away from the window, emptying the dregs down the logs and over the porch planking. When this stuff ignites he wants to be safely on the ground, in case the whole place blows. Gasoline is some violent shit. All those vapors, waiting to explode. He gives the container one last shake and tosses it aside.

BOOM

Something blasts at the barricade and glass shatters. He ducks jerkily, stumble-thumps down the steps. Crouches in the mud at the edge of the porch to peer up. A thin beam of light spears the night through a button-sized hole in the piece of furniture covering the window. Jesus, his head had been in that spot not even three seconds before. So sister has not only a light, but a gun. Why had she waited so long to use it? Just like a woman to waste the best opportunity. He had been a sitting duck with his arm hooked on the other side of the door, and instead of ending him when she had the chance, she had done exactly squat. Now she's just wasted one of her shots. Stupid.

But good for him. Time to get her out of there, see how she fares in a real gunfight. He still has four shots. That ought to be plenty. The seller touches the probes of the stun gun to one of the gas-splashed planks and presses the button.

54

Maya turns from the wardrobe, eardrums aching. At least she doesn't hear ringing, thank God. The shot from the bangstick hadn't been nearly as loud as the ones at the store. Maybe most of the sound went out the back of the wardrobe. Good. Let that bastard be the one who loses his hearing. Using the weapon wasted valuable seconds, but he was just outside, and she might not get another chance as good. Now it's time to vacate.

She ducks under the brace pole, runs for the open back door. Abby is already out, lowering herself off the porch into the waiting canoe. From the front of the cabin comes a sound, a sharp series of crackling pops that makes Maya think of—

Blinding yellow blooms behind her with a harsh *whump*, and for an instant the air pressure bears down hard enough to make her ears pop. A hot hand wraps itself around her. Squeezes. Then it's gone, and she's alone in the room with a ravening orange beast. Whirlwinds of flame engulf the wardrobe and roar up the wall. They fan out across the ceiling, greedily latching onto the timbers. Something in the firestorm whistles and squeals, and the blazing furniture pops like kettle corn. A rush of heat pushes her onto the porch through billowing gray clouds of smoke.

Abby has crammed herself into the prow of the canoe, and clings to one of the support columns so she doesn't drift away. She's already extinguished the light, without being told. Good girl, thinking ahead. Maya hands her the bangstick and scrambles into the back. The tiny boat sits low with both of them onboard, but it's better than she had expected. She sinks the push pole into the muck, shoves away from the burning cabin.

The sluggish water is less than three feet deep here.

"Can you reload?" she asks.

"I think so."

Maya leans into the pole again, digging deep enough to feel a twinge in the shoulder Abby hit with the tire iron not even an hour ago. It feels like a lifetime. She hears the *tink* of the shell casing hit the floor of the canoe when Abby unscrews the barrel mechanism. The boat begins to pick up speed, sliding away from the porch. The drizzle has ended and the clouds begun to tatter. Here and there stars peek through breaks in the foliage, distant and cold. Flickering yellow light from the cabin casts an eerie glow across the endless water, creating ghoulish writhing shadows. The low mist that clings to the surface cloaks the rotting stumps and cypress knobs and transforms them into hooded phantoms. Great cypress trees tower over them, draped in drooping stringers of moss like burial cloths. The thought that she'd banished Abby into this nightmare all by herself sickens her.

"It's ready," the girl says.

Something crashes in the underbrush near the cabin. Even though Maya can't see directly, she knows what it is. He's coming around the side, charging through vegetation so thick she hadn't even realized the water was here until they opened the back door. She pushes harder, harder again. Her shoulder sings. But she needs to get them further out, because his gun isn't limited to six feet the way hers is.

The canoe grates over a submerged stump. Abby yelps and grabs hold of the gunwales for balance. The bangstick clunks into the hull. One side lists alarmingly as the boat teeters. Maya slips off her seat, almost falls. Manages to catch herself. Water sloshes over the lip and splashes across the bottom. She brings the push pole around to the opposite side and stills the wobble.

The *crack* of gunfire echoes across the swamp and a plume sprays up ten feet off the bow. Abby cries out again and curls into a ball as low in the bottom as she can, between Maya's feet. Maya propels them further into the darkness, watching for obstacles but unable to see anything except the looming trees in the filmy mist. The next shot goes wide, slapping into the water twenty feet short. If he hits them now it will be luck, not skill.

"*Go!*" Abby cries.

Maya heaves against the pole, then risks a quick glance back. The back door of the cabin is an inferno too bright to look directly at. Flames seethe against the porch roof, tasting the beams, and curl upward around the edges. As long as they keep it in sight they can't get lost. Of their pursuer there is no sign. Except, she suddenly realizes, there is. Just upstream of the burning building is a spherical glow, floating in the haze. A face, lit from below. But the light isn't anything like a flashlight, it isn't bright enough.

A phone?

There's a secondary flash of light, lower. Waist high. A geyser of water spurts five feet from her. The sound of the gunshot rolls over them. *Shit.* She turns and digs in with the pole, her mind in a frenzied rush. Why would he look at his phone before shooting at them? At first, it doesn't make any sense, but as she reconsiders the last hour, the random thoughts begin to coalesce into a theory. What if he doesn't have the almost preternatural tracking ability she's been attributing to him, but a technological one? That would explain both how he found them at the store and followed them so easily through the woods. It makes sense.

Better, it feels *right*. The sort of thing a kidnapper would use, just in case his victim escaped.

Best of all, it's easy to prove or disprove in a matter of seconds. But not out here in the open, because they need light for this. Even though they're far enough out that he won't be able to see details, the less he knows, the bigger their advantage. She steers the canoe behind a thick cypress, its widening bottom and snarled roots providing almost complete cover, and brings them to a halt.

"Empty your pockets," Maya says, and reaches for the lantern.

55

The light is so bright after the dark of the swamp that Abby has to turn away, which she immediately regrets. Everywhere she looks, pairs of red eyes reflect the glow, gleaming in the gauzy mist. Another memory surfaces, a nighttime video from the handsome Floridian, coasting through the Everglades in a kayak, shining a flashlight all around to show how many gators there are. The blackness is filled with glittery crimson jewels in the video, even more than there are here.

But here is plenty bad.

She's suddenly terrified to move, afraid that any action will tip them over, the way they almost had a few minutes ago. It feels like there's a steel band around her chest, making it hard to take a breath. Slowly, eyes focused on the bottom of the boat, she checks each pocket of her shorts, finding only her keyring with her house and vacation rental keys and the Snickers wrapper. The sight of her housekey sends a pang of despair through her. Will she ever see home again? Attached to the ring is a keychain coin purse that her grandmother had given her for her last birthday.

She holds it out, but Maya shakes her head. "Open it."

Abby unclasps the pouch, which is modeled after a popular handbag and barely larger than a bar of hotel soap, and pries it open. She tips it toward the light, runs her fingers over the wadded bills crammed down into one side.

"That's all there—" she begins, falters. Concentrates. Something hadn't felt right with the money. It was ... stiff. A cloth divider separates the bag into two compartments, to keep paper and coins apart. She peels the fabric back. Tucked into the section she thought empty is a rectangle of black plastic. At first, she thinks it's a credit card, but when she pulls it out for a better look both sides are featureless.

"What is that?" Maya asks, leaning forward. Her brow is furrowed. She swipes the air in front of her face to scatter the mosquitoes that are swarming.

"I don't know. I've never seen it."

For an instant the woman's eyes seem to catch the light, glinting like those of the predators that surround them. The canoe is drifting, carried away from the tree by the sluggish current, and she uses the push pole to move them back.

"You're sure?" she asks.

Abby nods. "Positive. I bought a jawbreaker from the machine at Cracker Barrel this—er, yesterday—morning. I used my last quarter. It wasn't in there."

"Has the keychain been in your pocket since then?"

"Yes," she says ... but then she remembers Liam, and the water. The awful, *awful* beer. "But I left my shorts in the beach chair when I went out to the sandbar with the boy I met."

"For how long?"

Sh scrunches up her face, trying to remember. "An hour, maybe? I was supposed to be back by eight and got in trouble because I was late."

"That has to be it," Maya says. "I think that thing is some kind of tracking device. GPS, maybe, or Bluetooth."

The world seems to squeeze in around Abby like a starving constrictor. "Really?"

"It's the only thing that makes sense. Think about how easily he followed us to the cabin, straight as an arrow when we were zigzagging on the trail. There's no way he could have seen us. How did he do it? And when he was shooting at the boat. I saw him looking at his phone before he fired. Why would he do that? I'll tell you: because his phone was pointing him right at us, and probably telling him exactly how far away we were."

As Maya talks, a knot in Abby's guts seems to twist tighter and tighter. Everything feels like it's closing in around her, the way it does when she's about to puke. Electric spit floods her mouth. She has to get rid of the thing, to throw it as far away as she can so he can't follow them anymore.

But when she draws back to hurl the vile piece of plastic into the swamp, Maya stops her.

"Give it to me," she says. "I have an idea."

56

The seller hunkers at the edge of the land and peers across the misted expanse. In the eldritch glow emanating from behind a thick cypress in the distance, the flaring roots become a tattered dress, the lank strands of moss a shroud of tangled hair, giving the ancient tree the appearance of a leviathan sea hag lurching through the dismal waterscape in search of souls to claim. What are they doing back there? There's no ground he can see, no place to land a boat and escape to safety. Just the steaming water that goes on and on.

Fifty feet downstream, the cabin is engulfed in flames that reach ten feet into the trees. It's too wet—he thinks—for the fire to spread, but the rising heat whips the leaves above. Branches dip and sway. He can feel it from here, tightening the skin of his face. There's a hum near his ear, a tickle on the back of his neck. Another bloodsucker. The air is thick with them this close to the water. He slaps it.

In the distance, the light is extinguished. The canoe drifts from behind the tree, a dark smear made barely visible by the glow from the burning building. It's moving to the right, beginning to pick up speed. What are they doing? He checks the phone. Not quite two hundred feet away, and increasing ... but it looks like they're coming back to shore. He's almost certain of it. If they continue in a straight line, they'll make landfall about a hundred yards down from him. Closer to where the convenience store is, as the crow flies.

Yes.

She's making her move. They're going to run for it, gambling that the speed of their canoe will buy them enough of a lead while he fights his way through the thick undergrowth. He remembers the jug of antifreeze sitting in front of her car. The woman has high hopes in her, he has to give her that. Maybe he should just go back to the store now and wait for them to come out of the woods. Make his own move.

No.

That would put the product out of range. Invisible. And on the off chance he's wrong about their intentions, he might lose her for good. Better to intercept them as close to where they land as possible. Their own little Welcome Wagon.

The seller puts his phone away and pushes into the thick vegetation.

57

Maya levers the push pole in the muck and aims the canoe toward a spot on the shoreline about three hundred feet down from the cabin. That should give them plenty of time.

"I had you keep the tracker because we're going to use it against him," she says, her voice barely more than a whisper. "I'll take us ashore, far enough downstream that he can't see us. We'll leave it in the boat, push it back out. The current will keep it going."

Abby points out a jagged black stump rising from the mist and Maya guides them around it.

"We hide and wait for him to pass by," she continues. "When it's safe, we go back to the car and get the hell out of here."

"What if he sees us?"

"He won't." She hopes. "If he does, we have the bangstick and a whole box of bullets."

The humidity is even worse than the mosquitoes. She wipes her beaded forehead with her t-shirt and tries to feel as confident as she sounds.

The girl is quiet for a moment. Then she says, "I wish we could kill him."

Maya looks upstream for any sign of the kidnapper. They're skimming at a good clip. She glimpses white light, visible only for an instant, as he uses his flashlight to check for obstacles. A twinge of dismay turns the corners of her mouth down when she sees how far from the cabin he's already come. More than halfway to the point even with them. Too fast. Worry flutters in her chest. If they don't hurry, he's going to get within range and start shooting at them again. They're exposed out here. She sets the pole and heaves. Displaced water splashes to either side of the prow. A pair of cypresses reach for the night sky just ahead, limbs drooping into the surface mist.

"Get down, we're going through," Maya says. Abby scoots toward her and leans back.

The canoe cruises into the gap between the trees. Maya sweeps branches aside with her hand. A spiderweb, thick and crackling, cloaks her face and she hisses. Tries not to think about the size of the thing that calls it home, or where it might be now. She imagines the tickle of eight hairy legs skittering down the back of her neck and brushes at it, shuddering. They pass through the low foliage on the far side. Another glance back. He's lost ground. They're still fifty feet into the swamp, a hundred from the point she's picked to make landfall. She drives the push pole into the depths and—

Abby suddenly shrieks, begins to thrash in the bottom of the canoe.

Alarm stiffens her body. Her immediate thought is that Abby has been shot, but there's no gunfire. Ponderously, she leans forward, trying to see something, *anything*.

"What's wrong?" she cries, her voice sluggish and distant and muted.

Abby doesn't respond, continues to scream and fight. She scrabbles onto the lip of the hull and the small boat lists sharply to one side. Maya nearly tumbles out. She throws her weight in the opposite direction in a syrupy slow motion, trying to right them. Abby seizes one of Maya's legs and pulls, dragging herself along the gunwale, rear end hanging precariously over the water. Maya takes her arm and pulls with all her strength and the girl slides into her lap, tries to climb *over* her. The shrill cries cut through the wool batting that seems to enrobe her whole body, hurting her ears. She fumbles for the lantern. Gets it. Slaps the switch. The boat keels to the other side as Abby fights to get behind her, almost capsizes. Brilliance explodes, drives back the night.

An enormous banded black and brown snake as thick as her

upper arm is coiled in the bottom of the canoe between her feet. In the wash of light, it lifts its broad, triangular head and gapes its jaws threateningly, revealing curved fangs in a wide mouth as white as freshly picked cotton, before striking at her sneaker. It thumps hard against the rubber sole. Maya gasps, jerks her legs back. The movement causes the boat to list even more dramatically. Her stomach drops. One gunwale dips under the surface and murky water sweeps into the canoe, sucking it lower. She flails desperately the other way, trying unsuccessfully to get them righted. The lantern slips from her hand and plunges into the swamp. A bilious brown-green glow blossoms beneath them.

The canoe overturns.

Abby's screams are cut short as she goes under. The last thing Maya sees before the light goes out and water closes over her head is a sleek reptilian shadow, larger even than the inverted boat, hurtling toward them.

58

The seller has moved inland a little, where the vegetation is thinnest, and is making good time. He's not able to see the canoe from here, but it doesn't matter. In these conditions the tracker is better than his eyes. Besides, he knows exactly where they're going. The marker has traveled in a relentlessly straight line ever since the pair left the cover of the tree. Right now, the map says they're close, one hundred sixty feet. A little more than half a block. Literally a stone's throw.

A bloodcurdling screech of pure terror tears a hole through the night. He draws up short. That was the product. What the hell? What are they doing? The woman shouts, a short barking cry that almost sounds like a laugh. A panicky thumping fumble, and then both are screaming—but only for a moment, because a tremendous splash cuts them short.

All he hears now is the frogs, the faint hisses and crackles of the distant burning cabin.

On his phone, the red marker sits motionless. Intriguing. He picks his way toward the water's edge, until the brush grows too dense to proceed. He can't see shit. Another check of the map. Has she moved? He isn't sure. A tree leans haphazardly out over the swamp. He straddles the trunk, shimmies up high enough for a look. Maybe he's close enough to make something out.

There's no sign of the canoe. Other than the trees, the only things he sees in the misted water are scattered cypress knees and stumps. Perhaps Mother Nature has solved his problems for him and the fat gators are getting a little fatter tonight.

But then one of the stumps begins to move toward the shore. He's sure of it. As he watches, the shape shimmers in the cloak of mist. It separates into two dark humps. He checks the map. The tracker is definitely on the move again, but the course has changed. They're coming straight in.

The seller climbs back to the ground and goes to greet them.

59

Maya gets her feet under her and stands. Sinks. The thick sludge at the bottom is like quicksand, oozing over her shoes and ankles. The water is only hip deep, but because of the mud reaches her navel. Not as bad as it could be, but more than enough to hide the alligator she had seen.

Abby erupts beside her, gasping and spluttering. Before she can make any other sounds, Maya grabs her by the upper arm. Claps a hand over her mouth. The girl's smaller body tenses, thrumming with a terror that threatens to swallow her whole. For her, the water is deeper, all the way to her chest.

"Be still," Maya whispers. "And don't scream."

Abby makes a sound deep in her throat, the animalistic whine of someone on the verge of a full-blown panic attack. She squeezes her eyes shut. Reedy air whistles through her nostrils as she struggles in the grip of her fears. After a moment she relaxes, opens her eyes. Nods.

"We're okay," Maya says, her voice as calm and soothing as she can make it. She lowers her hand. "The alligators are more scared of us than we are of them."

She doesn't know if the words are true. Doesn't care. All she knows is that if she doesn't pull Abby away from the edge of the precipice she's on, their situation is only going to worsen. She needs the girl to be engaged, and ready to run like hell once they reach the shore.

Her mind goes to the row of stuffed heads in the cabin. The gaping jaws, the rows of teeth. All the better to crush you with, my dear. And to the man she knows is close—too close, now—relentlessly pursuing them. A cursory scan of the shore for a sign of his flashlight or phone screen reveals nothing. But he's there. Tracking. Coming for them. She'll figure out what to do about him soon enough. Right now they need to get out of the water.

The hull of the inverted canoe is barely discernible several feet away, rocking gently. A lost cause. Even though the two of them might be strong enough to right it, there's no way they'll be able to empty it out. Not in the middle of the swamp. With sudden hopelessness she remembers the bangstick, ammo, and light are all lost, too. They have nothing. Just the tracker and their wits.

She wants to give up. Refuses to, because then he wins, and that's unacceptable. Not until she's done everything she can to get them out of this.

"We're walking to shore," she whispers. "Take my hand."

Abby's eyes flash white as her gaze flits around them like a caged bird, but she remains outwardly calm. Reaches out.

Maya tries a step. Getting her foot dislodged from the mud is harder than she expected it would be. She staggers, almost falls. The stuff pulls and clings, fighting to hold her back. Maybe they need to swim instead of walk. No. That feels like it would attract alligators, would make them more like prey.

And she's damn tired of being prey.

Something nudges her hip and her heart stutters. A scream swells in her chest, but before it can escape she recognizes the bangstick, bobbing vertically because the handle provides enough buoyancy to keep the firing attachment from sinking. She wants to shriek with delight, to find whatever genius designed this miraculous thing and kiss them. Of *course* it floats! It would be stupid for something made to kill creatures in a swamp not to.

Maya lets go of Abby's hand long enough to pull the pin that acts as a safety. Now if Mister Gator comes calling, she has an answer. And if not, she has a solution for their two-legged problem.

60

Abby holds tightly to Maya's hand and lurches toward the shore. The muck around her feet is like wet concrete weighing her down, making each step slow and plodding. Part of her wants to try to run anyway, to take huge bounding leaps and make it out of the water before something gets her. Another part wants to stop, to just shut down and let whatever is going to happen, happen. But if she does, Maya will hate her, and she doesn't think she can bear that.

So she walks. It isn't far. One step at a time. She's got this.

Her foot catches in a root and she trips. Maya pulls on her hand and keeps her from falling. The thought of going under again makes her shudder. Ugh. Her breath hitches.

"You're doing fine," Maya murmurs. "Almost there."

Abby nods and swallows the lump that's risen in her throat. The water *is* shallower now, not much higher than the top of her shorts. The shore is close enough that she can discern the sprawling spread of tangled roots concealing dark hollow spaces where nightmares live.

And they have to climb over them to reach the land.

There's a sudden sensation of motion down by her knees, turbulence in the water as something passes. Something big. Panic plunges icy fingers into her scalp, down her back. Worries about the shadowy roots flee in the face of this new terror. No matter what Maya said about the alligators being scared of them, she doesn't believe it, because this is the kind of place where nothing is scared except the people who don't belong. She remembers tons of TikTok videos from the handsome man with the good smile. All the times the great beasts charged him. How he explained the way they roll you over and over underwater to disorient you until you drown, then stick your body under a submerged log or in one of those awful hollows behind the cypress roots until you decompose because their teeth aren't made for tearing and you have to be rotting to be nice and soft and *tasty*.

"Maya," she squeaks.

Maya stops and turns, instantly alert. "What's wrong?"

"Something's here."

"Where?" Her voice is sharp. She raises the bangstick, peers at the rippling surface.

Abby points, but there's nothing to see. If anything is with them, it's moving along the bottom, because the monsters always keep hidden until it's too late. Everyone knows that.

"Come on," Maya finally says, and gives her hand a squeeze. "Twenty more feet. Just ten steps. You can do this."

They reach the bank without further incident a few moments later. Maya helps her up and over the roots—nothing reaches for her from the darkness beneath—and she collapses on the mossy ground, trying to get her breath back.

Maya climbs ashore and crouches beside her. "Do you still have the tracker?"

Abby sits up and reaches into her pocket, wraps her fingers around the slim piece of plastic. Hands it over.

Maya whispers, "Do you trust me?"

She nods. Of course she does. More than anyone.

"Stay here. I'll come back for you."

"What are you going to do?"

She raises the bangstick. "I'm going to kill him."

61

Maya walks swiftly into the woods, her eyes peeled for any sign of the kidnapper. She wants to break into a run, wants desperately to bolt into the darkness at full speed and lead him as far from Abby as possible. But she can't risk tripping and falling again. Not when he's so close. She only has one opportunity to get this right. The cotter pin is back in the bangstick to prevent a misfire, the tracker tucked safely in her pocket. To lose the use of either at this point would be catastrophic.

The sharp crack of a branch to her right grabs her attention. She ducks behind a stubby pine, peers around. In the distance, the burning cabin appears only as flickers of yellow through the intervening forest. The flames dance with sinuous grace, and the light seems to ebb and flow. As she searches for the source of the sound, a shadow detaches itself from one tree and creeps furtively to another. Human. Her heart hammers at her ribs. He can't be more than fifty feet away, coming right for her. The fear that floods her and dries her mouth obliterates any fleeting exhilaration over being right about the device in her pocket.

She pulls out the tracker. Crouches and moves away from him in the straightest line she can, hoping that he's watching on his phone, or at least checking at regular intervals. Trying to make some noise. If he thinks she's fleeing, his guard will be down. She'll have the element of surprise. After a minute she stops and flings the tracker in the same direction. Then she hunkers behind a live oak and eases the cotter pin out of the firing attachment. Closing her eyes, she focuses on trying to quell the hurricane of emotions that rages within her. Terror, hope, anxiety, anger, anticipation, guilt. Each vies for the helm.

He's drawing near. She hears him. The squelch of his shoes in the soggy earth, the rustle of wet branches as he pushes through them. Louder. Louder still. And then he's passing by so close she can reach out and lay a hand on his shoulder if she wants to, bid him a warm how-do. She holds her breath, terrified he's going to hear her pounding heart, turn his head and see her there. Shoot her before she has a chance to thrust the bangstick into him.

But he doesn't.

His back is broad and strong, a perfect target. All she has to do is poke him right in the center of it, chest high. No matter what the shot hits on the way through—heart, lung, spine—it'll put him down, dead or wishing it, and they can end this hellish adventure once and for all. She steadies her nerves and wills her trembling hands to still.

It's time.

Maya steps away from the tree and raises the bangstick.

62

The seller slows. Makes more of an effort to hide his approach. On the barely lit phone screen, the red marker is thirty-six feet dead ahead. It isn't moving. They've found themselves a hiding spot to hole up in, never having the slightest inkling he can find them *anywhere*. Well, anywhere within three hundred feet. He slumps to make a lower profile, so he won't stand out against the burning building.

Twenty feet.

The forest falls silent, as if the creatures of the night sense the imminence of the confrontation. He slides the phone back into his pocket, withdraws the pistol from the waistband holster. Double-checks to make sure the safety is off. It wouldn't do to surprise them, only to squeeze the trigger and have nothing happen. He doesn't know if the woman still has her gun, but if there's going to be a firefight he can't be caught flatfooted. He pauses, listening for the soft susurration of their respiration, an uncontrollable whimper of fear. Not even a peeping frog or humming mosquito breaks the stillness. It's as if the entire swamp is holding its breath, waiting in anticipation.

The flashlight! He'll blind them. Spotlight them like deer and pick the woman off before she knows what hit her, then pop the product with the butt of the pistol or his fist and haul her back to the Mustang for delivery. And his money. He's earned every single penny. But as he unsnaps the holster, a terrible, growling *roar* fills the night, followed an instant later by the screams of the girl, nowhere near where he thought she was.

63

Maya stands frozen, rooted to a spot five feet behind the kidnapper, her bowels suddenly loose and liquid. The deep, resonant bellow seems to shake the ground itself as it reverberates through the swamp. It's a primal, guttural sound of unbridled power. Prehistoric, like something right out of *Jurassic Park*. Coming from her left, down near the water's edge.

Where she had left Abby all alone to run off and play hero.

A split-second later, a shriek of abject terror buffets her like a strong wind, cutting her to the core because the cry is a single word. Her name. Abby needs her. *Now*. Her first thought is to go ahead and employ the bangstick. Put the man out of her misery. Locate his gun, kill the alligator. Because that's what it has to be. She knows it in her bones. Nothing else makes a sound like that, so instantly recognizable. It's a gator and it's close and Abby is in even more danger from it right this minute than from the asshole right in front of her.

But what if she kills him and then can't find his gun? Abby dies. And even if she finds it, what then? She's not a gun nut, has no empirical knowledge of how to aim or use one properly. What if she gets it, faces down the alligator and pulls the trigger only to miss, or have nothing happen at all? Abby dies. What if by some miracle her aim is true, the shot perfect, and it isn't powerful enough to kill the thing? Abby dies.

The bangstick is a known quantity. It's too simple to screw up. She's fired it. It's capable. She's seen the pictures. The conclusion is obvious.

The next scream is different, a raw, agonizing howl. It's a dagger to her heart, and almost enough to make her forget the man entirely, to simply start running toward the girl. Anything to stop that *wounded* sound. But to do so would leave him at her back, with his gun. No way. He needs to be dealt with. Her resolve hardens to iron, because at the brass tacks this is his fault, not hers. Not Abby's. His. She silently inserts the cotter pin and draws the bangstick back.

Batter up, shithead.

The kidnapper straightens, beginning to turn, his attention drawn toward the water by the cries. Before he catches sight of her, Maya swings with every bit of her remaining strength. The metal shaft whistles through a wide arc, and the brass attachment smashes into the side of his head with a dull *whunk* she feels all the way up to her shoulders.

He crumples bonelessly.

Maya races for the shore, anguish twisting her insides. So dark. How is she supposed to kill something she can't even see? Knobby cypress knees rise from the sodden earth, trying to make her stumble and fall. Branches clutch and pluck at her. It's as if the forest wants to stop her from reaching the girl, to hold her back and force her to listen to every painful second of a violent, horrific death. She hears heavy thuds through the brush in the darkness ahead, the scrabble of chitinous claws on wood. It's big. Invisible. She's *blind* in here. Something heavy slaps the water, hard enough to whipcrack across the swamp like a gunshot. The next tortured cry is noticeably weaker, like Abby is losing consciousness.

Or worse.

A root catches the tip of her shoe and she goes sprawling. Holds onto the bangstick. She pushes to her feet and sprints. There! The dull gray of the water is just discernible between the trees. A hint of shadowy commotion. It's impossible to make out anything. The light from the fire doesn't reach this far. There's no moonlight, just the faint ambient radiance from the clouds. She screams in frustration. What she wouldn't give for—

Maya slows, paws frantically at her back pocket. Feels the pair of smooth, waxy cylinders and pulls one out. She tucks the bangstick under her arm. Pops the striker cover off the emergency road flare, then twists the cap off.

An eternity.

Abby is going to die. Is likely already dead. The certainty settles on her like a burial shroud.

But she has to be able to see in order to help.

She drags the tip of the flare across the striking pad, like a match. A spark. It catches with a cat hiss and comes to life. Brilliant red light floods the woods. Thin streamers of smoke rise into the night, smelling of spent fireworks. The flare sputters and splutters and spits, but the flame is strong, impossible to look at directly. Maya holds it away from her and charges into the underbrush. Fights against the prickling vegetation, screaming Abby's name. No response. Finally, she breaks through near the water's edge in a panic.

The alligator is massive, at least ten feet long, half in and half out of the muddy water. It has the girl by one thigh, powerful jaws clamped tight on the tender flesh. Ribbons of streaming blood are made black by the unearthly light. The beast regards her with its dead eyes, then swells and blasts another bellow in a wash of carrion breath.

Abby is still. In the sickly red glow she at first looks lifeless, as pale as a corpse in a freshly dug grave. But her eyes snap open at the sound of Maya's voice, and she raises her head from the thick cypress root she has her arms wrapped tightly around.

"Maya," she moans.

The alligator backpedals, trying to tear the little girl loose. Water is flung in sheets as it rolls its leviathan body, frighteningly fast. Abby is no match for its strength. Her fingers come apart and the monster drags her over the edge. The rising shriek is cut short as she goes under. Maya tosses the flare aside and reaches the bank in two bounding steps. She springs onto the root Abby had been holding, leaps without hesitation for the shadowy mass retreating from the shore, and splashes down beside the broad, tough back.

The alligator thrashes and rolls against her, rucking her t-shirt. Its rough humped scutes and thick hide scrape against her bared belly. Her feet sink into the mud, helping to anchor her. The flat head erupts from the water, tumbling Abby like a ragdoll. Maya yanks free the cotter pin and raises the bangstick overhead. Jams it into the glittering red eye that glares balefully up at her. The shot is deafening from this close. White fire erupts. Something viscous splatters her face.

The alligator goes limp and sinks into the murk.

She pitches the bangstick onto the shore and feels her way up the rough body until she finds the long, scaly snout. Abby struggles, whipping the muck at the bottom up in billowing blooms. Maya pries the jaws apart, grimacing, and the girl bobs to the surface, fighting to get to her feet. Maya grabs hold and lifts her. Abby throws her arms around her, sobbing and coughing and gagging. Nearly drags her down.

"You're safe," Maya says between great gasping breaths. "I've got you."

But they need to get out of the water. She doesn't know if alligators are like sharks, drawn by blood, but even if they aren't, there are probably a billion or more germs in every drop. That can't be good for an open wound.

"Can you walk?" she says.

"I don't know," Abby sobs. "It hurts so much!"

"Put your arm around my neck," she says. It feels like her heart is about to thrash itself out of her chest. "Let me help."

Together they climb the cypress roots and scramble onto the ground. While Abby rocks, squeezing her thigh with both hands above the injury to ease the pain, Maya retrieves the flare. She holds the light as close as she can and examines, wincing at the mangled punctures and the oozing blood. But blood is good. It helps clean the wounds. Relief makes her nearly giddy. She had expected gaping holes, missing flesh. Exposed bone.

"Does it feel broken?" she asks.

"I don't think so." Abby's voice is shaky through her clenched teeth. "Did you kill him?"

"I don't know. Maybe. I bashed him with the bangstick. He

went down hard."

"Good," the girl says fiercely. Her nostrils flare.

"Are you able to walk?"

Abby nods and wipes her tears away. Maya gets her under the arms and lifts, her mind on the man lying out there in the trees. In a movie he'd already be up, coming for them again, because one hit never takes out the bad guy. Everyone knows that. But life isn't a movie. People don't take a blow like that to the head and shake it off in a few seconds like a prizefighter returning for round two. They stay down, with concussions and brain bleeds and intracranial swelling.

And very often, without immediate medical attention they die.

He's unconscious, has to be … and he has a phone. A two-minute detour on the way back to the store, and she can be calling for help. Even if it has a lockscreen. And if there's no service? Then they aren't any worse off. There's still a plan. But there's service. There has to be. Especially if he put some kind of tracker on the Trans Am, like he did with Abby. How else could he have found them? A device like that would be cellular. She's sure of it. It's the twenty-first century, and as remote as this place feels, they're only a few miles from the very real civilization of Slidell, and only a few more from New Orleans. Plenty of coverage.

More than a phone, though, he has a gun. Right now they have no protection. Just the spent bangstick, which is useless against anything more than a spiderweb. In one fell swoop she can disarm him and give them the upper hand. Worst case, if he attacks and she can't figure out how to shoot him, she can throw the pistol into the woods. Even up the fight a little. There's still the bangstick, as minimal as it may be. Her pepper spray. But best case? She puts a stop to him permanently.

Either works for her.

And while she's at it, she'll take his light, too. See how the bastard likes being out here with nothing but his wits.

"Lean against me and use this for support," Maya says,

handing Abby the bangstick. She holds the hissing flare high to light the way, flame tipped to the side so liquid ash doesn't drip on either of them. "Let's get out of here."

64

Slowly and carefully, Maya helps Abby away from the waterline. The flare gives everything an ethereal look, transforming the woods into a surreal, unsettling landscape. The tall cypress trees, bathed in the crimson light, stand like sentinels blocking the way out of the underworld. Branches clutch at them, and the ferns and bushes cast long, distorted shadows. A light breeze makes the foliage whisper secretively.

She looks around, trying to get her bearings. Everything had been so balls to the wall, so full-throttle frantic when she ran through here moments ago that it's just a blur. The man should be somewhere nearby, but where? It was so dark then that now the light from the flare is useless. Nothing looks familiar, because she couldn't see anything except for the flames through the trees. She looks in that direction, gauging the distance to the cabin, and decides they haven't come far enough inland. If she doesn't see him soon she's giving up. The flare is already half gone, and it hasn't even been ten minutes since she sparked it. Then there's the kidnapper himself, current status unknown. The more time they waste looking, the more opportunity there is for him to wake up. She's not willing to bet their lives on her earlier assumptions about brain bleeds and concussions.

Every few steps, Abby stumbles as her injured leg tries to fold under her weight. Poor thing. Maya would give anything to be able to carry her out, but she's simply not strong enough. Abby is only a few inches shorter than she is, no more than thirty pounds lighter. It isn't in the cards. Each time the girl falters she catches her, bears her weight until her footing is sure. It's the least she can do. Her face burns with the shame of leaving Abby alone by the water. Why hadn't she moved her away from the shore before taking off, or helped her into a tree? Abby had even warned her there was an alligator in the water with them, and yet off she went. She wishes she could go back and do things differently, but she can't. All she can do is keep moving forward and try to stop obsessing over her failure, at least until they're safe. Distractions are deadly here.

She doesn't see the motionless man until they're almost on top of him. His dark t-shirt and jeans blend seamlessly with the dirt and crumbling leaves in the unsteady red glow, rendering him almost invisible. Maya draws up short, stops Abby before she can take another step. The girl's sharp inhalation is the only sign of her alarm at the sight of him.

He's face-down, snoring thickly. The flickering light makes it impossible to tell if he's faking, pretending to be unconscious while he waits for her to make a mistake. She's trembling with terror and adrenaline. What had she been thinking? Such a stupid idea. They should turn and go. Hoof it back to the store as fast as they can and forget about him.

But the gun is right there, inches from his outstretched hand. The phone is surely in one of his pockets, the flashlight in another. Maybe he even has a wallet crammed full of identification for the police.

All she has to do is get close enough for him to grab.

A bird is loose in her belly, flapping spastically. She wants to bend over, puke her guts out. Set it free.

But she doesn't. She says, "Can you stand on your own?"

"I think so."

She steps away from Abby, ready to catch the girl if she starts to fall. Abby stares down at the man, her expression detached and unreadable.

Maya inches forward. Just out of his reach now. No movement. No sign of wakefulness. She extends the flare and rotates her wrist, tipping the flame. A droplet of fire falls from the burning stick and plops onto his bare arm, white-hot. She imagines she can hear the sound of his flesh sizzling, can see the wisp of smoke.

There's no reaction. He isn't faking.

Moving at a glacial pace, her eyes never leaving the still form, she kneels beside the kidnapper and retrieves the pistol. It's much lighter than she expected. Almost like a toy, not something capable of taking a life. The metal is cool against her hot palm. She imagines pressing the barrel to the back of his head. Firing it.

Instead, she places the flare on the ground to continue her search.

"You should kill him," Abby whispers. "I wouldn't tell anyone."

"That's murder, and not who I am," Maya tells her. "We have his gun. Let the police deal with him. Or the animals."

Abby doesn't reply, just looks down at the kidnapper with the same shrouded expression, like she's distracted.

Keeping the pistol aimed at the man's back, she runs her hand around his side, feeling for the telltale rectangle of the phone through the denim. When she slips her fingertips into a front pocket and pinch-pulls it out, he doesn't move. She sets it beside the flare. His wallet is next, easy to find. She wants to open it. Check his ID. Know his name. Doesn't. Not here or now. Puts it with the phone.

The flashlight is on his other side, she discovers, in a snap holder on the waistband of his pants. When she thumbs the switch it crackles with electricity, a tiny blue-white arc popping between two leads on either side of the bulb, and she's so startled she nearly drops it.

"A stun gun," she murmurs. "Class act all the way, aren't you?"

There's a second switch. Pressing it engages the light, which she hands to Abby to direct while she checks the rest of his pockets. Her next find is a flat, folding leather case. At first, she thinks it contains knives, but they don't look right. More like the tools the dental hygienist sometimes uses to pick at a tough piece of tartar. Pick. Her mind goes back to the Trans Am, and how he had to get into the trunk without a key to stuff Abby in it. To the cabin, and the heavy clatter of the padlock on the front porch. His taunting voice. *Hear that, sister? That was your protection.* Of course this asshole needs lock picks in his line of work, just like the tracker. They join the growing collection. Her loot.

"*Hurry,*" Abby says.

The fourth pocket is empty. No keys. Pity. It would have been nice to take those, too. Leave him stranded while they take his car and get away from here. That makes the most sense. At least they might be able to get the Trans Am running, because waiting around for the police with him still out here is just *begging* for things to go south. They need to get on the phone, stay on the phone, and fill the radiator. If the police arrive before they get the old car going, good. If they don't, start walking to the interstate and provide directions to the 911 dispatcher. They have his weapons, his phone, and his identification. All that's missing is distance.

"Put these in your pocket," Maya says. She hands the wallet and lock picks to Abby, takes the light in return. They have no more need for the flare, so she taps the dwindling nub against a tree to knock the flame off and stamps it out. Leaves it with him. Collects the rest of his stuff.

Abby is bleeding. Crimson tracks streak her leg. She still has that spacey look, like her mind is in another place. They're not out of the woods yet—metaphorically *or* literally—and she could slip into shock at any time. Might already be there. Worry gnaws at Maya. The trek back to the store shouldn't be far, not even a quarter-mile, but how long will it be until Abby can be seen by medical professionals? The sooner they get some distance from him, the sooner she can call 911.

65

Abby bites her lip, puts most of her weight on the makeshift cane, and takes another step. Each time the muscles of her thigh flex it's like being stabbed by twenty knives at once. But she doesn't cry. She's done enough of that. Maya probably thinks she's the biggest baby in the world by now. The realization hurts even more than her leg.

Shadows twitch wherever she looks, brought to life by the bobbing light in the woman's hand. In each she sees another alligator, ready to attack. She tries to think about home, about her mom and dad and brother, but her mind keeps returning to the horror of the monster exploding out of the water, hurling itself onto the shore practically at her feet. The teeth and claws, cold scaly skin. She thought nothing could be worse than when the bad man snatched her, or when he touched her between her legs, but neither of those hold a candle to the alligator. Even the thought of kissing Liam isn't enough to drive the mental image away. She. Nearly. Died. Like, for *real*!

Her shoe catches on an exposed root and she almost falls, but Maya catches her upper arm and holds her up. The bangstick bumps her hurt leg. A sudden burst of pain elicits a grunt. Her eyes sting and her throat tightens. Not crying, she thinks, blinking rapidly.

In the eye of her mind, the alligator scuttles clickety-clack over the roots connecting the land and the water, a tree trunk on four legs. Each step quakes the ground, and its terrifying roar fills the world. She screams and crabs away, arms and legs flailing in a dreamlike slow motion, like the final girl in a horror movie trying to escape the deranged slasher. And then it's on her, claws raking hotly on her flesh as it moves in. The powerful jaws close on her leg so hard it feels like the sturdy bone is going to be ground into a fine powder and she screams again, not only from the agony but from the knowledge that her life is ending.

She shivers, suddenly chilled.

Maya senses the movement and stops, her face a mask of concern. She looks hard at Abby and says, "You okay?"

Abby nods.

"You're sure?"

"I'm sure."

"You understand why I couldn't just kill him, right? Even if he deserves it?"

"Yes." And she does. Mostly. But she has more pressing thoughts than the man somewhere behind them.

Maya stares at her for another moment, eyes probing and full of questions, but eventually looks away without saying anything else.

Abby remembers the sensation of being pulled apart like a wishbone as the monster tries to drag her into its watery lair, so it can tuck her away for later snacking. How all she can think about is the unfairness of it all. Her biggest worry should be whether Liam will try to hold her hand on the swamp tour tomorrow, only now she's in the worst swamp tour *imaginable*.

And then Maya appears like an avenging angel, charging at the alligator without a second thought. No one has ever done anything like that for her before. Not even her parents, and they're supposed to love her more than anyone else, ever. Single-handedly, the woman stopped the bad guy and killed the alligator, and then for an encore risked going back and taking his phone and gun! All that after choosing not to walk away when she had the opportunity. What kind of person would do that for a complete stranger? Suddenly the tears are back, filling her eyes and spilling down her cheeks. Something in her chest feels too large to be contained, like a light that wants to burst out of her and send the all the shadows running. She squeezes Maya's arm.

"What's wrong?" Maya says, alarmed.

Abby shakes her head. "Nothing. Just … thank you. For everything."

I hope I turn out to be like you, she wants to say, but doesn't, because Maya might laugh at her.

A smile brightens the woman's tired face and she puts her arm around the girl, pulls her close. "You don't need to thank me, sweetie. I never should have left you by yourself. I'm so sorry I did that."

"You had to. He was going to get us." How could Maya even think something like that? "You *stopped* him!"

The half-hug feels so safe, so much like home Abby wishes it would never end.

But it does, when both realize the sterile white light from the convenience store fluorescent bars is visible through the trees, just a couple of hundred feet ahead.

66

The seller groans. His eyelids flutter as consciousness seeps into him the way groundwater has seeped into his damp clothes, making his flesh cold and clammy. It feels like an elephant is standing with one foot on his back, pinning him to the forest floor. A relentless drumbeat pounds between his temples. When he tries to lift his head off the wet dirt a black wave of agony washes over him. He gags on the sweet metallic tang of blood in his mouth, retches. Soggy leaves cling to his cheek, the air ripe with their scent. He wants to close his eyes and go back to sleep, but he can't. That would be bad, because ... well, he doesn't know exactly why.

What the hell happened? His memories are ghosts in a foggy mirror, just out of reach. He concentrates, wills them closer. Images begin to flicker through the haze of pain like lightning in a thunderhead. The product on the beach, tasty in her swimsuit. Racing through the countryside with the cops on his ass. A pretty woman at a rest stop. Chasing shadows through the swamp.

No. Not chasing. *Tracking.*

Slowly the snapshots weave themselves into a tapestry of recollection. He had been on the verge of recapturing the product, only to discover she was somewhere else when she started screaming. After that, nothing. His thoughts want to wander like a herd of squirrels. It's a struggle to steer them. The woman must have found the tracker and used it to lead him on a snipe hunt, then hit him with something. He might have a concussion. *That's* why it would be bad for him to go back to sleep.

Gingerly he touches the side of his head, just over his left ear. Pain radiates from the spot like ringlets from a stone tossed into a pond, and he moans. The world spins, a giant carousel that causes his stomach to heave again. He hawks a blob of bloody spit. The tip of his tongue stings and feels raw. Bitten. And, weirdly, a spot on his sunburned arm stings like hell, as if he was standing too close to a pan of frying bacon and got splattered.

She did this to him. That stupid spic bitch.

The seller pushes onto his hands and knees. He's woozy and feels like hammered shit. Fresh blood trickles onto his face, but it's from the goose egg in his hair. The point of impact. Not his ears. Some old memory tells him that's a good thing. He crawls to the nearest tree and pulls himself to his feet using the trunk for support. His shaky legs want to buckle, weak as those on a newborn calf. How the hell is he supposed to walk like this? If it weren't for one hand on the rough bark for balance, he'd already be back on the ground.

But he's standing. And standing is a start.

He reaches for the flashlight to search the forest floor. The Kimber was in his hand when she hit him. It can't be far, the chrome easy to spot in the scattered wet leaves. But the holster is empty. What the...? Frantically, he pats each pocket. Finds nothing. She cleaned him out. A *woman*. Anger like a red flower blooms in him, an impenetrable veil that blots out every other thought. His stuff doesn't matter. Not anymore. Only one thing does.

Holding to the trunk, he shuffles around the tree until he locates the yellow-orange glow from the cabin, then turns until he's facing in the direction of the convenience store. It's so far! He can barely stand, even with the cypress to hold him up. Then he glimpses a quick flash, far away. His flashlight. It has to be.

The seller finds that with a little motivation, he's able to walk after all.

67

"Just a little further," Maya says, trying to keep the worry out of her voice. Abby is fading fast. Over the last three or four minutes they've slowed dramatically as she struggles to stay on her feet. Even with Maya holding most of her weight, her breath has taken on an awful ragged rasp, like she can't get enough air. In the backwash from the flashlight her face is pale, shiny with sweat. Maya once more finds herself wishing she could pick the girl up, carry her the rest of the way to the car like an infant. Maybe that would assuage some of the guilt.

"'kay," Abby gasps.

Maya shuts off the light and pockets it. They're close enough that she can make out the straight lines of the store now. A few more steps and they'll be out in the open, able to see the unobstructed sky again. Thank God. She takes out the phone, wakes it. Presses the *Emergency* button on the lock screen.

Makes the call.

When the ring comes through loud and clear, without a hint of static, she nearly bursts into tears.

"It's ringing!" she says.

It might be her imagination, but Abby seems to stand a little taller, step a little livelier.

"9-1-1, what is your emergency?" The dispatcher is a woman with a pronounced drawl.

"I need the police and an ambulance right away."

"Location?"

"Um, we're at a convenience store called Peepaw's. I don't know the road, but it's the first exit on I-10 after you cross into Louisiana."

"You're in Louisiana?"

"Yes."

"This is Hancock County dispatch in Mississippi. Please hold while I transfer you to St. Tammany Parish."

"There's someone trying—" she begins, but it's too late. The woman is gone. All she hears is the soft hiss of dead air. She wants to scream.

They've reached the thicket at the border separating grass and forest. Maya tucks the phone between her head and shoulder, and uses her freed hand to push branches and brambles and vines aside so they can shove their way through. As they break free into the blessedly clear night Abby falters, goes down onto one knee. She hisses and grabs at her wounded leg. Maya carefully lifts her to her feet.

"Almost there," she says. The Trans Am waits patiently for them no more than fifty feet away, gleaming in the castoff light from the store windows. The air smells of oil and asphalt. Humanity. She thrills to the sight of the clear sky painted with thousands of stars. Two blinking airplanes traveling perpendicular to one another. A rind of moon smiling down. The forest had been so *close*, so oppressive.

"Hello?" The new dispatcher is a man. "I have your location as Peepaw's Gas and Snaks. Correct?"

"Yes."

"Thank you. Sheriff patrols are en route, estimated time of arrival ten minutes."

Too long. *Far* too long. Got to get out of here. She says, "Okay."

"I've dispatched an ambulance from Slidell, ETA twelve minutes. What's your situation?"

"A man is trying to kill us. Me and a girl. Abby. He kidnapped her earlier. There was an AMBER alert. I think she's going into shock."

The story pours out of her in a disjointed jumble as they make their way to the Trans Am. She opens the door, helps Abby into the seat. The girl is even more pallid in the light. Her eyelids flutter erratically. Maya pulls the seatbelt across her, latches it.

"Listen," she tells the dispatcher. "I'm giving the phone to Abby. We can't sit here and wait. It's too dangerous."

When the girl whispers, "Hello?" Maya winces. Her voice is so weak!

She rolls the window down to follow as much of the conversation as she can, then pats Abby on the shoulder and mouths *good girl* before closing the door. Raises the hood, casting a nervous glance into the darkness beyond the fall of store light. Nothing. She takes out the flashlight and gives it a quick shine in that direction. Still nothing. Probably being paranoid. She extinguishes the light, sets it on top of the radiator. Moves on around to the driver side to work from there. The position is awkward, leaning so far in, but she'll be able to watch for him while she works, rather than stand there with her back to the woods.

Definitely paranoid. But alive.

The blue container of antifreeze is where she left it an age ago, ready to bring the old car back to life. She hopes. Before she picks it up she takes the pistol from her back pocket and sets it beside the flashlight. Easy to get to. A quick peek through the windshield shows Abby still conversing with 911. She looks marginally more alert, more with it.

Maya reaches for the antifreeze, but a sudden flurry of movement at the periphery of her vision catches her attention and stays her hand. Time seems to dilate as she turns to look, moving so slowly she can hear the tendons in her neck creaking like old floorboards. A shadow against the trees coalesces into the man when he lurches into the spill of light, his face a glistening mask of blood. Rage twists his features into a death mask. He bellows something incomprehensible, spittle flying. Panic tries to seize her, to sink its claws into her flesh.

Succeeds.

"Abby!" she screams, scrambling for the pistol. Touching it. She thinks for an instant she's screwed the pooch, that the cursed thing is going to skitter off the radiator and tumble into the engine compartment, but then her fingers close around the handgrip and she raises it.

He thunders across the parking lot, feet scuffing the wet pavement and kicking up trash from the overturned can. Reaches for her. Maya swings the gun around. Tries to aim. Her hands refuse to be still.

BOOM!

The kidnapper crashes into her full-tilt, crushing her into the pinching space where the raised hood meets the body of the Trans Am. She both feels and hears the brittle *crack* of ribs breaking. White-hot agony explodes along the side of her chest. The pistol spins away. Her left arm is wrenched around behind her by his momentum, twisting the shoulder already injured by the tire iron, and her face smashes into the underside of the hood.

With a guttural moan the man staggers back a step, clutching at his side.

"Shot me, you *cunt*," he rasps.

Maya tries to push away from the car, fights to get her footing. There's still the stun gun. But her legs refuse to obey, and the weapon is no longer where she left it. She sags against the quarter panel. Can't breathe. Nothing but short gasping wheezes, more coming out than going in. Something crackles in her throat.

The kidnapper tucks his arm against his belly and comes for her. She digs frantically for the pepper spray in her pocket with her good hand. Can't get it in time. He grabs the waistband of her jeans and drags her away from the Trans Am, drops her on the blacktop. Straddles her with his knees pinning her arms, teeth bared in a rictus of rage and pain.

"He's *killing* her!" Abby shrieks. "Please tell them to hurry!"

She's gotten out of the car and now stands at the rear watching in horror, still on the phone.

Run, Maya tries to shout, but there's not enough air. There's no air at all.

Then his fist descends, filling her world, and the screams of the girl chase her into a black fog.

68

The seller relishes the sensation of the blow connecting solidly, the way the soft flesh yields under the force of his fist, mashing and distorting the woman's pretty petite features into a caricature. Her eyes roll back to show nothing but white, cheek already starting to darken and swell. *Yes.* The feeling is almost sexual in its intensity ... so powerful and overwhelming it's a salve to the spot in his abdomen where the bitch shot him. And this is only the first punch. Payback for the pepper spray earlier. He looks forward to collecting on each of her transgressions, and only wishes he could remove the gloves and feel her skin on his. To slap her into consciousness and look into those brown eyes as he chokes the life out of her for shooting him. No. For disrespecting him.

For *disobeying* him.

The wound hurts like hell, but he doesn't think it's life-threatening. The hole is nearly even with his navel, but far to the right side. A couple more inches and the bullet would have missed him completely. He's no anatomist, but can't remember anything especially essential way over there. There's no sensation of his life draining away. No dizziness, and only a little blood. He feels pretty good, actually, except for all the places he's hurting. But he can deal with that after he gets paid. The injuries aren't as important as finishing what he started.

As he draws his arm back to break the woman's dainty nose for running a hook through his forearm, a shrill cry slices through the wildfire of retribution that threatens to consume him. The product, screaming. Something in it stands out, catches his attention. What? He forces himself to concentrate, to replay the frantic sounds, this time processing and absorbing.

Not sounds, he realizes. Words.

Tell them to hurry.

Tell *them*. Tell who? Them.

His gaze sharpens on the girl, hovering at the back of the woman's car, not tasty at all now but muddy and bleeding and wretched and screeching into a phone. *His* phone.

Someone is coming. She wants them to hurry.

He knows who. Trouble. Johnny Law. But when? How long has she been talking? No idea. He strains to hear the wail of a siren, but can't hear a damn thing over her banshee keening. She needs to be silenced. The woman can wait.

When the seller tries to get to his feet, the white-hot flash in his side staggers him, and he leans against the Trans Am for support. Jesus, it hurts! He presses his palm over the hole, which backs the pain off. A little. The product reels away, trying to run out to the road where the help will arrive. She moves like a wounded baby bird, dragging one blood-crusted leg as she begs the person on the phone for help.

Gasping through gritted teeth, he gives chase. He reaches her before she's made it much past the Mustang, catches hold of her by the neck and jerks her back. Wrenches his phone out of her hand. She slaps at him, punches at him as he checks the screen, but the feeble blows barely register. 911. Of course. He disconnects the call to terminate their access to the device's detailed location information. Make the bastards use signal strength to approximate where he is, at least until he's close enough to New Orleans to turn the damn thing off and blind them. Best they can do without the connection is one or two miles from the actual location. Plenty of wiggle room since they have no idea what he's driving, and there's no way the product would have told them.

He stuffs the phone into his pocket. She's on the run again, hobbling as fast as she can, thin arms flapping for stability. She really *does* look like a little bird, he thinks, grinning. His golden goose. Ought to still be able to get one fifty for her. Maybe even one seventy-five if the buyer cleans her up a little, uncovers some of that raw potential. Let him see what she has cooking under that grime and gore. Even in her current state he can see it shining through like a sunburst, ready to bring the heat. Make it two hundred. Hell, he should get full price for taking most of the fight out of her. Surely the customers might appreciate someone more … docile.

It takes all of ten seconds to run her down. He seizes one thin shoulder and spins her around.

"Not so fast, princess," he says. "We have places to go and people to meet."

The only response is an ear-piercing shriek that stokes the embers of his anger into flames, but a slap shuts her up. Probably just cost him another ten grand, but the shocked expression and her tears are worth it. He likes to see her cry.

The seller drags the feebly struggling product across the parking lot with one hand, the other clamped tight over his injury. All the movement is raising holy hell with it. He needs to sit down and rest. Soon. At the rear of the Mustang he makes a fist and pops her on the temple. Not too hard, not too soft. A Goldilocks punch, just right for knocking her out without ruining her looks. He lowers her to the wet pavement and fetches the keys from the cupholder in the front seat console, grateful in retrospect they hadn't been in his pockets when the bitch one-upped him out there. Chalk one up for the good guy.

He stows the product in the trunk, regretting the decision to toss the zip ties at the welcome center. They'd come in pretty handy right about now. Oh, well. It doesn't matter. What does is getting the hell out of Dodge.

As soon as he settles a debt.

He pauses to listen for sirens again, hears nothing. Slams the lid down. Glances over at the shadowy Trans Am.

The woman is gone.

He shambles to her car, clutching his side, looking in all directions. She can't have made it far. Down onto his hands and knees to check underneath, wincing, even though it's impossible for her to fit in the narrow space. Not enough clearance. The Kimber is lying behind one of the front tires. He picks up the empty weapon, disengages the release lock, and holsters it.

Briefly, he considers checking inside the store. See if she's hiding in there. But would she? He wouldn't. Too easy to be trapped. If he were the one hiding, he'd be out in the high grass again. It's the best spot to watch from. She's hurt worse than he is. Has to be. That tackle was one for the NFL, a bone-crunching slam that *must* have done some damage. The followup punch was just icing on the cake. She's out there, for sure, eyes on him. Scheming. He feels the weight of her stare. Too bad he doesn't have his light anymore. Put a spot on her and go finish her.

The paramount word being *go*. He needs to. If he stays and continues his search, all is lost. That's probably what she wants, anyway. Lure him all over hell and creation on a hunt until the cavalry arrives and saves the day. Screw that. His payment is more important than vengeance right now. Besides, he still has her phone. All he has to do is find someone to unlock it and open all that sweet, juicy personal information. Friends. Family. Home address. Socmeds. Pay her a visit at his leisure, when she thinks he's long gone. He can be down with that. For now, let her live with the knowledge that she almost won, almost saved the girl ... and failed.

He takes one last look around, squinting into the darkness. No sign of her. As he turns to go, the gallon of antifreeze catches his eye, patiently waiting to be poured into the radiator. All her hope in a shiny blue container. It might *still* be her hope, he realizes, but not as a way out of here.

As a way to follow him, if it occurs to her.

Yeah, right. *If.* He harbors no doubt that she'll try, if given half the chance. She's resourceful, that one. Earlier, he had admired the quality. Now he feels threatened by it.

The seller bends to knock the canister over, to pour out all that hope in an iridescent puddle on the pavement, but a sudden thought stays his hand. Spilling it isn't enough, because it doesn't solve his problem. She'll just fill the empty jug with water and put that in the radiator. Not as good as the coolant, for sure, but maybe good enough. Better to just take it. Slow her down, make her have to scavenge in the store while he's hauling ass away from this hellhole. He lifts the container and holds it up, sneering at the concealing weeds where she has to be hidden. The effort stirs serious—almost worrisome—pain in his guts. He bites the inside of his cheek. No matter how much it hurts, never let it show.

"So sorry, sister!" he taunts. "Too bad your best shot wasn't enough."

He pauses at the rear bumper of the Trans Am to retrieve his GPS tracker, then stores the gallon of antifreeze in the passenger footwell of the Mustang. The backpack he took from the woman's trunk is in the seat. He uses it to brace the canister, so it doesn't spill. Once the car is running, he wakes his phone and charts a quick course for New Orleans. The road in front of the store connects with his old friend highway 90 some fifteen miles yon, he discovers, and from there it's a straight shot. He won't even need to get back on the interstate. Barely more than a half hour, and that's if he goes the speed limit. Piece of cake.

The seller peels out of the parking lot and drives away into the darkness.

IV

FRED ANDERSON

69

Maya lies curled in the shadowed back seat of the Trans Am, hugging herself in a vain attempt to dampen the pain each shallow inhalation brings. Her cheek is hot, the skin drawn tight, and it's hard to keep her eye open. The throb in her shoulder is like a rotted tooth. Hurt blooms in it with every heartbeat.

She wants to draw great gulps of air. Her body is slowly starving for oxygen. She refrains, not only because of the agony it would bring, but because she knows to do so would draw the attention of the kidnapper, standing just outside the driver window. From this low vantage all she can see of him is his head, not even ten feet away. He's staring toward the trees. Looking for her. Considering. Perfect. That's what she wants. There's no way she can fight him. Not now, with only her bare hands. She'd be dead in seconds. Just climbing through the other window while he was chasing Abby had been an exercise in torture that nearly made her faint. Her only hope is to outsmart him. Use his anger against him.

So she hides and watches, willing him to take the bait. To go looking for her. Finish what he started, as he obviously wants to do. And while he does, each passing second brings help a little closer. If she's lucky, the police have put two and two together and are running quiet, no lights or sirens to warn him of their approach. She had made it clear to the dispatcher that he was still here, still trying to hurt them. Maybe this one thing will go right. Where *are* they? It feels like hours have passed since she first placed the call.

The head turns, looks down at something on the ground.

Drops out of sight and reappears a second later. The man raises her jug of antifreeze with one arm, like the severed head of an enemy, presenting it to the trees. When he does, his expression transforms from one of mockery to a grimace. She knows that look, knows it well. He's hurting.

Good.

He goads the woman he believes is in the grass with the blue container, but Maya barely registers his words, focusing instead on the last thing he said to her. *You shot me.* Between the possible concussion and a gunshot wound, he has to be slower now. Weaker. Maybe already a dead man walking. But he doesn't look close to death. He looks pretty lively, like being shot pissed him off more than anything.

The man turns in the direction of his car and disappears. How much time had her ruse bought? One minute? Two? It isn't enough. Help isn't here. Her thoughts go to Abby, once again his prisoner despite her every effort to keep the girl safe. The ache in her soul is even worse than those in her body. They went through so much together, and for what? Abby is right back where she started, locked in a trunk. His intentions are clear. That he hadn't killed Maya while she was unconscious beneath him, at his mercy, speaks volumes. He abandoned her in his moment of triumph because he was afraid the *real* prize might get away. Now he's going to leave with his spoils, and once they're gone Abby is lost forever.

If that happens Maya thinks she might be lost forever, too.

She struggles to sit up. Looks out the back window. He's on the passenger side of his car with the door open, leaned over the front seat. The blood coating his face makes him look inhuman under the dome light. He slams the door and comes around, hand pressed to his side. She needs to distract him again, now, even if it means her life. He can't leave.

"Hey asshole," she croaks, but her voice is weak, so small there's no way it made it through the open window and all the way over to his car. A person standing at the gas pump next to the Trans Am would have had trouble hearing it. The effort causes a rush of pain makes her head swim.

The kidnapper climbs into the Mustang, closing himself off even further. His phone flares to life, bathing him in blue. Maya stretches, reaches for the door handle. Moans when her chest makes contact with the folded front seat. The other car wakes with a growl. Her fingers snag and she yanks. The door opens enough to activate the interior light. She wills him to notice it. To realize he had overlooked what was hiding right under his nose.

"Come on!" she screams, and now there's more power in her voice. More life. Maybe enough to be heard. She fights her way over the seat, grunting. Gets a foot on the concrete. Wriggles. Pulls. Falls out onto her hands and knees with a gasp that feels like shards of glass in her lungs, just in time to see the Mustang accelerating down the wet road, carrying Abby to whatever fate the man has planned.

A sob tears itself from her. Why had she hidden in the car? Why didn't she run for the grass, like he assumed? She could have called out from the dark, teased him and taunted him and kept him occupied. But she hadn't. She anticipated *exactly* what he would do, and blew it, because in the heat of the moment she took the easiest way out. Why? Because she was a chickenshit. Too scared of the big bad man to act. Worse, she stayed put and kept quiet until it was too late. At any time she could have tapped on the window. Could have said, *hey asshole, I'm right here beside you.* But she hadn't, and now Abby is gone.

Jesus, what is taking the police so long? They're supposed to serve and protect, not show up for the cleanup, to scribble a few notes and cluck sympathetically while doing absolutely nothing. But that's how they are, perpetually five minutes late to do any good. She might as well forget all about Abby. They won't give two shits. When they ask, she should point vaguely and tell them, *oh yes, officer, he went thataway. Now if you'll excuse me I have a car I need to deli—*

The Trans Am.

In her head, Moretti's voice. *The car has LoJack installed.*

Followed by *I can monitor its location.*

Ending with *I'll be keeping an eye on my property.*

But would he be doing that in the middle of the night? No. What sane person would? Sane people are sleeping right now. The man's phone had shown the time to be three-fifteen when she stole it. Except, she realizes, it's an hour later in Atlanta, which means closer to sunup. It's summer. Plenty of people rise that early. Maybe Moretti is one of them. And even if he's not monitoring himself, *some*one might be. He can afford to pay for something like that. In the gig economy you can hire anyone to do anything.

Like drive a car to Baton Rouge for five thousand dollars.

There's another gallon of coolant in the store. She can see it in her mind's eye, coated with dust among the oil and flares and air fresheners. Waiting.

She's probably wrong. Moretti isn't watching, or keeping tabs. If he was, the police would already be here to find out why the car has been sitting in the lot of a closed convenience store in the middle of a swamp for ninety minutes. Unless he believes she got too tired to continue and pulled off for some shuteye, instead of trying to make it to the fancy hotel in Baton Rouge. That's possible. Barely.

Suppose she's able to get the Trans Am operational. What then? He'll have a lead of several minutes. She doesn't know where the road goes, only that his car turned away from the interstate. It could be anywhere. Moretti has to not only recognize the deviation from the planned route, but decide it's egregious enough to report. The police must locate both cars and rescue Abby without hurting her further.

All before the Trans Am overheats again, or she uses up what little gas is left in the tank.

Impossible outside Hollywood. Too much uncertainty.

But if she sits here and waits, the only certainty is this: Abby will be lost. Every second she dithers is another second the girl is further away.

Slouching to ease the pressure on her ribs, Maya pushes to

her feet and hurries toward the convenience store.

70

Broken glass crunches underfoot when she steps onto the tile floor. The automotive supplies are on the far side of the room, just outside the *Employees only* door. Maya remembers the way Abby's eyes lit up at the praise for spotting them.

Passing the front counter, a colorful spinning rack catches her attention. Single-dose packets of pain medication. She snatches two. Gulps the four pills with a shot of energy drink and collects the container of antifreeze from the bottom shelf. Before exiting she grabs a pair of candy bars. One to minimize the impact of the double dose of ibuprofen on her empty stomach, and one to give Abby after the police have stopped the kidnapper. Snickers, because she knows the girl likes them.

At the car, she has to force herself to pour slowly, so she doesn't slop the concentrated orange liquid all over the engine. She knows it needs to be diluted, but that takes time she doesn't have. If things work out, she won't be driving long enough to do any damage. If they don't, Moretti can go on the payback list, behind Peepaw.

Each passing second ticks off in her head like a whipcrack. Two minutes since the Mustang left. More than a mile, maybe as much as two. His speed likely depends on whether he knows about the call to 911, or spotted her as he drove away. The less threatened he feels, the slower he'll drive to keep from being noticed. Probably.

Another thirty seconds is lost by the time the last bit flows out. The two t-shirts Abby brought out earlier are still in a heap next to the gas pumps. Maya bends to pick them up, biting her lip when the embers in her ribs flash over to fire. She balls both together and stuffs them in. Good enough. The sound of the hood slamming shut marks three minutes Abby has been gone.

Keys out. Door open. An ungraceful flop, a quiet whimper.

The heavy rumble as she wakes the engine from its slumber.

Fifteen more seconds. She's at most three miles behind him. It might just be possible to catch up, if the road continues. If he hasn't taken a turn. If her car doesn't overheat or run out of gas.

This may be the stupidest thing she's ever done. There's only one way to find out.

Maya reverses away from the pumps, spinning the wheel. She drops the gear selector down to drive. Hits the gas. The tires fight for traction, catch, and the Trans Am slews out of the parking lot.

71

The seller cruises, trying to keep his burning eyes open. Trees crowd the wet asphalt from both sides, turning the two-lane into a long, monotonous tunnel. There's been no other traffic, no real signs of life. Just the endless black strip separating walls of greenery. In the ten minutes since he left the little store, he's nearly nodded off three times. Fatigue drapes him like a weighted blanket. It's been a hell of a long day, and there is still much to do. Once he hits the city, he has to find a suitable spot to leave the car and notify the buyer. He's never made a dropoff this late—this *early*—and doesn't know how the message will be received. If there's no response or no interest, he'll deal with the DNA under her nails and figure out what to do with her. Maybe find another swamp. This godforsaken state is full of them.

The pain in his side has spread across his middle, a dull ache that serves as a constant reminder of what the woman did to him. It needs to be seen by a professional, and he has no idea who to call or what to do. Reputable doctors are required to report gunshot wounds, and the kind of doctor who'd fix him up for an under the table cash payment isn't going to advertise. Possibly on the dark web, but that takes time. Days. By then infection might have set in. Not to mention the odds are high that he'd have to travel.

Would the buyer know anyone? All signs point to yes. The buyer deals with fresh products on a constant basis. He isn't going to tolerate sick or damaged goods. There must be a doctor in his contacts, probably on speed dial … but would he be willing to cross that boundary, to make a tangible connection with one of his sellers? Doubtful. If their roles were reversed, he sure as hell wouldn't. Too much risk. But it can't hurt to ask. Nothing ventured, nothing gained. Surely the sheer number of quality deliveries he's made over the last two years must count for something.

The map places him less than two miles from the intersection with highway 90. He'll be at the outskirts of the city in fifteen minutes. His mind turns to his day job. What others would call his *real* life, although today has felt more real than any open house, any closing on a home sale ever has. He needs some time off. To lie low, while he heals. Let the assistants handle all the heavy work. Can't have the customers noticing anything out of the ordinary during a showing or inspection. A week, no more than two.

Maybe it's time to think about retiring from that world anyway. From *both* worlds. Today has been a hell of an eye-opener, showing him how lucky he's been so far. With this payment—assuming he can get at least two hundred for the girl—he'll have almost three million socked away. He should hang up his hat. Sell the real estate business to an investor and get his face off all those billboards. Move somewhere cheap. Live in luxury until he dies of old age in a hot tub with a couple of bunnies who know how to treat—

The tires drop onto the shoulder and the car shimmies, jerking him back to wakefulness. The seller glances at himself in the rearview, wide-eyed and alert now, but what grabs his attention and blasts a jolt of adrenaline into his blood isn't his face. It's the far off headlights, coming fast. Not a cop, though, unless they're running without the light bar activated.

Her.

It has to be. Somehow, the silly bitch managed to get some water in her radiator, and now she's chasing him down. Her tenacity is almost admirable.

But why? What does she expect to accomplish? She has no phone, no way to reach the police. Just her emotions. Typical of women. A colossal screwup on her part, but one he can use to his advantage. Maybe his luck is starting to change. First the product, and now this. Looks like he'll get his chance with her after all. And there's a perfect spot for it not far outside the city.

All he needs to do is lead her there.

72

Abby groans and touches her temple. Each heartbeat pounds in her head, the pain compounded by vibrations that rattle her to her core. Her leg feels like a spiked steel band has been wrapped around it and cinched tight. She opens her eyes to a cramped space, bathed in an eerie red glow. Another flipping car trunk. But not Maya's, not this time. *His.* He must have put her in here after he hit her.

He hit her.

Just like he had hit Maya.

The memory of the woman's still body on the pavement beneath the bad man comes back in a rush that squeezes her chest and makes her forget her aches for the moment. *He's killing her!* The words screamed into the phone echo in her mind. What if Maya is dead?

She can't be.

Can she?

Abby shoves the thought aside before grief renders her immobile. Maya was alive the last time she saw her. Unconscious, but alive. Her throat feels like it's closing off. He was so *angry*. What if he went back for more? She can't bear to think about that. Can't bear to *not* think about it. Sweet, brave, *incredible* Maya who risked her life time and time again for a stupid kid she didn't even know.

He has to die.

Something is touching her hip. Maybe a possible weapon. But when she turns to look, it's just an old tire. Crud. Next to it is a thick, coated cable. Each end splits and terminates in a pair of alligator clamps. Ugh. Just the word, and the image it evokes, makes her shiver. The cable is worthless without a dead battery. Her dad has one just like it hanging in the garage at home he sometimes uses to start the riding mower. The final discovery is a wad of stretchy bungee cords. Also useless, unless she needs to tie something down. Hang on. That's not a bad idea, actually. If she can find the right places to hook or tie the cords, it might prevent him from raising the lid. For a while, anyway. Abby sets them aside for further consideration.

She isn't able to peel up the faux carpet beneath her, and there are no tools or metal rods to be found. This sucks. Unlike in Maya's car, these taillights aren't protected, but she has no way to knock one out to attract attention. No screwdriver to remove the screws she can feel. Despair threatens to consume her. He's eventually going to stop and open the trunk—even if she delays him with the bungee cords—and she has no way to protect herself.

How can there be a tire but no tools for changing it? Has she missed something? She double-checks the floor, lifts one edge of the tire to uncover a big fat nothing beneath. Maybe a storage compartment in the back for the tools? She rolls over to face the wall, which is covered in the same synthetic material she's lying on. Runs her fingers over it searching for a knob or handle, a seam that would indicate a panel. Nothing.

Wait a second.

Up near the top, where everything comes together and it's hard to fit her hand, she feels a cupped indention in the gap between the wall and the top. Inside it is a curved metal bar about as thick as a pencil, in the shape of the letter U. A second piece is hooked over it like a tab. When she pushes on the tab, it jiggles the tiniest bit. Odd. The position is awkward so she twists, straining, in order to force her hand a little further into the space. Pushes harder. First back, then up. With a faint *snick*, the tab pops free.

A section of the back seat folds down into the passenger compartment.

Fear coils in her like a venomous snake preparing to strike.

Cool air bathes her fevered face. The man is in plain view, straight ahead. Close enough to touch him on the shoulder if she wriggles forward just a little. Which she does ... but only far enough to stick her head through the opening, to look for a weapon.

"You've got balls, sister, I'll give you that," he says. "But playtime is over."

Abby freezes, terrified. But he can't be talking to her. She's directly behind him. There's no way he can see her. It's a blind spot. So who? She's the only other person in the car.

Then it clicks.

Sister. He said *sister*.

That's his mocking nickname for Maya, just like *princess* is hers. He said it in the parking lot, then again on the front porch of the cabin. She inches out a little further for a better look. Now the side of his head can be seen. He's watching something in the mirror.

The engine screams under sudden stress. A heavy thrum rocks the chassis, and the car leaps forward. Abby grabs the section of folded seat to keep from sliding back into the trunk. He's put the pedal to the floor. Like whatever he sees has spooked him, made him want to run. She feels like her heart is going to explode. A savage grin splits her face.

Because she thinks he might be looking at Maya.

73

The seller eases off the gas as he approaches the stop sign and the end of the road. Highway 90. According to the map, ten more miles to New Orleans. Three to his immediate destination. He checks the mirror. The other car is closer, less than a tenth of a mile back. She's falling for it. Hook, line, and sinker.

One other vehicle is on the highway, a pickup approaching from the direction of the city. Not a threat. He sweeps through the turn without stopping and begins to pick up speed. Signs of civilization show in the headlights. A jumble of houses, an apartment complex, a seafood shop. A bright parking lot for the apartments. Illuminated windows glow softly here and there. The Mustang passes these, climbing the rising arch of a bridge over an inky expanse of water. At the apex, the best thing he's seen all night. Like a constellation on the horizon, the glittering lights of New Orleans brighten the western sky. Almost there.

Behind him, the Trans Am slingshots onto the highway and straightens. The woman flicks her high beams rapid-fire at the oncoming pickup. It passes with no reaction. *That's right, sister*, he wants to tell her. *No one cares about your troubles. About you at all.* It's a cruel world, and for her it's about to become a little more so.

The seller wishes he'd held onto Brandon's gun, but it's like his father always said. *If wishes were horses beggars would ride.* At least she doesn't have one either. He doesn't know what the hell she fired at the cabin, when she nearly took off the side of his head, but it must be gone, or she'd have used it instead of his own gun to shoot him. Maybe when the boat overturned. So what does that leave her? The pepper spray, most likely. That's a pocket thing. It wouldn't have fallen out in the water. Possibly his stun gun. Not so bad. Forewarned is forearmed. She won't catch him by surprise.

The wound in his side concerns him. How much is it going to slow him down? Quite a bit, he thinks. But she's hurt, too. That tackle did a number on her. She has to have a few sprung ribs, at the minimum. He remembers the crunch. The *give*. If it comes down to a one-on-one fight, they're going to look like a couple of geriatrics trying to screw. However ... he has size and strength to his advantage, and is more than happy to use them.

At the nuts and bolts it's a simple plan, really. Force her to run hard until her car overheats again, then circle back and take care of her. While he can buy the idea that the shitty little store *might* have some automotive supplies, like the antifreeze he took, there's no way the place had a replacement radiator cap for a car more than forty years old. Just ... no. His credulity has its limits.

So that means she's rigged up some temporary measure, some limp-along stopgap that works but doesn't actually *work*. All he has to do is apply pressure and wait for the inevitable. If it doesn't happen quickly, he'll pivot from outlast to outrun and lose her. It won't be hard. The Mustang is ten years old, but it can still run circles around her antique. Either way he wins, collects his jackpot. Those are the kinds of odds he likes.

Two more miles.

The plan requires isolation. Someplace industrial or commercial. Unused, so there won't be any cops to intervene and mess things up, and derelict, with long stretches of road where he can keep his speed up. Force her to push the Trans Am past its limits. Fortunately, another nasty bitch named Katrina took care of that for him almost twenty years ago, when the levees broke and created the blighted landscape he sees every time he comes into the city from the east on I-10. Everything should have been razed to the bare dirt and rebuilt from scratch, like they did in the moneyed parts of town. Instead, the politicians bickered and complained and did jack squat, just like in the days before the hurricane made landfall. People in the city consider the area an eyesore, but to him it's beautiful in its own way. Haunting.

There's no way anyone will be around, not this early.

Which means no one to hear her screams.

74

A ferocious wind whips through the Trans Am and helps dry the sweat on Maya's face. All the windows are rolled down, the heater on full blast to bleed a few degrees off the engine. It's working. Sort of. The temperature gauge hangs just shy of the red line, but it's held steady there for the last couple of minutes. High, but not hot enough to cause another breakdown. Yet. More worrisome is the fuel gauge. The needle hovers a hair above empty.

But she's closed the gap. The Mustang is only a couple of hundred feet ahead.

It isn't good enough.

She pounds the steering wheel with a fist. No sign of the police anywhere. The lone vehicle she passed had completely ignored her frantic footwork on the dimmer switch to stutter the brights. Everything is about to come tumbling down around her. She's a fool for taking off without thinking ahead. Little Miss Jumps the Gun. Just like she did in the swamp.

Just like she's done her whole life.

The world passes in a blur outside. Trees and grass, the occasional house or neighborhood or business. No real signs of life, but they're rejoining society bit by bit. The highway is leading them into a city, one big enough to create a glowing dome ahead. New Orleans, she thinks. The view from the top of the bridge had been impressive, despite the distance. Only a few more miles if they stay the course.

She doesn't think the Trans Am has that many in the tank.

Ahead, brakes lights flare and the Mustang slows. She lets off the gas. What is he doing? There's a crossroad approaching, one busy enough for a traffic signal. Two gas stations and a thrift store. A metropolis compared to what she's seen since sometime in Mississippi. The Mustang hangs a hard left at the light and she follows. Her headlights sweep across a hotel gone to rot.

The road traverses a neighborhood. Streetlights throw pinkish cones on either side, and small houses elbow for room along the thoroughfare. Most appear abandoned, but the presence of automobiles in front of a few indicate at least some people make this place their home. As the Trans Am gathers speed, Maya lays on the horn in hope the long, discordant blasts inspire someone to call the police and report her. Soon the houses fall away and the wilderness returns, greenery to either side, interspersed with the occasional glitter of water.

Her mood is as empty as her tank.

What was she thinking? Did she really believe Moretti would call in the good guys, that they'd swoop in at the last minute and save the day? He isn't watching. No one is coming. Now she's going to run out of gas in a forgotten part of the world and be forced to watch him drive away with Abby all over again. Only this time instead of help already being en route the way it was at Peepaw's, she'll have to start all over. Find a phone and waste precious time trying to explain the situation from the beginning. By the time they even get started, the asshole will have disappeared in a city of half a million or more, plus who knows how many tourists. And what helpful information will she be able to provide? *He's in a dark Mustang.* Wow. Go, Maya. What a lifesaver.

The least she can do is try to memorize the license plate.

She gives it more gas and the Trans Am creeps closer to the Mustang. A hundred feet now.

Still too far.

75

Like a turtle retreating into its shell, Abby inches back into the trunk. She's seen enough. Over the last several minutes the interior has brightened as the car behind them draws closer and closer. The man keeps checking the mirror, but it's become apparent that he's not frightened. He *wants* Maya to follow him, has been taunting her under his breath, calling her a stupid b-word and telling her to *hurry up, sister*, oblivious to the girl eavesdropping just a couple of feet away. Especially just now, when he took a turn so hard it almost flung Abby all the way out, onto the back seat. But why?

To stop her. It's obvious. He's going to wait until Maya is right beside him and then jerk the wheel. Sideswipe her and shove her off the road. Cause her to wreck, so she won't be able to follow them anymore. Maybe not that exactly, but something close to it. She's certain. He's leading her on, pretending he's running from her so she doesn't realize she's walking—driving—into a trap. And once he's gotten her out of the way he'll be home free.

No. Freaking. Way.

Not if she has any say in it.

She has to warn Maya somehow. Let her know he's playing a trick and that she needs to keep her distance. Think. What would Maya do if their roles were reversed? That's easy. Anything and everything she could. She wouldn't be satisfied with simply sending a warning to back off. She'd also find a way to prevent the bad man from doing whatever he has planned, before he even realized she found a way out of the trunk. And for an encore, probably leave him hog-tied on the side of the road for the police. Because that's who Maya is. She always knows the exact right thing to do.

Abby relishes the mental image of her assailant trussed up on the shoulder, screaming his fool head off like a little baby, but her heart is breaking. She has no idea what to do next, other than the obvious. She can crawl out of the trunk and make herself known. Pop up like a Jack-in-the-Box in the rear window, waving and screaming and making sure Maya sees her. It might be enough. But if she does, what happens then? He'll know she's free. Will he stop the car or keep driving?

Duh. The latter. Has to be. If he continues, she's still his captive. This is a two-door. Freedom means going past him. She will have gained nothing except for alerting Maya. But if he stops, he's going to have to deal with both of them, because Maya will seize the opportunity the same way she has with everything else. It's how she's wired. The badass circuit. He's not going to want that. Which means that instead of just raising an alarm, she needs to figure out a way to make him stop the car.

That's what Maya would do.

Slowly, Abby returns the seat back into its upright position, lifting the latch out of the way, so it doesn't make a noise and alert the man. She moves the spare tire aside and scoots over to the other seat. Unhooks the matching tab. Lays the seat down. Must. Be. Careful. It's much easier for him to notice her now that she's no longer in his blind spot. If he turns his head the slightest bit, she'll be in plain view. But she has to do it this way because she needs the other seat to sit in, buckled up.

She creeps through the opening on her belly to keep the lowest profile. Slithers to the edge of the seat, then partway into the footwell, avoiding contact with the front seat. Once her clenched fists are on the floor she swivels, so she can cross.

"What the hell are *you* doing?" the man bellows, his furious moon face suddenly looming between the bucket seats.

Her heart skips. She lunges for the safe space.

The car swerves hard. Abby feels a big hand on the small of her back, searching for purchase. He manages to get his fingers under the waistband of her shorts and seizes hold. Drags her onto the seat. She flails, trying to wrench herself out of his grasp. Her bitten leg bangs into the back of the passenger bucket and everything goes white. Blinding pain forces a scream out of her. Rocking on its springs, the car slaloms down the road, veering from one lane to the other as the two struggle. Her feet make contact with the far side wall. She kicks away, as hard as she can. The movement twists his arm behind him and he spits a litany of curse words.

But he lets go.

She falls between the seats and scrambles to the space at his back, where he can't reach. It doesn't stop him from trying. His hand swipes through the air and she makes herself flat. Pulls herself into the seat and scrunches into the corner, legs up, so he can't sneak his other hand through on the door side and grab her. Yanks the seatbelt across and latches it in case they wreck.

The light in the passenger compartment flares as Maya engages her high beams. She's right behind them, not even ten feet off the rear bumper. The man punches the gas and the car leaps ahead. Abby makes a fist, thumb up. Raises it into the bright light, so Maya will see that she's okay. Hears an answering honk over the tandem thrum of the engines. Teamwork. She wants to cheer.

Instead, she leans forward and loops a bungee cord over the man's head, jerking back with all her might once it's across his neck.

76

The streetlights are further apart here, sentinels guarding a divided and empty road with no signs of civilization as far as Maya can see. Swarms of bugs tick off the windshield like sleet, and the air whirling through the cabin is thick with the nose-stinging chemical stink of burning plastic. It's been at least a mile since she passed a house, and she's only seen two cars since they left the highway. Both ignored her frenzied honks and flickering brights. Every failed business that flashes by is covered in graffiti, given over to ruin. The cars rocket through a wasteland.

But none of that matters because it's over. The needle on the gas gauge has dropped frighteningly below the line marking empty. Teaspoons. That's all the Trans Am has left. Despite her best efforts, she's going to be hamstrung by a lack of fuel, and not the radiator she worked so hard to fix. At least she has the number from the Mustang's tag. She recites it over and over, aloud, so she won't forget it. Even though it's too little, too late.

Meet the new Maya, same as the old.

Forty feet in front of her, the Mustang jinks wildly to the right. Recovers an instant before the tires slam into the curb. An instant later, it arcs toward the median. What the hell? A sudden notion fills her equally with terror and sadistic joy. Maybe the bullet is finally doing its job, and she's witnessing his descent into death. As much as she'd like to see that—would in fact relish it—if he crashes Abby will be ricocheted like a pinball inside the trunk with no protection. Severely injured, or even killed. *That* thought is unbearable.

The Mustang continues to careen between the two curbs. Is

he seizing as he dies, foot stuck on the pedal ... or is he playing some kind of game with her? At this point it doesn't matter. The Trans Am is running on nothing more than good intentions. If he's dying, this is her last chance to help Abby. Try to get around him and bring both cars to a stop.

And if he's waiting to strike? Then let the asshole give it his best shot.

Miracle of miracles, when she gooses the pedal there's still some oomph left in the tank with the fumes. The Trans Am advances to the rear of the other car. If he taps his brakes she's going to ram them. But the kidnapper is distracted, reaching over the seat with one reddened arm for something in the back. His face shines in profile, twisted in fury. She taps the dimmer switch to light him up ... and screams in exultation when a blonde head appears over the rear deck, very much *not* in the trunk.

She watches Abby hurl herself into the corner, directly behind the asshole. Good girl! As if she heard Maya's thought, Abby raises a hand and gives her a thumbs-up. Maya slaps the horn and sounds a triumphant bleat, then floors it. With a feral roar the car leaps ahead. She jigs the wheel to the left, greasing alongside for an even better look. In an instant her mind catalogs the snapshot image.

The kidnapper, clawing desperately at his neck with one hand, trying to steer with the other.

Abby, holding what looks crazily like a set of reins in her fists, pulling back as though trying to stop a runaway stallion and oh, dear God, is she *choking* him with something? The shoulder strap across her torso is taut, pinning the girl to the seat.

The Trans Am falters, engine sputtering. Starts to fall behind.

The girl's words echo in the halls of her memory. *Promise you won't let him get me. I'd rather be dead.* She had given Abby her word.

Praying she's doing the right thing, Maya snaps the wheel to the right before he pulls away, and steers into his quarter panel with her bumper. With a queerly elegant grace, the Mustang pirouettes across the front end of her car. She catches a glimpse of the man's terrified face in the glare, then the other car slams sidelong into the median curb and skips into the air. A dissonant cacophony of receding heavy thuds and crumpling metal assaults her through the open windows as the Trans Am hops the opposite curb and sideswipes a tree, coming to rest amid a stand of cattails in several inches of water.

77

Maya throws the door open and splashes through the muck to solid ground, shoving reedy stalks aside. She lurches into the road, screaming for Abby. Her chest, which the medication had begun to muzzle, wakes like a raging beast. The path taken by the cartwheeling Mustang across the median is evident in the feeble light. Swaths of black earth stripe the grass like monstrous claw marks. Broken pieces of molding and splintered fiberglass litter the crash zone, and pebbles of tempered glass decorate the opposing lanes. A glowing rectangle at the far edge of the pavement catches her eye. His phone, the screen glazed with cracks but still mostly intact, open to a map. She snatches it up, barely breaking stride.

The battered car is resting upright in marshy undergrowth about thirty feet off the shoulder, not far from a narrow side road that disappears into the trees. The hood is missing, and steam rises from the ticking engine. It reeks of burning oil. Maya tosses the phone on the dented roof and wrenches the passenger door open, terrified of what the interior light will reveal.

A sickly sweet stench rushes out to greet her. Antifreeze. The orange liquid seems to coat every surface, and drips from the headliner. Her backpack is on the front seat, slimy with the stuff. The blue container is upended in the lap of the kidnapper, who sits belted and slumped behind the wheel, breathing slowly. A bungee cord is draped over one shoulder. His door is caved in, crushing him against the center console.

She ignores him and slams the seat forward to clamber into the back with Abby, who isn't crushed or mangled but blinks at her in a stupor, feebly struggling to rise, incognizant of the restraint holding her in. Oily speckles dot her skin and clothes. The rear passenger seat is folded down and Maya climbs onto it.

"Hang on a second," she says, reaching for the seatbelt latch. Visions of shattered bones and internal bleeding fill her head. "Don't move. Are you injured?"

"I hope when I'm older I'm like you," Abby says dreamily.

Maya feels her face grow hot. She wants to correct the girl, to tell that's the *last* thing she should want. Impetuous and headstrong are not traits anyone should aspire to. Instead, she asks, "Where do you hurt?"

The man groans. Coughs. Mutters something under his breath.

Her pulse quickens. For an instant she considers taking the bungee cord from his shoulder and lashing him to the seat. No. To get even closer is to borrow trouble. He might be playing possum, hoping to fake her out so she drops her guard.

Not a chance.

Abby's eyes clear and she focuses on Maya.

"Everywhere," she says, then smiles weakly. "But not bad. Mostly my leg, but that hurt already."

"Can you move?"

"I think so." She tests each limb. Twists in the seat and shrugs her shoulders. Nods.

Maya takes Abby by the hand and helps her out of the car, keeping a wary eye on their assailant.

"Hold onto the door, I need to check something," she says.

She snaps the passenger seat upright. The bastard had a pistol, and he carried a stun gun. Maybe he took them back, or has something else stashed in the Mustang. He likes weapons. It would be foolish not to check while he's incapacitated. She's already learned one lesson tonight on how long it takes help to arrive when you're desperate for it. Squatting, she feels under the seat but discovers nothing more than sticky antifreeze. She wipes her hand on her jeans and pops the glove box. There's no weapon within, but what she finds elicits a small rush of joy. Her cell phone in its yellow case, undamaged, resting on some paperwork. She lifts it out of the cubby and—

The man lunges, snarling, but is stopped short by the seatbelt when it locks. His slick, greasy hand closes around her wrist. She bucks wildly, trying to yank loose, but her strength is no match for his and she's drawn inexorably back into the car. Into his space. As he reaches for her neck with his other hand, she ducks and jams a thumb into his eye, trying to scoop it out like a melon ball. The man screeches something incoherent and lets go, clapping both hands to his face. Maya falls out the door and scrabbles away through the mud and water, almost bowling Abby over in her haste. Somehow, she's still holding her phone.

911. Right now.

But when she stands and presses the button to wake it, nothing happens.

The click of a seatbelt latch draws her gaze from the black screen. The kidnapper skitters over the center console like a spider, one eye puffy and streaming. Abby screams, shambling away from the open door. Maya pockets her phone and swipes the other one off the roof of the car as he worms across the slick seat, dragging his legs from the cramped footwell.

He pulls himself out the door, struggling to stand.

"Lean on me," Maya wheezes. The pain is a knife in her lungs. "Like we did in the swamp."

Abby throws her arm around Maya's neck, and they hobble for the barren road.

78

There's no traffic in either direction, just equidistant streetlights in the median as far as she can see. Behind them, their pursuer staggers away from the corpse of the Mustang, hunched like a troll with a hand on his wound and one leg dragging. At his back, the lights of New Orleans form a luminous gray dome over the treetops.

Maya needs to call 911 again, even though she knows it's futile. They're still too far out. Help isn't going to reach them in time. She remembers the run-down buildings, the empty houses. Now that his car is totaled and hers is out of gas, he has no way to escape with Abby. No reason for him to try. Game over. By the time the police make it they'll both be dead unless they can outrun him.

She knows they can't.

Knows they have to try.

Holding tight to keep Abby from falling down, Maya prepares to make the call. The map has kept his phone awake, and before she dismisses it to dial, takes a quick look at the screen. Just in case. Maybe there's someplace close they can reach before it's too late. Sanctuary.

There isn't.

More than a mile to the north is the last neighborhood she passed. Boarded and broken windows, barely any vehicles in the driveways. Graffiti tags on every surface. Even if by some miracle Abby made it that far on her injured leg and they managed to stay ahead of the kidnapper, what are the chances a resident in a place like that would open their door to a stranger banging on it?

The unlighted side road less than a hundred feet south

of them appears to be the entrance to an office complex, a scattering of blocky buildings around a loop just on the other side of the trees. Abandoned, for sure. They don't turn off the streetlights otherwise. Lots of places to hide, if they can gain some distance. If. But that's not what sparks faint hope in her, it's the intersection of an interstate and its spur the map shows on the far side of those buildings. A union of two arteries for the metro area, guaranteed to have traffic no matter the time of day … and it's barely more than a quarter-mile from where they stand.

"Through there," she says, tipping her head. "It's about as far to the interstate as it was to get back to the store from the water."

Except it's further, she thinks. And Abby had been on the verge of collapse by the time they exited the swamp. At least here they won't have to fight their way through brush and brambles and sludge.

"Okay," Abby murmurs.

"We can do this. Girl power, right?"

"Right." Except her voice is listless. Exhausted. Maya wishes there was time to stop at the Trans Am for the candy bar she brought.

But he's coming.

She dismisses the map and thumbs open the dialer as they start for the secondary road. Dials 911.

"That's right," the man cries. "Keep running! See how far it gets you out here."

Maya hears the scuffle-scrape of shoes on the pavement and risks a look. He's twenty-five feet back, standing straighter now. Like the thought of getting his hands on them renews his strength.

"Faster!" she hisses. In her ear, a ring.

Someone asks what her emergency is, the voice barely audible over the staticky pounding in her ears. Abby whimpers, but picks up her pace. Each limping step causes her to bump into Maya's side, thumping her ribs. Pure hell.

As they take the corner and the road enters the trees, she

relays their situation to the dispatcher between shallow panting breaths. The two-lane is cloaked in deep shadows. Crowding branches overhang, and clumps of weeds erupt from the cracks that craze the asphalt. Maya and Abby reel like zombies in a horror movie, trying to stay one step ahead. A series of concrete Jersey walls have been arranged across the road to prevent vehicle entry. She wants to scream. Not *probably* abandoned. Definitely. And they can't turn around now; he's blocking the way out.

Unless they want to detour into the swampy woods.

Hell no. Been there, done that. Never again.

"Please tell me you can find us," she gasps into the phone, assisting Abby around the end of one of the barriers. "I don't know where we are. Can't stop to look. Can't talk. Need my breath."

"I have your location," the dispatcher says. "Police and emergency services are en route. Save your breath, but don't hang up."

The kidnapper heaves himself over the concrete, cries out. Twenty feet back. Desperation and despair fight for control of her emotions. How is he gaining?

"Almost there," she tells Abby.

Tells herself.

Holding the phone at her side, she rushes the girl headlong down the lane. But after a few steps she realizes the folly of her faux optimism. There's another barrier blocking the way, this one a thousand times worse. An eight-foot cyclone fence, crowned with coils of razor wire to discourage climbing, disappears into the trees in either direction. Spanning the road is a pair of similar gates, secured with chain and padlock.

She feels her spirit break. They're going to have to wade into another swamp after all. And she doesn't think she can do that, even if Abby is up for it. She slams a foot into one of the link panels in frustration. It moves a little. A narrow gap opens between the gates before the chain pulls taut.

Too small for her, and *definitely* for him, but Abby...

"Try to squeeze through," she tells the girl, pushing the phone into her hand. "Go! I'll slow him down."

Ducking away, Maya turns and charges the man.

79

His limp is so pronounced staying vertical is a challenge, each step a barely controlled fall that propels him down the spalling road. He's hurt worse than she thought. Too bad the wreck hadn't done more. A compound fracture, for instance. Jagged bones sticking out through his pants, glistening wetly in the moonglow.

But she can work with this.

In two steps she knows what she'll do.

Ten feet. Five.

The fence rattles behind her. There's a clink of metal on metal. She just needs to buy Abby a little breathing room. Give her a chance to slip through the gates, where he can't go. Despite the thunderous pain in her chest and the thrum of her shoulder, she feels good about her chances. Get in and get out. Fast, before he can get his hands on her. Her legs are solid. No injuries there. Plenty strong.

As he shambles into reach, she pivots to his left, skips once, and drives a heel into the side of his knee. He folds, snorting through clenched teeth like a bull, but doesn't scream or even whimper. The hate in his gaze is enough to melt steel. Turning so that his bad leg is away from her, chuffing from the torment, he balances on his good knee. Beckons.

"Come on," he says. His voice is constricted with barely controlled rage. "Wetback bitch. Try it again."

A clank and a scuff behind her. The jingle of chain.

Maya barks a peal of humorless laughter. "Is that supposed to make me lose my cool? To trigger me? I got news for you, asshole. Better people have called me worse."

"I'm through!" Abby cries excitedly. "Come try, Maya. It's wider than it looks!"

Maya spins and bolts for the gates, chased by the pitiful sounds of the kidnapper trying to gain his feet.

The girl waits inside, spreading the panels apart. The gap is tiny. There's no way.

"I won't fit," Maya says. "But that means he can't, either. The police will be here soon. Just back away and be ready to run if you have to."

"But you *will* fit!" Abby insists. "It's wiggly, especially at the ground. Look."

She bends, and when she tugs on the bottom of one gate, the opening widens. Maybe enough.

Maya drops to her hands and knees, puts her head through. Twists. Squirms until her shoulders slip between. Pressure mounts on her chest and back as the bars squeeze. She hears the grate of the man's shoes on the pavement. His suppressed moans and mewls as he tries to rise. She wriggles. Pressure becomes pain. Becomes torture, an Inquisitor grinding glass into her lungs. She can't catch a breath.

"Pull harder," she wheezes.

Abby puts the phone down and uses both hands to prise the metal tubing apart, putting all her weight into the effort. A final bright red flash of pure agony, and Maya gets her ribcage free. Tremors wrack her body. The relief is palpable. She drags herself the rest of the way inside. Wills herself to breathe slowly, shallowly. A small worry niggles at the back of her thoughts as she recovers. Can he force his way in? The cheap fencing is one grade above flimsy. If a child is able stretch the gap enough to allow a grown woman through, what can he do with his superior strength? They have to go. She stands.

Gawps for precious seconds as she processes the view before her.

The road terminates in a long, narrow rectangular parking lot. Saplings and shrubs sprout from the disintegrating blacktop, and pools of stagnant water fill the low spots.

A hundred feet ahead, weak moonlight reveals a columned pavilion at the lot edge, set behind a black fence with gaping gates. A line of brick booths is arrayed underneath, separated by turnstiles designed to funnel people in like cattle. The silhouette of a once majestic Ferris wheel rises against the glow of the city, distorted by missing spokes and on the verge of collapse. A number of cabins dangle crazily from broken axles. Conical roofs jut from the encroaching growth like ice cream cones, and a trio of sky lift support pylons reach for the stars. Towering over the ruinous tableau, the serpentine hills and tight curves of a behemoth roller coaster fill the sky, swaths of greedy vegetation slowly reclaiming its skeletal latticework.

Is there anything in this damn state that isn't horrifying?

"We need to keep moving," Maya says in a low voice. Then, with sudden panic, "*Abby!*"

The kidnapper crashes into the gates and thrusts his arm between, reaching for his phone.

Abby lunges, stumbling when her injured leg gives out. Almost falls. Catches herself on the chain link panel and manages to send the device skating with one sneaker before he gets it. He snarls and grabs for her, but she's already out of harm's way, so he immediately attacks the bottom of the fence, trying to bend the metal tubing.

Maya supports Abby as the two cross the parking lot. Updates the dispatcher. "We're going to hide in an old amusement park. Next to the interstate spur. Tell them to hurry!"

She leaves the call connected, but before slipping the phone into her pocket she opens the settings and disables the lock screen in case they're cut off and 911 calls back. They're almost to the entrance when his taunt reaches them. "Coming for you, sister. You hear me? Coming for *you*."

The wail of a far-off siren rises into the night sky, not close enough to cover the dragging scrape of approaching footfalls.

80

The turnstiles spit them onto a promenade so littered with debris it's nearly impossible for Abby to pick her way through without tripping. Lumber and litter and broken pieces of concrete from the dilapidated buildings flanking the walkway threaten each labored step, and she's so tired she thinks if she falls she might not be able to get back up. She's acutely aware of how much she's slowing Maya down.

They pass beneath balconies decorated with elaborate ironwork as Maya peers through tall, broken windows for a place they can hide. Graffiti covers the walls, which look like they were brightly colored and beautiful once upon a time, but are obviously faded and weathered even in the dark. A furtive clatter and crunch causes her to look over her shoulder in time to see the bad man emerge from the pavilion, limping, into the moonlight. Breathing down their necks already. Because of her.

"He's here," she whispers, and Maya starts. Checks. Grimaces. She hoists Abby a little higher and grunts as the girl bumps into her side.

"Can you walk any faster?"

"I'll try."

Abby doesn't know if she can. Her leg is getting worse. It's swollen, all the way to her knee, and stiffening up at the hip. Each inflamed puncture wound burns down to the bone, and there's a deeper hurt underneath that she believes might be something serious. She doesn't think Maya has noticed, and she's not going to say anything. After everything Maya has done for her, she'll walk until it falls off if she needs to.

They pick up the pace as the path forks around an overgrown

lagoon. Maya leads them to the right. Some heavy beast scuttles away among the palmetto trees and splashes into the water. Abby shivers. A swing carousel looms on their left, chairless chains dangling. The crown of the structure looks like a pie with several slices missing. Just past it, the floor of the bumper car arena shines with standing water. Some past visitor has dragged one of the cars out into the walkway, bent its hot rod almost double. Maya steers them around it. More sirens join the chorus. It sounds like the whole police department is coming.

But Abby knows they're not going to get here soon enough.

81

The park was built over a swamp, and now the swamp is reclaiming its own. That much is obvious to the seller. Mankind tried to tame the wilds, to layer on concrete and metal and New Orleans Colonial architecture to give the place a veneer of the legendary French Quarter, but nature has peeled back the mask and revealed its true countenance. It's a good place for killing, he thinks, with enough cover that he might even be able to elude the police once the bitch is dead.

She needs to be taught that butting in has consequences.

He accepts now that the product is a lost cause. That's okay. She's been crawling through mud and taken a swim in a swamp. There's a chance—a pretty good one—that his DNA has been swept away. She can go home to mommy and daddy and live happily ever after, for all he cares. As long as he gets his hands on the woman. At this rate, it won't be long. The pair is navigating a leftward curve forty feet ahead, just passing a half-collapsed building with a weatherworn SpongeBob SquarePants that grins toothily down. There's a stink of moldering upholstery hanging in the air. His knee hurts like a son of a bitch, but the thought of ripping the life out of her renews his energy. So much, in fact, that he's made up nearly every bit of distance they gained at the front gate.

The seller plucks his shirt away from his side, making a face. The coolant soaking his clothes makes his skin sting like hell, especially the wounds in his arm and belly. As soon as he's dealt with her, the next order of business is to clean the shit off. One more source of pain that can be laid at her feet.

He can't wait.

It sounds like a whole platoon of cops is coming. Earlier, the realization would have sent him running for the hills. Not anymore. Not until she's dealt with. If they corner him, so be it. He's had a good run. Made a lot of money. Is *outstanding* at delivering quality product. Going out on a high note is a thousand times more appealing than landing in prison. Everyone knows people in his line of work don't fare well behind bars, whether they partake of the merchandise or not. Better to suicide himself by cop if it comes to that. But he doesn't think it will, because by the time Johnny law makes it through the gates and into the park, the woman will be dead, and him vanished into the wind.

Twenty-five feet.

82

Maya and Abby are close enough to hear the sounds of intermittent traffic on the interstate spur ahead. Elevated headlights wink at them through the beams and latticework of the towering roller coaster as oblivious drivers almost within spitting distance pass on the way to the rest of their lives.

It might as well be a thousand miles.

The back of the park is a lowland, and here the swamp has taken over. Where the thoroughfare arcs to the left and parallels the berm and freeway outside, it disappears into still, shallow water. Massive concrete pylons bearing the coaster supports sprout from the muck like crooked teeth. The narrow path that marks the ride entrance on their right still has a faded statue of a leering jester standing guard, one arm outstretched in invitation to riders.

Strobing blue lights paint the structure from the far side as a wailing police car approaches. Slows. A brilliant spotlight jitters over the trusses for a moment, then dips down to play across the surface of the water. Creatures scramble for the cover of darkness before the light shuts off and the car moves on, as if the officer realizes the futility of trying to assist from out there.

"Ain't that some shit, sister?" the kidnapper crows. "When seconds count, the police are minutes away, can I get a hallelujah?"

He sounds near. Fifteen or twenty feet. She doesn't look. Can't. The promenade is a minefield of refuse and rubble waiting to trip them up. It's going to be even worse if they try to ford it and loop back around to the front, where all their help is apparently being sent despite her telling the dispatcher they were trying to reach the interstate. One misstep in that mess and he'd be on them. The jester beckons them in a direction overgrown and crumbling and leaf strewn, but the path appears solid, wet only from the rain. They might be able to make it all the way to the rear fence and find a way under. The lady, or the tiger?

Before she can decide, Abby pulls her toward the statue.

"Don't make me go back in the water," she says, tremulously. "*Please*."

"Never." She hopes she isn't signing their death warrants.

As they veer onto the smaller path Maya takes out the phone. Verifies someone is still listening.

"We're at the base of the roller coaster. In the back of the park," she says. It's hard to both breathe and talk, and the words burst from her in fits. "Next to the interstate spur. I saw a police car out there, but it left. The man after us is catching up. *Please* tell them to hurry. We don't have anywhere else to go."

The walkway carries them under what had once been a canopy to shield waiting riders from the weather. Now all that remains is the metal frame, engulfed in climbing vines. It angles slightly upward as the path becomes a ramp leading to the boarding pavilion. From here the perimeter fence and berm beyond are visible. Maya's heart sinks when she sees the standing water that blocks the way. A tractor-trailer snores past in plain sight, close yet unreachable. The cacophony of sirens has reached a fever pitch, still too far away to do any good because they're all on the other side of the park. Scuffles and scrapes and ragged exhalations from the rear. She imagines the heat of his breath on the back of her neck.

They ascend the ramp at a snail's pace. Even so, when she risks a glance from the entrance to the boarding pavilion, he's further away than she expected. Twelve feet. Interesting. It has to be his knee. An incline would force him to use it more ... and would not only slow him down, but likely cause him considerable pain.

Which delights her.

The floor of the boarding pavilion is treated wood, and their footfalls echo hollowly as they duck between the rails of the queue line, crossing to the boarding area. Dried leaves protected from the elements crunch underfoot. Maya kicks something hidden among them and it rolls away. A piece of safety railing, similar in appearance to the pipes of the front gate but coated in enamel and considerably thicker. Sturdier. A weapon.

She picks it up. Swings it. Hell yes.

"I have an idea," she says, looking ahead. "Can you dig just a little deeper? One last push to hold him off until the police get here?"

Abby nods. Sweat shines on her face, and her breathing is dangerously erratic.

I hope when I'm older I'm like you.

The first words the girl had said after the accident come to Maya now, as they hurry alongside the track and exit the darkened building onto a walkway of buckling planks suspended several feet above the swampy mess. After everything she had been through, her first thought was something nice about the very person who put her through all of it. So guileless and trusting. A lump in her throat makes it hard to swallow. She'll die before she lets him get her.

Directly ahead, the coaster track ascends into the night sky. The ancient chain lift mechanism is still in place between the rusty rails, an endless series of teeth ready to bite. To the right of the track is a disintegrating wooden staircase, no more than a foot wide, that seems to reach nearly to the stars.

Maya lets Abby take the lead and places herself between girl and man, and they begin to climb.

83

The seller tests each tread before putting his weight on it. It's old lumber, soft and springy despite being pressure-treated back in the day. He doesn't trust it. Probably been exposed to the weather for twenty-five years, and unmaintained since the hurricane closed the park for good nearly two decades ago. There's a banister, constructed from the same punky wood. Spindly two-by-twos support it every four feet, secured with rusty bolts. Janky as hell, but he leverages it for support to minimize the burden on his bum knee. His ascent wouldn't be possible otherwise. Each time he leans on it, he wonders if this will be the one where it tears loose—with a rotting purr instead of a sharp crack—and pitches him over the side. He's already at the level of the treetops. Falling from this height is more likely to be fatal than not.

A fact he's counting on.

Twenty feet upslope, the bitch prods the product, trying to get her to move faster. Backing them both into a corner. Go right ahead. If they make it to the crest, what then? There's no staircase on the downhill side, and if they try to descend using the bents supporting the track, well, gravity will do his job for him. Disappointing, but he can live with the outcome. His hope is that she wants a showdown. One on one, may the best man win.

And he will.

She may have the higher ground, but she lacks what it takes to finish the job. Otherwise, she would have killed him when she had her chance, while he was out cold. So let her have the high ground, because all he needs is a couple of quick shoves and goodbye sister, goodbye product. Hello freedom. But first, his phone. Always the phone.

Holding fast to the shaky rail, the seller continues up the stairs.

84

The kidnapper isn't falling behind the way Maya expected him to. If anything, he's gained. Her great plan is crumbling like the rides arrayed in and around the swamp beneath them. She already regrets her snap decision, but what can she do now? Nothing. They need to pick up the pace. Buy some time to prepare for him. Looking toward the top of the incline, she thinks she might see a way to keep Abby safe.

"Take this." She taps the girl's arm with the pipe she found in the pavilion. "Use it like a cane. One hand on the banister, one hand on that. Let your arms do most of the work, not your leg. It'll help you climb faster."

Abby doesn't reply, but she takes the length of metal and uses it for support. Her face is drawn and tight. Running on fumes, Maya thinks. The same way the Trans Am had been at the very end. And just like the car, the girl seems to dig deep, to find the gas to go just a little faster. Maya prays it holds, because the next ask is going to be a whopper.

They're almost to the summit. A stiff breeze pushes her, whips Abby's hair. The massive structure beneath them creaks and seems to sway with every step. From here Maya can see police cars lined up at the barricades blocking the entrance drive. Three so far, two more approaching on the road where the cars crashed. They look like toys. Flashlights bob in the desolate parking lot, headed for the ticketing area. She pulls out the phone and updates the 911 operator with their location. To her right, New Orleans stretches to the horizon, a sea of diamonds, and she wonders if the officers can see the drama unfolding up here, silhouetted against the city's glow.

The stairs terminate at a maintenance platform at the top of the lift hill, no more than two feet by three. When Abby reaches it she sits, clinging desperately to one of the support posts. Her eyes are squeezed shut against the unsettling view. A catwalk continues over the peak, an arc of ten-inch planking with toeboards at regular intervals, joining a matching work area on the drop slope. The banister here is broken away, leaving behind only jagged spindles and a single post marking the highest point.

Maya stops, puts her hand on the girl's shoulder. A knot of anguish and terror writhes in her belly. She's asked for so much already ... and now there's one last thing, because this is the end of the line for her.

"You need to keep going, Abby," she says. It feels like a giant hand is clenched around her heart. "All the way to the other platform. Crawl. Don't try to walk. Hold onto the track."

Abby's head whips from side to side. She doesn't open her eyes. "Can't."

"You have to, sweetie. He's too big and heavy to make it across. Not with his leg."

"You can stop him."

Maya wishes she felt as confident. She takes back the length of guard rail and presses the man's phone into the girl's hand. More than anything, she wants to pull Abby close and tell her that no girl should ever have to go through the things she has tonight. That none of this is her fault, and in a better world this would have never happened. She'd spend her night sitting outside with the boy she met without a care in the world, her only concern a lecture from her mother.

But there's no time.

85

Abby wants to curl up in a ball and die. Why is Maya making her do this?

"I hope I *do* stop him," Maya tells her. "But no matter what happens, you can't give up. Then he wins."

Abby shakes her head again. A tear forces its way out and runs down her cheek. How can she keep going all by herself?

"Stay right there if you want, princess," the man says, so close there's a whiff of antifreeze on the wind. "Don't let her tell you what to do."

She opens her eyes. He's not even a dozen steps down from where Maya stands facing her, dragging himself up. What she wouldn't give to wipe the smirk off his stupid face.

No. Don't focus on him. Look at Maya. Be strong, like her.

Abby nods once.

"Kick his ass," she says.

She swivels onto her hands and knees and sticks the phone in her pocket, then crawls onto the catwalk, gripping the cool steel track so fiercely her left arm tries to cramp from the strain. High places terrify her, and this is worse than her worst nightmare. Her knees barely fit together on the warped board, forcing her to swing her injured leg over the void with each movement. The gusty wind snaps her t-shirt, and makes her think she's going to blow over the edge at any moment. Groans and pops rise from below. The entire hill gently rocks from side to side, like a cradle. As much as she tries to concentrate all her attention on the plank before her, her eyes are drawn to the gap between it and the track. The ground is so far away it makes her dizzy.

But if Maya can face him, she can face this.

Abby continues to crawl until she reaches the peak, where a lone support strut points at a sky yet untouched by the coming day. Here. This is far enough. There's something she needs to do. Holding tight to the post, she carefully rotates until she's sitting on the track, with her feet on the catwalk. She doesn't look over at Maya, because she's afraid of what she'll see. That would be unbearable.

The city before her is a glittering expanse of lights nestled around the black curves of a river, and as she retrieves the phone she thinks about all the people out there sleeping, content in their lives. What she wouldn't give to be among them.

But she's not.

"I have to call my parents to say goodbye," she says to the 911 operator. "Tell the police we made it to the very top of the roller coaster."

She ends the call, cutting the surprised dispatcher off midsentence. When the breathless, harried voice of her mother interrupts the first ring, Abby begins to sob.

"Ab?" Hysteria tinges the word. "Where are you, baby? Are you hurt? Tell me and we'll—"

"Mom, listen," she says. Far away is the voice of the man, saying something to Maya that she's unable to make out over the wind and her hitching breaths. He doesn't matter anymore. "I can't talk long because things might get … bad, and I don't want you to hear that."

Her mother tries to break in, panicky and crying, but Abby doesn't give her a chance.

"I want you to know that I love all of you, and I'm sorry. For everything." She disconnects the call.

When Maya cries out in pain a short time later, Abby discovers she's able to look after all.

86

Maya watches the girl crawl away for a moment to make sure she isn't going to freeze up, then raises the pipe and turns to face their pursuer. He's about ten feet down, supporting himself with the guard rail, hate-filled eyes on her as he pulls himself one step closer. In the eastern sky the only sign of the approaching day is the slightest lightening of the dark at the horizon. Far below, flashlight beams flicker through the trees on the path around the lagoon. Two minutes away. No more than three, assuming word of their location has made it through the police grapevine, or the officers think to look up. She can't hold him off that long. Why hadn't she said something to the 911 operator before giving the phone to Abby?

"Up here!" she shrieks at the approaching lights. The wind flings the words back into her face. A bolt of pain lances her chest and she grimaces. Why isn't Abby trying to get their attention? But she can't look back to see what the girl is doing. Not now.

"Save your breath, sister," the man says. "They'll hear you screaming soon enough. Or can I call you Maya? I feel like we're pretty close after everything we've been through."

She says nothing.

Letting the rail bear most of his weight, left arm curled across his belly to apply pressure to the hole in his side, he moves up another step. Underneath the mask of fury that twists his features, the hurt is clearly evident. The climb *has* worn him down, like she hoped. Just not enough.

She weighs her options. The knee is the obvious choice for an attack, but it's simply not possible. She's on the high side, making any swing by necessity downward and low and awkward. Too easy for her to miss, or lose her balance and fall right on top of him. A recipe for disaster. The gunshot wound is also an appealing target, but it's on the side of the railing. Protected. No way to get any kind of swing. That leaves his head. Good enough. She's already softened it up with the bangstick. Now it's time to crack the egg and make an omelet. Kick the bastard down the stairs if he doesn't go over or through the rail.

Maya steps down, eyeing him warily.

"Let's do this," he says, trying to straighten. Cords pop on his neck from the effort.

Down again, landing her in the sweet spot. Too far for him to reach without lunging—and with the state of his knee something she doubts he's able to do, anyway—yet close enough to hit with the pipe.

An excruciating twinge on her flank nearly staggers her when she draws the weapon back. Can't stop now. Fight through it. But as she follows through with the swing, something in her chest pops in a bright flash of agony. She sags against the guard rail, suddenly unable to take a breath. He blocks the weakened blow easily with his forearm.

Then he grabs hold of the metal shaft and jerks it out of her hands. Flings it away, out over the trees.

"Nice try," he says. A smirk surfaces through the discomfort, there and gone. "But I think this should be a little more *intimate*, don't you?"

He hoists himself up another step.

As she counters his movement with one of her own, her gaze jumps to the path below. She can see the officers now, three dark shapes behind lights rounding the bend. They're about to discover the water over the promenade. *Look up!* she wants to scream, but there's no air left. Each attempt to draw breath is torture. So be it. If the only way to save Abby is to latch onto him and pull him over the side, she will. He can't win. *Won't* win. At least the sound of two bodies hitting the ground will get their attention.

Get their attention.

The thought echoes in the chambers of her mind. It's important. Why?

He lurches a step closer … and it comes to her. She already *has* a way to alert them, in her pocket. Maya reaches back, wincing, feeling for the second road flare. Finds it. She pops the striker cap and rakes the ignition button across the rough surface. Red sparks fly.

With a sibilant hiss, crimson fire blooms in her hand.

A shout rises from below.

But it's too late. He's *right* here. Before she can retreat another step his fist lashes out, hammers her ribs. Maya collapses on the staircase, screaming without awareness. The pain is unimaginable, a hot poker rammed through her. She wields the sputtering torch weakly in front of her, trying to resist him, but he bats her arm out of his way.

One hand seizes her by the throat, the grip tight enough to trigger her gag reflex. The other shoves roughly between her legs, scooping under her buttocks. He lifts her, face painted red by the eerie glow. The chemical stink of the antifreeze is overwhelming. Faintly she is aware of the thunder of racing footfalls on the walkway to the entrance ramp. With a ferocious roar, the man raises her to his chest. Turns to heave her over the rail.

And for an instant, the gunshot wound is exposed through a tiny hole in his wet shirt.

Maya thrusts the incandescent tip of the road flare against his side. Hears the sweet sizzle of frying flesh. She twists her wrist viciously, trying to grind the burning ember through the skin and into his belly.

The effect is galvanizing. With a shriek of outrage and pain, he drops her on the guard rail. The rotted wood gives way. She thumps heavily to the steps in a cascade of splinters, half on and half off. The flare pinballs down through the latticework in a shower of ruby sparks. As gravity beckons and she begins to tip almost dreamily over the edge, her only thoughts are for the safety of the girl. She's done her best, and that's all anyone can ask. The police are here, and Abby is safe on the other side of the narrow catwalk. Game over, asshole.

Except Abby is grabbing her by the upper arm, so she doesn't fall. Not safe on the far platform at all but right freaking *here* where he can still get her. Maya wants to scream for the girl to get the hell away, to ask her what she's thinking by coming back, but of course there's no time. She throws a leg onto the stairs, and with the extra helping hands manages to heave herself the rest of the way up. Something grates in her chest as she tries to push to her feet and she moans. Dying. That's what it feels like.

But when she turns to face the kidnapper, his attention isn't on them at all. He's three or four steps downslope, frantically slapping himself all over with both hands, like he stumbled over a hornet's nest and is fending off an angry swarm of stinging insects. An instant later she realizes he's enveloped in rippling blue flames, so pale as to be nearly invisible, fed by the coolant soaking his clothes and nurtured by the wind. His face is a rictus of quiet panic. The breeze reeks of burning chemicals. He grabs fistfuls of his shirt in an attempt to peel it over his head and ease the suffering, but loses his balance. His shoe catches on the steel track and he falls, crashing hard on the cross ties that separate the rails, which disintegrate and do little to slow his descent. He manages to catch hold of the rusted lift chain and hangs, dangling over the abyss. Glaring at her. Translucent flames climb his face, blistering the flesh. His hair ignites. Thin tendrils of foul smoke are snatched away by the breeze.

Then he's gone.

After an eternity Maya hears a sharp *crack* almost like a gunshot, far below. She slumps over her knees, trying to lessen the agony in her chest, and leans far enough to see between the track rails to the swamp below. The whole lift hill shakes from the weight of the three burly policemen bounding up the stairs. One notices her looking and pauses long enough to shine his flashlight through the trusses, revealing a blocky pylon rising from the shallow water, the concrete dashed with bright blood and gore. A body, facedown in the muck. She sits up and watches the officers climb, trying to catch her breath.

"I knew you would do it," Abby says.

She reaches back and takes the girl's hand. Squeezes it, but doesn't speak because she's afraid the tears will come, and if they do, she doesn't know if she'll be able to stop.

87

Maya sits on one of the concrete barricades blocking the amusement park entry, looking on as the paramedics lower the stretcher and lift Abby—who appears to already be asleep—into the back of the waiting ambulance. A second is on the way for her, siren warbling to warn the building traffic to get out of the way. Across the divided road, the Trans Am rests silently in the marshy undergrowth. All the damage from the tree is on the unseen side, and from where she sits the car appears pristine in pre-dawn light.

There are so many people she needs to contact right now, before the whole day is lost with doctors and the police. And sleep. Lots of sleep. Soon, please and thank you. She powers on her phone. No texts from Moretti questioning the location of the Trans Am, no missed calls. Nothing. She locates his number in her contacts and calls it.

"Maya," he says after three rings, his voice thick with sleep.

"I'm sorry to wake you, but I have some bad news."

"What's wrong?" Alert now, fully awake. Concern tinges his words. "What happened?"

Flashing red lights appear around a curve a half-mile away.

She doesn't know where to begin.

"There was an accident. The car is banged up, and I have to go to the hospital. Then probably interviews with the police. Or the FBI. I need to sleep. I'm not going to make it to Baton Rouge on time. I'll pay for all the repairs, I swear."

She realizes she's babbling and shuts up.

"Never mind the car, how are *you*? Are you hurt? I hear sirens."

"I'm okay. Cracked or broken ribs, I think, but not from the accident. It's a really long story I promise I'll tell you as soon as I'm able. If the Trans Am can be driven, do you want me to deliver it or bring it back to you?"

"I'll call AAA and have it towed to a shop there. Bring it back if it's cleared. I want to see it. Otherwise, rent a car and I'll cover it." He pauses. Adds, "Did you say the FBI?"

It's getting too hard to hear him. EMS is nearly there. She stands, swallowing to quell the emotion that constricts her throat.

"I have to go, Mr. Moretti. I'll call you as soon as I can and tell you everything. I'm so very sorry I let you down."

His response is drowned out by the siren, and she ends the call as the tears she's been holding back finally begin to flow.

88

Abby shifts in the armchair in the corner of the rental house bedroom, trying to find a comfortable position. The pain medication is wearing off. Despite sleeping much of the day she's dozy, and if she takes another of the pills it's going to put her out. It'll be dark in a couple of hours. She'll take one then. Maya should be stopping by on her way back to Atlanta soon, and she wants to be alert because they never got a chance to talk. Everything after the roller coaster is a blur of police and paramedics. She was zonked even before the ambulance made it to the hospital. After all the examinations and scans and suturing, her parents had shuttled her back to the house for some much-needed rest ... except someone from the FBI was waiting when they arrived. She had to answer the same questions all over again. Talk, talk, talk. That's all they wanted to do.

She checks her phone for the hundredth time in the last half hour in case Liam replied to any of her texts, but he hasn't. Not even to the picture of the sick stitches in her leg. Ghosted, obviously. It's hard to blame him. She knows how her mom can be a queen b-word sometimes, and it's all too easy to imagine the kinds of things she must have said to him in the heat of the moment last night.

As soon as she had asked for her phone at the hospital to text him, her mom had started in, calling him a troublemaker and saying *fourteen years old, and what is he doing? Drinking beer and luring you out of the house in the middle of the night.* Abby had said *this isn't his fault* and nearly fallen out of the hospital bed when her mother agreed. *It isn't anyone's fault except for the man who did it,* she said, *but that boy isn't the kind of influence you need, Ab. You're not an adult yet, no matter how much you want to be.*

So, yeah. She understands if he's salty. That doesn't make it any easier.

The deep rumble of an engine out front pulls her from her thoughts. Maya! Abby rises and limps down the hall to meet her at the door, but her butthead little brother beats her to it. Her parents are already in the front room, teary-eyed and thanking the young woman—cleaned up and decked out in a pair of pink surgical scrubs—all over again, generally being dorks about everything. Good grief. Embarrassment is written all over Maya's face as she tries to downplay their effusive praise.

"I can't stay long," she says, when Abby's father offers her a seat. "I just wanted to check in. Say goodbye. I'm going to try to make it to Birmingham tonight. No sense sitting around in a hotel when I can do the same in the car and make progress."

But Abby sees something in her eyes when she speaks. Maya wants to put distance between herself and everything that happened. She gets it. Boy, does she.

"I'll walk you out," she says, slipping past her parents. At the door, she elbows her brother aside and follows Maya onto the tiny stoop.

"So ... are you going to show me your stitches, or what?" the woman says, smiling. "Let's see those bad boys."

Abby lifts her leg and hikes up her shorts. In the orange light from the setting sun the bruises around each puncture are especially magnificent, and Maya nods appreciatively.

"Awesome, right?" Abby says.

"Totally badass."

They walk down the sidewalk to the idling Trans Am, and Abby asks, "Did the FBI talk to you?"

"For hours. I didn't think it was ever going to end so I could get some sleep." Maya considers for a minute. "I gave them his phone. They said it looked like he wasn't working alone. Like he might have been part of ... I don't know, a ring or something."

Despite the heat of the day, Abby feels a chill. That sounds so much worse than what she thought the bad man had planned for her. "I hope they put them all in jail."

"They seemed optimistic. To the point of mentioning a reward for us." She doesn't spell it out, but Abby knows what any reward would be for. All the other girls who weren't as lucky as her. Who didn't have a guardian angel.

Maya turns and reaches through the car window for something, which she holds out. A Snickers. "I picked it up for you last night and never got the chance to give it to you because of … you know."

Abby wants more than anything to hug Maya but doesn't, because she knows how much it would hurt her ribs. "Thank you. For everything."

"Come here, you," Maya says, and holds her arms out.

The embrace feels just as safe as it had in the swamp.

"Can we get a selfie?" Abby asks afterward, sniffling. She swipes her eyes. Maya positions herself at her side and throws an arm around her shoulders.

Abby readies the phone. "Should we say *cheese*?"

"No," Maya tells her. "Say *girl power*."

89

The white mansion gleams so brightly in the Saturday morning sun Maya has to lower the visor when she turns between the brick pillars at the end of the drive. Moretti sits on the front steps, elbows on his knees, watching the Trans Am approach. As she turns around and backs under the *porte cochère* next to her waiting Miata, he stands and stretches, and by the time she shuts the engine off he's waiting at her door.

"Do you need help?"

"I've got it," she says. A twinge along her flank as she climbs out of the bucket seat makes her grimace, but the nerve block is still performing admirably.

Moretti whistles at the sight of her black eye. "Damn, he got you good, didn't he?"

"It looks worse than it feels."

"How about the rest of you?"

"Sore, but it's already not as bad. They numbed the nerves around my ribs in the ER Friday. Advil and Tylenol for the rest."

"And the girl?"

"She's mending." Maya smiles, remembering Abby in the rearview mirror, nomming happily on the candy bar. Her greatest hope is that time will heal more than just the visible, physical wounds from the previous night. "Proud of all the stitches she got for the alligator bite."

"Good," he says, nodding, then turns his attention to the Trans Am. "So where's all this damage you warned me about?"

"On the passenger side."

"That? That's a few dings and scratches. You made it sound ready for the junkyard when you called."

They walk around the rear of the car, so he can inspect more closely. Moretti squats at the door, runs his fingers along the scraped indention where the car skipped off a tree.

"This is nothing," he says, rising. "A new door, a little filler and paint on the fender, and she'll be good as new."

"You think so?"

"I know so. This is cosmetic. I don't need to get underneath and check the frame to be sure it's still straight."

"I'll pay for the repairs. Just let me know what it costs."

"Bullshit," he says, matter-of-factly. "I'm the one who pushed you into the situation in the first place. The car is insured. Besides, if I decide not to use a body shop, all you've done is given me an opportunity to spend more time with Alex fixing her up. I should be paying *you* for that."

She isn't sure if he's glossing over the damage and reimbursement out of some sense of male ego or kindness or guilt. Peepaw—her first stop on the drive back to Atlanta—had been the same way, brushing off her apology for breaking into his store and leading the kidnapper straight to his hunting cabin. The old man had told her she did what she had to, then gone so far as to *laugh* when she offered to repay him for the supplies and window she broke. If that's how they want to play it, who is she to disagree? She made her apologies and has a clean conscience … but can't help wondering if they'd be as adamant if she told them about the reward the FBI mentioned.

"Speaking of," he continues, "Are you sure I can't give you something for your time?"

She shakes her head. "I wouldn't feel right. You hired me to deliver a car and I didn't do that. Since you won't let me cover the damage, let's call it even. Fair enough?"

He cocks an eyebrow at her, then extends his hand. "Fair enough."

As she's about to step into her Miata, Maya pauses.

"If you still need it delivered once the work is done, give me a call."

ACKNOWLEDGEMENTS

The following people were indispensable during the production of this book:

Robyn, my wife, who had to listen to my musings about Maya's trials and tribulations in terrible places.

Michelle Lynn, who not only tolerated an INSANE number of emails from me without telling me where to put them, but read each chapter in its infancy and offered suggestions that sent me in better directions.

Vonnie Rosnick, who received the book in chunks as I finished them and provided thoughtful feedback that helped improve the story, especially the ending.

Gina Churchill, Kerry Nadeau, and Amanda Waske, who read the completed book and shared their thoughts.

BY THE SAME AUTHOR

Run All Night
Saving Grace
The Witch
Charnel House
The Convert
No Limit

Visit fredanderson.org for more information